THE BLACK MASK LIBRARY

THE EARLY YEARS (1920–26)

The Man in the Shadows: The Complete Black Mask
Cases of Terry Mack *by Carroll John Daly*

Zigzags of Treachery: The Complete Black Mask Cases of the
Continental Op, Volume 1 *by Dashiell Hammett*

THE SHAW YEARS (1926–36)

Blood on the Curb *by Joseph T. Shaw*

Black Harvest: The Complete Black Mask Cases of Jules Tremaine *by Norvell W. Page*

Boomerang Dice: The Complete Black Mask Cases of Johnny Hi Gear *by Stewart Sterling*

The Case-Hardened Samaritan: The Complete Black Mask
Cases of Dal Prentice, Volume 1 *by Roger Torrey*

Dead Evidence: The Complete Black Mask Cases of Harrigan *by Ed Lybeck*

Laughing Death *by Raoul Whitfield*

Luck: The Complete Black Mask Cases of Oscar Sail *by Lester Dent*

Murder Maze: The Complete Black Mask Cases of Jerry
Tracy, Volume 2 *by Theodore A. Tinsley*

The Price of a Dime: The Complete Black Mask Cases of Ben Shaley *by Norbert Davis*

Somewhere in Mexico: The Complete Black Mask Cases
of Jerry Frost, Volume 1 *by Horace McCoy*

South Wind: The Complete Black Mask Cases of
Jerry Tracy, Volume 1 *by Theodore A. Tinsley*

That's Hollywood: The Complete Black Mask Cases of
Bill Lennox, Volume 1 *by W.T. Ballard*

White Talons: The Complete Black Mask Cases of Tex of
the Border Service *by Katherine Brocklebank*

THE LATER YEARS (1936–51)

Dead and Done For: The Complete Black Mask Cases of
Cellini Smith, Volume 1 *by Robert Reeves*

Dog Eat Dog: The Complete Black Mask Cases of Cellini Smith, Volume 2 *by Robert Reeves*

The Hound with the Golden Eye: The Complete Black Mask
Cases of Luther McGavock, Volume 2 *by Merle Constiner*

It Happened at the Lake *by Joseph T. Shaw*

Let the Dead Alone: The Complete Black Mask Cases of
Luther McGavock, Volume 1 *by Merle Constiner*

Murder Costs Money: The Complete Black Mask Cases
of Rex Sackler, Volume 1 *by D.L. Champion*

Murder on the Midway: The Complete Black Mask Cases of
the Human Encyclopedia, Volume 1 *by Frank Gruber*

Murder Pays 7 to 1: The Complete Black Mask Cases of
Rex Sackler, Volume 2 *by D.L. Champion*

THAT'S HOLLYWOOD

The Complete

Cases of Bill Lennox

1933–34

W.T. BALLARD

introduction by James L. Traylor

illustrations by Arthur Rodman Bowker

cover by Jes Schlaikjer

BLACK MASK

2023

Table of Contents

Introduction

MANY OF THE hardboiled writers of the *Black Mask/Dime Detective* school have had short story collections reprinted. In the 1940s and 1950s fans of the private dicks could obtain copies of Paul Cain's *Seven Slayers*, Frederick Nebel's *Six Deadly Dames*, George Harmon Coxe's Flash Casey, several collections by Raymond Chandler and the Dashiell Hammett short stories collected by Ellery Queen.

There were even several famous anthologies which offered stories by otherwise unavailable authors: Joseph T. Shaw's *Hard-Boiled Omnibus* (both the longer 1946 hardback and the somewhat shorter 1952 paperback edition), Ron Goulart's valuable collection *The Hardboiled Dicks* (1965), Herbert Ruhm's *The Hard-Boiled Detective: Stories from 'Black Mask' Magazine 1920-1951* (1977) and Bill Pronzini's *Detective and Mystery Stories from the Great Pulps* (1983).

Yet with all these collections available, there was not a single short story by W.T. Ballard in print. It's quite true that Tod Ballard's most famous character, Bill Lennox, is not strictly speaking a PI. Still, he has all the elements except for carrying the license and he was one of the most popular characters in *Black Mask*, appearing twenty-seven times between 1933 and 1942.

This volume is just a sampling of Bill Lennox, a selection for both the connoisseur of crime and the lover of good, fast-moving crime/adventure stories. As the title of Lennox's first adventure—"A Little Different"—indicates, by 1933 even Cap

Shaw was aware that the hardboiled formula needed enhancement. By this time, Hammett was no longer writing for Black Mask; Raymond Chandler had not entered the field; Carroll John Daly was showing signs of declining popularity (at least with the editors); and Erle Stanley Gardner was concentrating on his new Perry Mason novels. Shaw himself would edit *Black Mask* for only three more years before becoming an agent.

Of course three Bill Lennox novels were available to the public in the 1940s and sold quite well. Even so, the short story appearances of Ballard's Hollywood Troubleshooter have a different sort of charm from that of the novels. *Black Mask* writers often spoke of their freedom to develop character in their tough guys. There is a sense of immediacy with Lennox; the reader likes Lennox. He's hardboiled enough to satisfy all but the fringe element, yet has a respect for women which is atypical of the normal pulp orientation. One of Tod Ballard's achievements as a pulp writer is his ability to portray realistically a sense of love between characters. There are chiseling harpies and heartless bozos in these stories but these types are not protagonists. Lennox is as warm a pulp character as can be found. He romances girl friend Nancy Hobbs through nine years in the pulps and eighteen more in novels, obeying all the dicta against a hardboiled character's marriage, yet still revealing the real commitment which is a characteristic element of a Ballard PI. His stories quite often conclude with the "happy" ending of a marriage proposal, following closely on the identification of the murderer who has been trying to keep the protagonist from such a marriage declaration.

The stories in this collection present Bill Lennox at key points in his career. We first see him in his debut appearance in *Black Mask:* "A Little Different" (September, 1933) and "A Million-Dollar Tramp" (October, 1933). In these stories, we find all the now familiar characters of the Ballard created Hollywood milieu: Sol Spurck (the egotistical but mostly benign movie studio mogul), the seemingly unchanging actors and actresses who wage their fierce little battles over roles and image (the names change but the character types rarely do), Nancy Hobbs ("pert and chic, plainly pleased with Lennox," his long term and long suffering girl friend/lover who spends most of her time trying to get Bill to quit the studio and write the great American novel), Jake (one of a long line of studio minions who help Lennox get studio hams and vapid female stars out of trouble, usually murder) and Sam Marx (the archetypal Jewish attorney). In "Tears Don't Help" (April, 1934), we meet Captain Floyd Spellman (the not so dumb cop who regularly appears as Lennox's friend and nemesis).

The final Lennox short story, "Lights, Action—Killer!" (May, 1942), shows Ballard planning his character's first book appearance. This story, while having all the characteristic pulp touches (one of the characters is murdered by being sliced in two in a sawmill), marks a change in emphasis. There is even more characterization than usual with Ballard. We learn that Lennox was a student at Northwestern and had been a newspaperman in Chicago, the same facts which Ballard reworked into his first book appearance in *Say Yes to Murder* (1942). Ballard correctly believed that people read stories about believable people. All his stories, no matter how pulp in orientation, have this common element of humanity.

Lennox succeeds for this reason. He is comfortable territory, a likable character in fast moving, literate, yet tough stories. The stories display a confident sense of period, reflect their era very well, yet retain a timeless sense which makes them accessible. The original *Black Mask* readers enjoyed and highly regarded them. You will too.

A Little Different

Bill Lennox, studio trouble-shooter, finds real trouble and the shooting not so good

1

BILL LENNOX NODDED to the gateman and climbed on to the shine stand, just inside the General gate. The shine-boy grinned, his white teeth flashing in his dark face. "When is you all gwine tuh star me, Mister Lennox?"

Bill said, absently: "Pretty soon, Sam. Lean on that brush, will you; I'm in a hurry."

"I'se leaning." The boy ducked his head and went to work briskly. A big gleaming car came through the gate. Bill could see the woman on the rear seat, a dazzling blonde with dark eyebrows. He watched the car sourly until it halted before the star's bungalow dressing-room. The blonde descended, assisted by her maid, and disappeared. Lennox said something under his breath, found a quarter, which he tossed to the boy, and climbed from his seat.

Sol Spurck, head of General-Consolidated Films, put his short fingers together and stared at Lennox as the latter came into his office. "Where was you yesterday?"

Lennox looked at him without visible emotion. "Out, Sol. Out doing your dirty work."

The short figure behind the big desk shifted uncertainly. "I told you that you should watch out for that dumb cluck Wayborn. He's in a jam."

Lennox shoved his hands deep into his trouser pockets and sat down upon the corner of the desk. "What, again?"

Spurck seemed to explode. "Again—again! Always that guy—"

"Save it." Lennox's voice was very tired. "What's he done now?"

"Am I a mind reader—am I?" Spurck had come to his feet and was bouncing about the office. "What is it that I pay you for—what is it? Must I do everything—everything? I tell you that Wayborn's gone. Fifty thousand they want—fifty thousand for that—"

Lennox said: "Remember your arteries, Sol. Who wants fifty grand and for what?"

Spurck was wrenching open the drawer of his desk. He pulled forth a dirty scrap of paper and shoved it at Lennox. "Find him—find him quick. Are we half through shooting *Dangerous Love?* I ask you. Can we shoot without Wayborn? But fifty thousand for that *schlemiel.* I wouldn't pay fifty thousand for Gable yet, and they ask it for a ham like Wayborn."

Lennox said: "You wouldn't pay fifty grand for your grandmother," and stared at the piece of paper. On it were printed crude letters with a soft pencil. They said:

We've got Wayborn. You've got fifty grand. Let's trade. Go to the cops and we drop him into the ocean. More later."

Lennox looked at his boss. "Where'd this come from?"

Spurck threw up his hands, appealing to the ceiling. "He asks me riddles yet. Mein Gott! He asks me riddles."

Lennox said, roughly: "Cut it. Where'd this come from? Who's seen it?"

His voice seemed to quiet the little man. Spurck returned to his chair and lit an enormous cigar with care. "No one has seen it," he said in a surly tone. "I found it on the floor of my car this morning."

"How long has Wayborn been gone?"

Spurck shrugged. "Yesterday, he was here. Today, he is not. Find him? Yes—but fifty thousand—no. Ten maybe. Not one cent over ten."

Lennox said: "I suppose you know what this will mean? The picture is half in the can. If we don't find Wayborn, we shoot it over and Price is three days behind schedule now."

Spurck's eyes were narrow. "Why did you let me use Wayborn? That ham—what is it I pay you for?"

Lennox said: "Because I'm a fool"; he said it bitterly. "Because I stick around this mad house and keep things going. Some day, Sol, I'll quit this lousy outfit cold. I'll sit back and watch it go to the devil."

Spurck grinned. He'd heard the threat before, many times. "Find him, Bill." He reached across and patted Lennox's shoulder with a fat hand. "Find him, and I take you to Caliente. That's a promise yet."

2

BILL LENNOX, TROUBLE-SHOOTER for General-Consolidated Studio, walked through the outer office. Trouble-shooter wasn't his title. In fact, one of the things which Lennox lacked was an official title. Those in Hollywood who didn't like him called him Spurck's watch-dog. Ex-reporter, ex–publicity man, he had drifted into his present place through his inability to say yes and his decided ability in saying no.

His searching blue eyes swept about the large waiting-room. A world-famous writer bowed, half fearfully. A director whose last three pictures had hit the box-office paused for a moment to speak to him. Bill grunted and went on. As he walked down the line towards the row of dressing-rooms he was thinking quickly. Wayborn was gone. They needed him for *Dangerous Love*. No one seemed to know anything about him.

Lennox paused before the door of the third bungalow and knocked. A trim maid opened the door. Her eyes were uncertain when she saw who it was. Bill said: "Tell Miss Meyer that I want to see her."

The maid's eyes got more uncertain. "I don't think—"

His voice rasped. "You aren't paid to think. Tell Meyer that I want to see her at once."

Elva Meyer's eyes were cold, hostile beneath her dark brows as he walked through the door. She was seated before her dressing-table, but there was as yet no greasepaint on her face. "Well?" Her voice was colder than her eyes.

He was staring at her blond hair. "I'm not so hot," he said, helping himself to a chair. "When did you see Wayborn last?"

The eyes flecked, glowed for an instant. "I told you some time ago that I was perfectly capable of looking after my affairs without your help."

"Yeah?" He'd found a loose cigarette in his pocket and was rolling it back and forth between his strong fingers so that the tobacco spilled out at both ends. "Well, sweetheart, it so happens that I'm not sticking my schnozzle into your playhouse at the moment. You and Wayborn were at the *Grove* last night; then you turned up at the *Brown Derby* about one—"

She pushed back her chair, noisily. "I'm not going to stand this any longer—your jealous spying is driving me insane. I'm going to Mr. Spurck."

He said, "Nerts! You'll get damn little sympathy from Sol today, honey. He left it at home, wrapped in moth-balls—but you're getting ideas under that peroxide-treated mat of yours. I'm not checking on you because I'm still interested. I'm washed up, baby, washed up. You're not the first chiseling tramp that forgot my first name after I boosted them into lights, and I don't suppose that you'll be the last. I always was a sucker for a pretty face with nice hips for a background; but this is strictly business. *Dangerous Love* should be in the can by the last of the week. It won't be unless Price can shoot."

She said: "I've been here all morning, waiting." She said it in the tone of one who does not like to wait.

Lennox grinned. For the first time in days he was enjoying himself. "You're good, baby." His voice mocked her. "You're plenty good. You should be. I found you, trained you, but you aren't good enough to play love scenes by yourself. Wayborn isn't around. He's been snatched."

She made her eyes wide. "Snatched?" she said, slowly. "You mean—"

His voice rasped with impatience. "Quit acting. You read the papers. You know what snatched means. They want fifty grand and they won't get it."

She sank back into her chair as if her legs suddenly refused to support her. "This is terrible. When did it happen?"

His eyes were sardonic. "That's what I'm asking you, sweetheart. You were with him last night. He hasn't been seen this morning."

Her eyes blazed and she made two small white hands into little fists. "You're lousy, Bill Lennox. You can't tie me into this." Her voice threatened to break. "Ralph took me home at one-thirty. I haven't seen him since."

His eyes searched her face. "I guess you're in the clear, kid." He sounded almost regretful. "Wayborn's boy says that he came in around two, but that he went out again, without his car."

She gained assurance at his words. "But what will Spurck do? He'll have to pay the fifty grand."

"Will he? You don't know Sol, sweetheart."

"But he can't junk the picture. Why, he's spent more than that on publicity."

Lennox shrugged. "We'll reshoot it if Wayborn doesn't turn up." He was on his feet; the girl came out of her chair.

"But he can't leave Ralph to—to—die. It isn't human."

Lennox's voice grated. "Want to pay the fifty grand yourself?"

She stared at him. "I pay the fifty thousand? Don't be absurd."

"There's your answer," he told her. "That's the way Sol feels, and Wayborn isn't Sol's boy-friend."

She said, angrily: "You're getting nasty again; but Sol will have to pay. I'll go to the papers, to the police."

"Do that," he suggested, "and you and me will be going to one swell funeral; that is—if they find the body."

3

NANCY HOBBS WAS eating in Al Levy's when Lennox came through the door. She nodded to the empty chair, and he sank into it. "Hello, brat."

She smiled at him. "You look worried, Bill."

He ordered before he answered. "And you look swell. Why don't you go into pictures instead of writing about them?"

She said, "Because I know too much. You have to be dumb to get by, like Elva Meyer."

He scowled. "Seems I saw an interview in a fan magazine where you said that she was just a home girl—"

Nancy laughed, not nicely. "She is. Anybody's home girl. Look at the ones she's wrecked."

He said: "Lay off! I'm trying to think. I can't when you chatter."

She was silent with no sign of resentment. He broke a piece of bread savagely. "Wayborn's been snatched."

Her eyes were narrow. "What is it? A publicity gag?"

"I wish to —— it was. The dumb cluck is gone; someone wants fifty grand."

Her eyes were still suspicious. "I don't trust you, Bill; not since you pulled that burning-yacht stunt."

He didn't grin. "I'm out of that racket, sweetheart. I've got to find Wayborn. The picture's half in the can and the big slob looks like a million. Sol is howling his head off."

She said: "Why don't you chuck it Bill—pull loose? You used to be a decent pal; now you're nothing but a two-timing mugg.

Get loose. Shove off to New York. Write that book. You've been writing it in your mind for ten years."

His mouth twisted with a shade of bitterness. "What would I use for money, sweet?"

She stared at him. "You're getting three fifty—"

He spread his hands. "It goes—I'm living on week-after-next now. Sol lets me draw ahead."

"Sweet of him. He knows that he can hold you as long as you're broke. Listen, Bill. I've got a few dollars that aren't working their heads off. I'll stake you. Get the Chief tomorrow and get the hell out of this town."

For a moment he was silent, then he patted the back of her hand. "It won't work, babe. I gotta find Wayborn. I gotta get that damn' picture into the can; after that, we'll talk about it."

She sighed, knowing that she had lost. "This Wayborn thing? It's on the level?"

He said: "So help me."

She sat there, playing with her fork, thinking. Finally she looked up at him. "Better see Red Girkin."

He stared at her. "Who's Girkin? What is this?"

She said, in a tired voice: "I'm helping, pal. Helping as I always do. Go on. See Girkin. He's got an apartment on Van Ness off Melrose." She gave him the number.

He said, roughly: "What do you know, babe?"

She shook her head. "Just a hunch. Go see him. Stall." She gathered her bag and gloves and rose. "You can pay my check, that is, if you have enough."

He said, absently: "My credit's good, but, Nance, what's the—"

"For a smart guy, you ask plenty of questions. You wouldn't believe me if I told you."

She was gone, leaving him staring after her. Lennox said something under his breath, then went on with his dinner. Afterward he took a taxi.

The cab dropped him at the corner of Melrose and he walked to the apartment house. A row of brass-bound mail-boxes stared at him from the tiled lobby wall. One of them, number five, had the name W.C. Girkin. There was another name, but Lennox did not notice it. He pushed the bell viciously. The door at the bottom of the carpeted stairs buzzed as the catch was released from above. Lennox pulled it open and started up the steps. At their head a man in a light, close-fitting suit waited.

The man said: "What the hell?"

Lennox stared at him and said: "Hello, Charley."

Charley took a thin hand out of his right coat pocket and wrapped the fingers around those of Lennox. "I'll be a so-and-so. How are you, pally? How'd you know that I was in this burg?"

Lennox started to say that he hadn't known, then stopped. "I know things." He grinned. "What's the matter? Cops in the big town get rough?"

The other shrugged. "Pal of mine had a doll out here. I drifted out with him. Jeeze. What a country!"

Lennox said: "Some of us like it. You ought to have blown in a year sooner. Could have used you in a gangster picture."

Charley said, "Me?" and made his eyes very wide. "You've got me wrong, pally. I'm just a businessman with ideas. But come on. Red will think they've put the finger on me." He turned and led the way towards the door of number five. The door was closed and he knocked, three knocks all together, another after a slight pause. The door came open and Charley said: "Okey, just a pal. Meet Red Girkin. This is Bill Lennox."

The red-headed man said hello without evident pleasure. He was big, with heavy shoulders and a rather short neck. He sat down on a chair before the small built-in desk and went on with his game of solitaire. Once he swore to himself and turned over a pile of cards to reach an ace. Charley said: "What are you doing in Suckerville?"

Lennox laughed. "That's one for the book. You'd make a swell gag man."

The other nodded slowly. "There's money in these hills, Pal. Like to cut you in."

The red-headed man at the desk said: "Shut up." He made it sound vicious.

Lennox looked at him with narrow eyes, then back at Charley. "Your friend doesn't like me."

The thin man grinned. "Don't mind him; it's just the bad booze. Lemme have your number. I might put you on to something swell."

4

BILL LENNOX SAID to Spurck, "I haven't found the slob yet, but I know who's got him."

Spurck was excited. He came out of his chair and bounced around the corner of the big desk. "You know—you know, and you don't go to the police yet?"

"Listen, Sol. Why don't you try thinking once in a while before you open that mouth of yours? I know who's got Wayborn, but I don't know why and I don't know where he is."

"Who's got him?"

"That's one thing that it isn't wise for you to know. These boys are tough, Sol. It don't mean a thing to them that you're the biggest shot in the industry. They'd as soon rub you out as look at you. In fact, they'd a little rather. You never won any beauty contests, you know."

Spurck sat down at his desk again. "What do we do, then?"

"We pay fifty grand."

"You're crazy!"

"Sure, I got that way, working for you. We pay the fifty grand, finish the picture, and then I try to get it back. If I don't, we spread the story all over the front page and charge the fifty grand to publicity. What the hell else can we do?"

Spurck swore. He raved. He almost cried, but Lennox paid no attention. "Take it and like it," he said. "You've spent more than that on New York flops and kept nothing but the title. Have you heard from the gang?"

The little man pulled out his desk drawer and found an envelope which he handed to Lennox. "They want I should bring the money down to Redondo, in a suitcase. I should bring it myself, and I should not bring the cops; no one but me and my chauffeur."

Lennox said: "Okey. Go to the bank and get the dough in small bills as they say. Don't be a sap and mark them. Then take a ride to Redondo tonight."

Spurck rolled his eyes. "It ain't that I'm afraid, you understand; but I don't like it, I'm telling you."

Lennox grinned. "I'm your chauffeur, Sol. I wouldn't miss this party for a lot."

At seven o'clock Lennox swung the Lincoln town car out of the driveway of Spurck's Beverly Hills home. Dressed in brown livery borrowed from the chauffeur, he was hardly recognizable as he cut across towards Inglewood and picked up Redondo Boulevard.

In the back seat Spurck, with a black bag clutched between his fat knees, was nervously watching the passing traffic. Lennox stepped the car up to sixty and watched the back road in the rear-view mirror. At Rosecrans Avenue a Chevrolet coupé swung in behind them and followed them through Manhattan and Hermosa. Lennox slowed down to twenty and the coupé slowed down also. As they reached Redondo city limits, the Chevrolet speeded up and ran them to the curb. Two men were in the coupé, hats drawn low over their eyes. Lennox saw that the one beside the driver carried a riot gun across his knees.

For a minute, the road was empty, no traffic coming either way. The man with the riot gun said: "Keep your hands on that wheel, mugg."

Lennox obeyed, a thin smile twisting his lips for a moment. He knew that voice, knew it well. The man with the gun said to Spurck: "Toss the bag over, quick!"

With trembling fingers, Spurck obeyed. The driver of the coupé opened the bag, inspected the contents. "If these are marked, guy, it's curtains for you. Okey, Charley."

The man with the gun nodded. "Keep driving through Redondo and up through Palos Verdes till you come to where the road ends and another road goes off to the left and into Pedro. Drive out in the field at the end of the road. You'll find your ham along the top of the cliff, tied up. We were set to push him over if you didn't show up." The coupé's motor speeded up and they jerked away, swinging left at the next street.

Spurck moaned: "Fifty thousand!" He sounded out of breath.

Lennox put the Lincoln in gear. They went through Redondo, climbed the hill beyond and skirted the ocean until they came to the road's end. Five minutes later, with the aid of a flashlight from the tool-box, Lennox found Wayborn. The actor was tied securely, lying flat on his back so close to the cliff's edge that had he made any effort to free his bonds, he might have rolled off. Aside from chafed wrists and stiff ankles, he appeared none the worse for his experience, nor was he even thankful. "You might have gotten here sooner," he told them, in a peevish voice. "I assure you that it was far from comfortable lying here, bound hand and foot."

Spurck exploded. For five minutes he called the actor everything that he could think of. Wayborn listened silently, then climbed into the car. Lennox grinned to himself as he turned the Lincoln towards town.

5

STAN BRAUN, SPURCK'S nephew, walked back and forth across his uncle's office. He was slight, with black curly hair and long eyelashes. He looked like an actor and wasn't. He was production manager for the studio.

"It's strange," he said, "that Lennox advised you to pay that money. I wish that you'd have asked me about it." He pouted as a small boy pouts when his feelings have been hurt.

Spurck threw his hands wide. "Ask you? What good does asking you get me? Does it bring back Wayborn? Does it catch Price up with his schedule? It was you that wanted Wayborn —— that ham. It was you that held up the schedule three days, changing the story. Maybe you would have got him back and saved us fifty thousand—you—"

Braun said, harshly: "At least I'd have marked the money. You say Lennox wouldn't let you do that?"

Spurck's face became crafty. "Which shows what you know. Me, I got a list of them bills from the bank. Every number. A copy I have made which Lennox takes. If we had marked the bills, they might have killed Wayborn when the picture is only half shot, to say nothing of retakes. Such ideas you've got."

Braun's voice was stubborn. "You could have hired private detectives."

"A swell idea, when the barn door is closed and the horse is—"

"Anyhow," his nephew's voice rasped, "I've hired some. They're waiting outside now."

Abe Rollins and Dan Grogan came in. Grogan was big with a flat Irish face. Rollins was small, dark, with shifty eyes and too white teeth. He said: "Please tuh met yuh, Mr. Spurck. Braun's been telling us about your trouble. Don't worry, we'll turn these muggs up." He examined the two notes from the kidnapers. "I'd like to talk to Lennox," he said. Spurck hesitated, then pressed one of the buttons at the side of his desk.

Bill came through the door and nodded slightly to Braun. His blue eyes narrowed as they went over the two detectives; then he looked at Spurck. "What's eating you now, Sol?"

Spurck explained. As Lennox listened, his eyes got narrower. Then he looked at Rollins. "Okey. What do you want me to tell you?"

The man cleared his throat with importance. "Did you recognize either of the men in the Chevy?"

Lennox hesitated, then said: "No. Their faces were shadowed by their hats. I couldn't have recognized my grandmother."

"Yet you told Mr. Spurck that you knew who had Wayborn?"

Lennox said: "Yeah, I also told him that I'd try to get the fifty grand back, if he let me work it my way. I didn't figure that he'd run in a couple of lame brains to mess things up."

Rollins' face got red, Grogan shifted his feet. "Don't be too smart, fella," Rollins warned. "You're not in the clear on this thing, not by a damn' sight."

Lennox said: "Now isn't that just too swell? You'll be telling me next that I framed the whole play and got the fifty grand myself."

"That's not such a bad idea," Rollins snapped. "Maybe you did. As I remember it, you advised Mr. Spurck to pay the money."

"That's right, Bill, you did." Spurck sounded excited.

Lennox looked at him. "So you got me tagged as a kidnaper, too. Okey, Sol, get your own fifty grand back. I'm quitting, washed up." He swung towards the door. Rollins' voice stopped him.

"Not so fast, punk." The detective's hand was in his coat pocket, shoving the gun forward against the cloth.

Lennox shrugged. "You seem to be running the set." He turned back into the room.

Spurck said: "Just a few questions, Bill. Don't get sore."

Rollins said: "Isn't it true that you are always broke?"

"Ask Sol," Lennox advised. "He's my banker."

"And isn't it true that you told Mr. Spurck that you knew who had Wayborn?"

"What of it?"

"You may be asked to explain that statement at the D.A. office." Rollins' voice was threatening.

"Nerts!" Lennox found himself a cigarette and lit it.

"And isn't it also true that you offered to drive the car to Redondo? I should say that you insisted that you be allowed to drive; yet you made no effort to follow the kidnapers after the money had been passed?"

Lennox shrugged. "Go right ahead, bright boy. Wrap me up in cellophane and deliver me at San Quentin; but while you're talking, the muggs are spending Sol's dough." Spurck groaned, and Lennox laughed.

6

NANCY HOBBS SAID: "So you finally quit." She said it in the tone of one who hears about a miracle and does not believe.

Lennox nodded. "Can you feature that? After all I've put up with from that fat slob he accuses me of kidnaping. There's one of his funny-looking dicks outside this joint now. I'm getting important."

She said: "Now's your chance to get out of this town. No," as he started to speak. "I know you're broke, but I've still got a stake."

He was silent and she read refusal in his silence. "Too proud to borrow from a woman?" There was a jeer in her voice. "You've done worse."

He said: "It isn't that, Nance. You're a pal. I could borrow from you, but I can't scram with this hanging over my head. I'll get Sol's fifty grand back; then I'll take a powder; but I can't go until I do. I said that I'd find that dough and I will."

"Don't be a fool." Her voice was hoarse. "These boys play rough. If they get the idea that you're gumming their game, they'll plant you in a ditch."

He looked at her with narrow eyes. "What boys, Nance? You seem to know a lot about this play."

"I know plenty about this town that I don't print in fan magazines," she told him. "I get around."

"Words." His voice was harsh. "Why not pass out some names."

She said: "Girkin. I gave you that once."

"Where's he tie in? A cheap New York hood."

"He used to hang around the New York club where Elva Meyer undressed," she said, softly. "That wasn't her name then, but she's the same girl that you promoted into lights."

"Is this straight?"

"Did I ever give you a wrong steer, Bill?"

Lennox was silent for a moment; then he shrugged. "That's nothing to keep me awake nights. Girkin may be a big shot in New York, but he doesn't rate out here."

"Doesn't he? I saw him on the boulevard yesterday with French and they didn't act like strangers."

Lennox swore softly. "French of the *El Romano Club*, huh? Nice people."

The girl smiled with her mouth, but her eyes were serious. "Friend of yours, isn't he?"

Lennox shrugged absently. "So long." He rose. "I'll be seeing you in New York."

She rose also. "You're not losing me, Bill Lennox. I'm in this if you are." She followed him into the street. He grasped her thin wrist in strong fingers.

"Don't play the sap, sweetheart. It would be just that much tougher, having you along."

A cab cruised by. He let go of her wrist and jumped to the running-board. The next moment he was inside. "Go ahead fast," he told the startled driver. The cab lurched forward. Lennox peered through the back window. He saw Grogan cross the pavement and wave wildly to an approaching taxi. Lennox found a five in his pocket and passed it to the driver. "There's a guy following us. Lose him."

The driver grinned and turned sharply into Vine, right on Sunset, left at Highland, crashing a signal. Finally, at the corner of Arlington and Pico, he pulled to the curb. "Where to?"

Lennox said: "Take me to Melrose and Van Ness." The driver shrugged and turned towards Western.

Lennox got out at the corner and walked to the apartment house. He rang the bell of suite five, got no answer, tried nine and was answered by a buzz from the door. He jerked it open and started up the stairs. A woman's voice called: "What is it, please?"

Lennox said: "I pushed the wrong bell. Sorry." Her door slammed, and he paused before number five. He knocked without response, then tried the knob. The door was unlocked. He opened it cautiously and stepped into the small hall. For a moment he stood listening. There was no sound in the apartment. He closed the door softly and went along the hall to the living-room door. There he stopped and said something under his breath. The door was partly open. Through the crack he saw the figure of a man sprawled in the middle of the rug. His quick eyes went about the room; then he pushed the door wide and crossed to the body. The face, twisted with fear and pain, was that of Charley, and he was very dead.

7

BILL LENNOX FOUND nothing in the apartment that interested him. There were no papers in the desk, nothing, in fact, except a soiled deck of cards. He went into the bedroom and looked through the closets. Two suits hung there, flashy garments of extreme cut, nothing more. He walked back to the living-room and stopped just inside the door. There was a man looking at the body, a man with a gun in his hand, who said: "Now isn't this swell?" The man was Grogan.

Lennox didn't say anything and the private dick laughed.

"Imagine finding you here." His voice held a note of gloating self-satisfaction. His gun came up so that it bore on the second button of Lennox's vest. "Get the paws in the air, nice boy."

Lennox obeyed, and Grogan picked up the phone. "Gimme Hollywood station, and make it snappy." His eyes never left Lennox's face, the gun did not move. "That you, Bert? Grogan of Rollins and Grogan. Yeah, listen. Is Lew there? Swell. Let me talk to him, will yuh? Hello, Lew, Grogan. Listen. There's a stiff in an apartment on Van Ness." He gave the number. "It's close to Melrose, apartment five. Yeah, I got the mugg. He's standing against the wall with his hands in the air. Make it snappy." He hung up and grinned at Lennox. "Nice weather we're having."

Lennox didn't say anything. He stood there with his hands in the air. They stood there seven minutes, then a siren moaned below, heavy feet made noise on the stairs, and three men in plainclothes came in. The leader nodded to Grogan and looked at Lennox, then at the huddled body on the floor.

He said: "What's going on here? Who's the stiff?"

Grogan shrugged. "I don't know who he is. I was trailing this bird. He came up here and I sneaked up after him. When I got here, he was searching the joint."

The city detective's eyes went to Lennox. "Well, what's the story?" His voice sounded bored, uninterested.

Lennox shrugged. "When I got here, Charley was on the floor with a knife in his guts. That's all I know."

Grogan pursed his lips and made a funny sound of disbelief. The homicide man said: "Charley who?"

"Bartelli."

"Where's he from?"

"New York."

Two other men came through the apartment door. One said: "What's going on here, Lew?"

The other looked at Lennox and said: "Hello, Bill." Lennox recognized Alder, of the *Post*.

The city detective said: "So you know this guy?"

Alder's eyes widened. "Sure, everybody knows him. He's Bill Lennox of General-Consolidated. What's it all about, Lew?"

The city man looked hard at Grogan. "Thought you said that you were trailing this dude?"

Grogan shifted his weight from one foot to the other. "I was, Sol Spurck's orders."

Both reporters looked interested. Lennox snapped: "Be careful, you fool."

The city detective looked at him. "When I want to hear you talk, I'll ask you. All right, Grogan. Go ahead with the story and don't skip anything."

Grogan said: "Well, yuh see, it's this way. Ralph Wayborn was snatched—"

"Snatched?"

"Yeah." He went on and told the whole story. The reporters looked at each other. "So I was trailing Lennox to find where he had the dough planted, and I walked in on this."

The city detective said: "So we've got a kidnaping charge on you along with a murder rap."

Lennox said, in a tired voice: "That man's been dead hours. If you birds would think before you open your mouths, you'd know that. Grogan here is my alibi. He can swear that I wasn't in this place five minutes before he walked in." Lennox smiled sweetly at the now silent private detective.

8

NANCY HOBBS SAID: "So you wouldn't listen to me and you get yourself into a worse jam." They were seated before the Hollywood Station in her car. "Will you go to New York now?"

"Such ideas you have, brat. I'm going to get that fifty grand."

"You'll probably get a knife about where Charley got his."

"At least that would be a new experience. Who was it that said there is nothing new under the sun?"

She swore whole-heartedly and stepped on the starter. "Where do we go from here?"

"You don't go anywhere," he told her.

"I suppose I'm to hang around, ready to bail you out?" Her voice was sarcastic.

He grinned without mirth. "That's a thought," and unlatched the door at his side. "I'll be seeing you." He turned up the collar of his coat against the cold wind from the ocean and walked rapidly along. A block farther down he hailed a cab and climbed in.

"Know where the *El Romano Club* is?" The man didn't and Lennox gave him the address. Fog was beginning to roll in from the southwest. The street lamps looked fuzzy and the auto lamps glowed with funny rings. Lennox lit a cigarette, snuggled his chin deeper into his coat collar, and stared at nothing.

The *El Romano Club* was located on the top of a storage building. The attendant looked at Lennox, nodded and motioned him to the elevator. They shot skyward, stepped out into a hallway with blank concrete walls. There were doors off this hall. Lennox knew that some of them opened into storage rooms. The door at the end seemed to open automatically as he stepped before it. He said: "Hello, chiseler," to the man that stood aside for him to enter.

The man grinned in what he thought was a pleasant manner. "Evening, Mr. Lennox. How are you?"

Bill said: "Pretty lousy, Bert. Big crowd tonight?"

The man shrugged expressive shoulders. "Fair. What can you expect with the studios on half-pay?"

Lennox nodded and tossed his hat and coat to the hat-check girl, " 'lo, gorgeous."

She gave him a dimpled smile. "Hello, Bill. You look like the devil."

"Sure, that's because I've been working for him so long."

He went down the short, carpeted hall and into the main room. The room was large, high-ceilinged and comfortably filled. Three roulette wheels, set in line, occupied the center. In the far corner was a group of men and one woman about the crap table. Chuck-a-luck and the half-moon blackjack tables were ranged against the wall. Lennox crossed the room, conscious that people were turning to look at him. A blonde who a week ago would have rushed across the room to attract his attention presented a pair of too prominent shoulder blades for his inspection.

Lennox's lips thinned. "Just a friendly town," he thought. "When the knife falls, everyone helps you down into the gutter." He paused before the grilled window of the cashier's cage and, picking up a pad of blank checks, filled one in for five hundred.

The man behind the grille took it in his soft white fingers

and pretended to study it. Lennox watched him with narrowed eyes. "Don't you read English?"

The cashier said: "You're sure that this is good, Mr. Lennox?"

Lennox said: "Hell, no; it isn't good, and you know it, but you've cashed a hundred like it. I've never failed to pick them up, have I?"

The man shrugged. "Sorry. My orders are not to cash any more checks."

"You mean any more of mine?"

Again the shrug, as he pushed the check towards Lennox. Someone behind him snickered. A voice said: "Did you hear that Sol was getting himself a new office boy?" Several people laughed.

Lennox apparently had not heard. He said: "Is French here?"

The cashier shrugged for the third time. Lennox picked up the check, folded it carefully and slipped it into his pocket as he crossed one corner of the room, went around the end of the metal bar and through a curtained doorway. Before him was a wide hallway with a door at the end. A young man with too black hair was seated on a chair in the bare hall, reading a confession magazine. He dropped the magazine and came to his feet with cat-like grace. "You can't come in here, you."

Lennox said softly: "I'm coming in, lousy. Out of the way."

For the space of a half-minute neither moved. The black-haired one's hand was in his pocket. He said, slowly, distinctly: "You don't rate around here any more, Lennox. Take a tip and get out."

Bill's smile was very thin. "That's where you have your cues mixed, handsome. I still rate, plenty. I'm seeing French, and he's going to like seeing me."

The other's voice was confidential. "Why don't you get wise? When you're through in this town, you're through. Go out easy, pal. I wouldn't like to throw you out."

Lennox hesitated, shrugged, and half turned. The other relaxed slightly. Suddenly Lennox's right shoulder sagged, his left came up, and his right fist crossed to the gunman's jaw. The black-haired one went down with a look of surprise and pain. Lennox caught him, eased him to the floor, knelt on his chest, pulled the gun from the side pocket and got another from the shoulder-harness. There hadn't been much noise.

"Now I'll give you a tip," he said, in a low, grim tone. "This town isn't healthy for you. Remember that killing at San Clemente? The D.A.'s office might hear something about that if you aren't out of the village before morning."

He straightened his coat, pocketed the two guns, and went on down the hall to the door. Looking back, he saw the gunman get slowly to his feet. Lennox stuck a hand into his pocket. The man looked at him once, then disappeared into the gambling room.

There were voices in the room beyond the door. One that Lennox knew said: "But, French. How was I to know they had a list of the numbers?"

"You fool! That's what you should have found out. A hell of a help you are. Why didn't you tell me sooner?"

"Because I couldn't get away sooner. My uncle kept me at the studio until late. He's half-crazy."

"Yeah." French's voice had a biting quality. "Now get out of here and don't let anyone see you go. I'll call you when I want you."

A door closed somewhere within the room, and Lennox retreated down the passage towards the gambling room. His eyes were narrow, but there was a thin, half-mocking smile about his lips. The voice he had heard belonged to Stan Braun, Sol Spurck's nephew.

He came back along the passage, taking pains to walk heavily.

"Hello, handsome," he said to the empty hall. He didn't shout, but his voice was loud enough to carry to the room beyond. "The boss in? Yeah, well, don't move, rat. This thing in my hand isn't an ornament."

He covered the remaining distance to the door in quick strides. It wasn't locked and he pushed it inward, only far enough to slip through. A man was just stepping around the flat-topped desk, a man with a young, cold face, and gray hair. He stopped when he saw Bill, his face showing no emotion, his eyes very narrow.

"Hello, Lennox! Didn't Toni tell you that you weren't wanted?"

Lennox's smile was almost child-like. "He did mention something like that, but I didn't believe him."

The gambler took a step backwards and sat down in the desk chair. "Maybe you'll believe me?" The direct, prominent eyes measured Lennox carefully.

Bill walked slowly towards the desk. He took his hand from his coat pocket, calling attention to the fact by doing so very slowly. "The cashier turned down my check. I got the idea that it was your orders."

The man at the desk shifted his weight slightly. "We've had plenty of trouble with your paper, Bill. That bank account of yours is like a sieve, a rubber one."

Lennox said: "You never howled about my paper before. It's always been covered."

The other shrugged expressively. "Spurck always took care of that. I hear that he isn't taking care of it any longer."

"Meaning?"

"Just that. You're off the gold standard as far as Spurck is concerned. Sorry, Bill. If ten will help you?" He drew a large roll from his pocket and hunted through the big bills slowly, insultingly.

Lennox grinned. "Thanks, French, but I'll eat tomorrow." He turned towards the door, then said, across his shoulder: "Don't mind if I hang around a while? I always did like raids."

The man at the desk laughed. "So you'll have me raided. Your mind's getting twisted. You've got yourself mixed with someone important. There isn't a cop in town that would dare touch this joint."

"Like that?" Lennox's voice sounded interested.

"Like that," French told him, blandly.

9

LENNOX WENT BACK into the main room. Toni, the slick-haired gunman, was not in sight. Lennox stopped before the bar and spun a half dollar on the polished surface. The white-coated bartender shoved across a scotch and soda, with a twisted bit of lemon peel in the bottom. Lennox tasted his drink; then, hooking his elbows on the edge of the bar, he considered his next move. The blonde, who had given him her back when he first came in, swept past with a black-haired youth in tow. She turned her head.

"Why, it's Mr. Lennox. My dear, I didn't recognize you."

He said, sourly: "It's your age, sweetheart. Age dulls the eyes."

Her face reddened beneath the rouge and she moved hastily away. Someone tugged at Bill's arm. He turned to see Frank Howe. He'd gotten Howe a job in the publicity department six months before. Howe was a little drunk, but it affected neither his speech nor actions.

"Listen, Bill." His voice was a hoarse whisper. "I heard that lousy cashier hand you the runaround. This is my lucky night. Beat the wheel, I did." His hand disappeared into his pants pocket and came out with a crumpled stack of bills. "Money's no use to me. Never had any, don't know how to handle it— hey, bartender, a drink. I'm burning up."

Lennox said: "Thanks, kid." He was genuinely touched. Out of a hundred people in the room that he had helped at one time or another, Howe was the only one who seemed to remember. "No can do. Get you in trouble with Spurck."

Howe said: "To hell with Spurck. To hell with the whole lousy industry. Swell job. You take some tramp from behind a lunch counter and build her up until she's writing autographs instead of orders."

He shoved the bills into Lennox's hand and went away from the bar, his drink forgotten. Lennox watched him go. The bartender brought the glasses. Lennox drew a crumpled bill from the wad in his hand and started to hand it over. Then he stopped, stared for an instant at the number on the bill and put it into his pocket. He found some loose silver, paid for the drinks and drank both of them.

That done, he crossed the room and disappeared into the men's lounge. There was a shine stand in the wash-room. He crawled onto the stand and watched the kinky head bob as the boy applied the brush. After a moment, he drew a sheet of paper from his inside pocket and compared the numbers on the bills with those on his list. Five of them tallied. He put the five bills into his breast coat pocket, and shoved his white silk handkerchief on top of them, then thumbed through the rest of the roll.

As he counted them he whistled softly. There were four hundred dollars left. Certainly Howe had been lucky. Lennox knew him well enough to know that the ex-reporter seldom had four dollars at any one time. He paid the shine-boy and climbed from the stand. As he emerged into the main room a newspaperman with two girls walked past.

Lennox said: "Know Frank Howe?"

The man nodded.

"Didn't notice which table he was playing at a little while ago?"

The man nodded again. "Yeah, the center one. He was on thirteen and it came up. He let the money ride and she repeated."

Lennox said: "Thanks," and looked about.

A man came out of the passage which led to French's room. Play stopped at the first table while the man exchanged cases of money with the croupier. This was repeated at the other tables. Lennox frowned. He started forward, then stopped. For perhaps a minute, he stood, undecided, then moved towards the center table. He had the idea French was withdrawing the bills which bore numbers that were on Lennox's list.

As he stepped to the table, the rat-eyed croupier glanced at him sharply. Lennox apparently did not notice. He watched for several minutes, then bet twenty dollars on black. Red came up and he bet forty, only to be rewarded by double-O. He switched and played the middle group of numbers, won and let it ride. He won again, and shoved the whole pile onto black. Black appeared. He gathered up his winnings and moved towards the crap table.

The lone woman had the dice when he reached the table. He put twenty on the line and watched the green cubes dance across the cloth to turn up a five and six. He picked up his winnings and transferred them to no-pass. She threw snake-eyes.

French came through the curtained door at the end of the bar. He stood for a moment just inside the door, a striking figure, his shirtfront gleaming, his gray hair carefully brushed; then he walked across to the crap layout, just as Lennox picked up the dice.

"You're through, Bill."

Lennox turned slowly, deliberately to face him. The room was suddenly quiet. Everyone was watching, breathlessly. Lennox said: "Meaning?"

"Just that." French's voice held a flat quality which was almost metallic. "We don't want your play here. We don't even want you."

The dice rattled in Lennox's hand. He shoved the whole pile of currency onto the line and sent the green cubes dancing across the table with a twist of his wrist. They turned up six and one. Lennox's eyes met the croupier's. "Pay off, mister."

The man hesitated, his eyes went to French. The owner nodded imperceptibly and the man counted out bills beside those which Lennox had laid on the board. Bill gathered them up slowly, stripped two tens from the pile and tossed them to the croupier, then folded the rest and slipped them into his pocket.

"Okey, French. I thought that you were yellow." His voice carried across the silent room. "Now I know."

He walked calmly towards the door. No one said anything, no one moved. He got his hat from the check girl, slipped into his overcoat and tossed her a folded bill, then he rode down in the elevator. The elevator man said:

"Take it easy, Mr. Lennox." There was a gun in his hand.

Lennox grinned, "You, too, Mac?"

The man shrugged. "Orders." He stopped the car at the second floor and opened the door. Two men stepped in, one of them was Toni. He smiled when he saw Lennox. "If it isn't my little boy-friend." He ran quick hands over the other's coat and removed the guns. "Come on, mugg. This is where you get off."

Lennox obeyed. They went along a poorly lighted passage

and down a flight of stairs. Lennox said: "I never knew how French got rid of people he doesn't like."

Toni grinned. "There's lots of things you don't know. One of them is how to keep your mouth buttoned. In there." He pushed open a steel door and shoved Lennox into a curtained touring car. "Hey, Frank!" he called to the driver. Lennox turned his head a little and the gunman brought the barrel of his automatic crashing down on Lennox's skull. "That's for clipping me on the jaw," he muttered, as he shoved his way into the car.

10

CONSCIOUSNESS CAME BACK slowly. Lennox groaned, moved slightly, then lay still for several minutes, his eyes open, staring about the dark room. To the right, a window gave an oblong of lighter sky. Morning could not be far away. He raised a hand to the side of his aching head, felt the knob there, the hair, matted with dry blood. Sounds from another room reached him indistinctly. A cry, a thump as if a heavy object had been thrown against the wall, then the door opened. Instinctively, Lennox closed his eyes. Light showed against his lids.

French's voice said, from a distance. "Take the —— in there and let him think it over."

Heavy feet made noise in the room. There was a groan, a hoarse laugh, and the door slammed. The groans continued. Lennox opened his eyes. The room was again in darkness. Cautiously he swung his feet from the couch and sat for a moment, his head in his hands. Then he rose, swayed and looked about. There was a huddled shape in the chair beside the window. Lennox blinked at it and said, cautiously:

"Who're you?"

The groans ceased. The room was quiet except for the labored breathing from the chair. Lennox moved closer. His head was clearing.

"Come on!" His voice was louder than he intended. "Who *are* you?"

His hand fumbled in his pocket and found a box of matches.

He struck one with fingers that shook. The match flared, and Lennox stared at the battered features of Red Girkin. He said: "My ——!" and let the match drop to the floor. "They don't play nice, do they?"

Girkin swore heavily, tonelessly. "Let me alone."

Lennox's voice got sharp. "Your playmates will be back in a few minutes to give you another dose. What do you want?"

The gangster said: "Go to hell!" He said it indistinctly, as if his lip got in the way.

Lennox managed a laugh. "Boy, you love punishment. Come on! Who decorated Charley with the chiv?"

"Charley?" There was a new note in Girkin's voice. "What about Charley?"

"Only that he's dead."

"Say, who are you?"

"A pal of Charley's. Don't you remember? Bill Lennox. I was up at your place the other day."

The man in the chair said slowly: "Yeah, I remember, and Charley's dead. You sure?"

"I found him on the rug with the chiv in his side."

"That damned French."

"So it was French?"

"I'm not talking."

Lennox got mad. "Listen, sucker! Why don't you get next to yourself? Do you think that they've been pounding your pan because they love you? It's a wonder that you aren't in a ditch by now."

The man in the chair found a laugh somewhere and managed to turn it on. It was a poor effort. "They'll keep me until they find out what I did with the ten grand, the dirty —— They can beat me, but I don't talk."

Lennox tried a shot in the dark. "Still figuring that Meyer will help you?"

The gangster started to swear again. "That tramp! She got me into this; then she tied a can to me."

It seemed that the floodgates had opened. He talked and talked; finally he got to repeating himself. Lennox turned away and walked towards the window, his lips very thin, his eyes bright.

Suddenly the door opened, a light switch clicked, and Lennox swung about to see Toni. The gunman said, with surprise: "Look who's come to. Hey, chief! The boy scout's awake."

French's voice growled: "Bring him in."

Lennox took a quick step towards the window. Toni seized his shoulder, forcing him towards the door. With a shrug, Lennox relaxed. "Okey! You win."

Toni said: "We win every time, mugg. Start walking."

French sat in a leather chair. His coat was off and the gray hair mussed. There were pouches under his eyes and he looked very tired.

"Well, Bill—"

Lennox said: "Not so hot. Your boy-friend here swings a mean gun."

French said: "Little boys who play outside their own yards get hurt sometimes. Why the hell can't you keep your nose clean?"

Lennox shrugged. "Mind if I sit down?" He moved towards a chair.

The gambler's voice cracked. "Stand still."

Lennox let his eyes widen slowly. "What is this?"

French said: "It's your show-down." He came out of his chair, and they faced each other. Toni shifted his feet, grinning loosely. "What did you tell Frank Howe?"

Lennox hid his start of surprise. "What did I tell Howe? When?"

The gambler growled: "Don't stall, Lennox. You and Howe talked it over last night at the bar. You gave him something and he went away fast. The boys didn't tell me about it until later. They haven't found him yet, but they will. Come on! What did you tell him?"

Lennox grinned. He was beginning to understand why he was still alive. French thought that he had told Howe something at the club, something about the money, perhaps. Lennox said: "I gave him some dough to take home for me, some dough to put in a safe place."

"You—" The gambler took a step forward, his hands clenching at his sides. "Where is he?"

"That's a little mystery you can solve for yourself." Lennox grinned carelessly, much more carelessly than he felt. There was a desk in the corner of the room. He stepped sidewise towards it. French said:

"Stand still, you."

Lennox nodded. "Okey, French, I wouldn't try anything with you." He took another step. "I'm in a jam; I know it. I've been around long enough to know when my number is coming up. What's it worth to you for me to get Howe on the phone and call him off? Does it buy me a ticket to New York?"

French said: "Yes," quickly. He said it too quickly. Lennox knew that New York meant a wash in San Fernando Valley, but—

"Okey! Gimme the phone."

French's eyes searched his. "Don't try any funny stuff," he warned.

"Would I try any funny stuff when Toni has his gun on me?"

He crossed to the desk and, picking up the phone, called the first number that came into his head. As he waited, his hand toyed with a heavy glass inkwell hidden by his body from the other men. Toni still stood beside the door. He had his gun, but he let it hang carelessly at his side.

"That you, Howe?" Lennox demanded, as a sleepy voice asked what the hell he wanted. The voice protested that it wasn't Howe, that he had never heard of Howe, and that if he did now, it would be too soon. Lennox paid no attention.

"Listen, boy!" he said, making his voice sound serious. "That money I gave you, you know, those ———"

He picked up the inkwell and half turned so that he could see both French and Toni. "What'll I have him do with them?" he asked the gambler.

Toni's eyes switched from Lennox to his chief's face for an instant and in that instant, Lennox dropped the phone and threw the glass inkwell. He threw it underhanded, threw it with all the force that he had.

It caught the gunman just above the temple and he went over onto the rug without a sound. Lennox sprang at French. The gambler was tugging at his coat pocket. He had his gun half free as Lennox's fingers closed about his wrist. French tried to jerk free, couldn't and struck Lennox in the face with his free hand. Lennox grabbed his throat and tried to force the gambler's head back. French was too strong.

Slowly, ever so slowly, his hand came from the pocket, bringing his gun with it. Desperately, Lennox clung to the man. French hit him again, squarely on the nose. Tears started from Lennox's eyes; his fingers sank deeper into French's throat. The gambler swung about, carrying Lennox with him, and then across French's shoulder, Bill saw something which almost caused him to relax his grip.

The door into the other room had opened. Girkin, on hands and knees, was crawling towards the gun which lay on the carpet at Toni's side. Even as Lennox saw him, Girkin's hand reached the gun, closed over it, and he reeled to his feet, his eyes burning with hate, staring at French.

The gun came up slowly. Lennox cried out. He was never sure afterwards exactly what he said.

"French!" Girkin's voice cut across the room.

Lennox's fingers slipped from the gambler's throat. Girkin's gun flamed and French stiffened. Lennox threw himself sidewise, out of the line of fire. French paid no attention to him. It was as if the gambler had forgotten his existence. He turned slowly and, as he turned, Girkin fired again. French staggered, went to his knees.

His gun came up, and Lennox saw a hole suddenly appear between Girkin's eyes. The gunman pitched forward without a sound.

French stared at him, coughed twice, bent over on his hands, and then settled to the floor. For a minute there was silence in the room, then Lennox bent above Toni, and noted that he was still breathing, but unconscious.

Lennox rose, found a handkerchief, and dabbed at his bleeding nose; then he looked around the room. Behind the desk, a wall safe, its door half open, attracted him. He crossed to the safe and drew out bundles of currency. In all, there were thirty-five thousand dollars. He found a newspaper, wrapped up the money and moved towards the door. Everything was quiet. Evidently there was no one in the house. He wondered vaguely why the shots had not attracted attention.

Outside, it was broad daylight. The house, he saw, was set far up on one of the hillsides north of Beverly. He walked down the long, curving roadway without seeing anyone. He walked for a long time, his head aching dully, the sun growing warmer on his back. Finally he reached a drug-store and called a cab.

11

THE SHINE-BOY LOOKED up as Lennox came through the General gate.

"Morning, Mr. Lennox."

"Hello, Sam." He went on across the lot towards the executive offices. Steps sounded on the concrete behind him. Nancy Hobbs' voice called.

"Oh, Bill!"

He turned and managed a grin. "How 'r' you, Nance?"

She said: "I've been hunting for you since I heard you were out of here, looking every— Your face! What's the matter? What happened?"

"I've been playing house with the boys." He grinned. "Come in while I see Sol, if you want some fun. Then you can drive me to the station."

She followed him towards Spurck's office. "So you're really going to pull out?"

"You said it. Just as soon as I see Sol."

"I'll wait out here," she said, stopping in the reception room. "And, Bill, don't let him talk you into anything."

He stopped also, and patted her shoulder. "Don't worry, sweet, I'm washed up." He went through into Spurck's office. Spurck's secretary was beside the big desk taking dictation. Spurck came to his feet.

"Bill?"

"Mr. Lennox to you," Bill told him. "Get Elva Meyer and that precious nephew of yours in here. I want to see them."

Spurck said, "But—your nose!"

"Never mind my nose. Get them."

Spurck swung on the secretary. "What is it you're standing there for? Get them—can't you? Must I do everything about this plant yet?"

"Yes, Mr. Spurck." The secretary bobbed, and disappeared.

Spurck said: "Where have you been? All night, I don't sleep, wondering."

Lennox clipped: "Save it until Braun gets here." He helped himself to a cigarette from the box on Spurck's desk and stood, rolling it between his fingers so that the tobacco spilled out a little at each end. The door opened and Elva Meyer came in. "You wanted—" She stopped when she saw Lennox.

Bill said: "Sit down."

"I—er—"

His voice snapped: "Sit down!"

She sank into a chair. Spurck looked at her, then at Lennox, started to speak, then changed his mind. Again the door came open and Braun entered the room. His face changed when he saw Lennox, losing its color; his lips grew almost pallid. "Hello, Bill?" he managed.

Lennox nodded. He crossed to the desk and tore the news-paper wrapping from the package. Money spilled out upon the desk. Spurck made a glad sound, deep in his throat. Braun and the girl exchanged quick, startled glances.

Lennox said: "There's thirty-five grand there, Sol. You'll have to take the rest out of Braun's salary."

Spurck, who had been fingering the money, looked up quickly. Braun made a strangled noise. "You can't—"

Lennox said: "Shut up! Listen, Sol! This relative of yours has been bucking the wheel. He dropped plenty to French. French had his paper for fifty grand and was threatening to come to you. Someone got the bright idea of snatching Wayborn and soaking you fifty grand to get him back. They figured that you'd call Braun in and let him handle it, but you didn't. You showed the letter to me." He stopped and lit the cigarette.

"Meyer here has been playing around with Braun when people weren't watching. He told her about his jam and the Wayborn idea and she put him in touch with Girkin. Girkin and Charley did the dirty work—"

"It's a lie!" Braun was on his feet.

Lennox said, coldly: "See this nose?" He touched it with his finger. "The man that gave me that is dead. Shut up!"

Braun sank back in his chair with a sick look.

Lennox went on:

"Girkin thought that Meyer was still his moll. He didn't know that he was washed up there. When he found out, he held up ten grand. I don't know where it is. Neither did French. They grabbed Girkin and tried to make him talk. They searched his apartment and stuck a chiv into Charley's ribs when he walked in on them. That's about all."

Braun said: "You can't prove it, you can't prove it."

Lennox looked at him. "For the first time in your life, you're right. French and Girkin are dead, but I don't have to prove it. Sol knows."

Spurck was looking at his nephew. "Loafer!" he shouted. "Loafer! Get out!" He waved his arms wildly. Braun tried to say something. Spurck moved around the desk towards him. Braun went out fast.

Lennox said: "That will be about all, Sol. I'm washed up here.

It's New York and some rest for me."

Spurck said: "But listen once, will you? I—"

NANCY HOBBS HAD been waiting a long time. She looked at her watch again, just as the door opened and Lennox came out. She told him: "You'll have to hurry. There isn't much time."

He didn't meet her eyes. "I'm not going today, Nance."

"Bill!" She was facing him, her hands on his shoulders, forcing him to look at her. "You've let Spurck—"

He shrugged wearily. "Sol's got a new idea for a picture. All about an actress who has her leading man kidnaped to raise money for her boy-friend so that he won't have to go to the big-house. Sol says that it's the best idea in years. That it is 'superb, stupendous, colossal.' That's just the usual bunk talk, of course, but I think that I'll hang around and see how it turns out. A few weeks won't matter, and this picture may be a little different."

A Million-Dollar Tramp

*Bill Lennox looks for a star, but
not of the shooting variety*

1

BILL LENNOX, TROUBLE-SHOOTER for the General-Consolidated studio, sat in the dark projection room and watched the rushes of their latest picture. When the lights came up he dropped his cigarette to the floor, stepped on it, and yawned.

Sol Spurck, boss of the West Coast studio, looked around his large cigar at Lennox. "I tell yuh, Bill, we got something. If that ain't an extra special feature, I'll go back to the fur business yet, and from what I hear, furs ain't what they once was, you understand."

Lennox yawned again. "Why shouldn't it be a good picture? If that back-stage story has been made once, it's been made a hundred times. MacNutt did the script. Arthur the dialogue, and Hendrix the music. Buzzy staged the routine, and you spent enough to buy the Chicago Fair."

Spurck ignored this. "Jean Hammond will wow them," he predicted. "I tell you, Bill, that girl is hot."

"She's been hot too long," Lennox said, as he rose, "but there's a bet in the picture at that; the little girl with the big eyes that steps out of the chorus and sings a number in the last reel. Who is she?"

Spurck shrugged. "Am I the casting director?" he wanted to know. "Always you are chasing girls with no reputation yet, no box office draw."

Lennox did not argue. As he left the projection room, he passed Carlson, the director. Carlson was big with bushy hair and heavy eyebrows. He said, "How'd it look, Bill?"

"Lousy; but it's box office. The exhibitors will probably send you an orchid. By the way, who's the lassie with the big eyes and the educated puppies that sang the number in the last reel?"

Carlson hesitated, then shrugged. "Just an extra. Billy Walters was slated for that, but her tonsils got tangled up with a knife and this kid begged me so that I gave her a chance. Not so hot, huh?"

Lennox did not bother to answer. He went along the passage to his own office and shoved open the door, violently. A girl seated at his desk looked up with wide eyes. "My gawd—Bill! Save the hinges."

He said: "Hello, Nance! What brings a fan writer out this way?"

She shrugged. "I came out for a bit of news, and then stopped to say howdy. I was hoping for decent company, but your mood doesn't seem to be right. Has someone been spoiling your temper again?"

He lifted her bodily from the chair, sat her on the corner of the desk, and took the place vacated. "They make me mad," he complained. "Here is a kid with looks, a voice, and educated feet. Add a little sex, and it spells wow, and neither Sol nor that dumb kluck Carlson can see her."

Nancy Hobbs looked at him with narrowed eyes. "I know the signs," she said, half to herself. "You're about to pick out some unknown tramp and educate her for pictures. I thought that you'd sworn off that pipe dream. Haven't you been burned enough?"

"But this kid has class. I tell you, Nance, the trouble with pictures is—"

She said, wearily. "I've been writing for fan magazines for three years, and you try to tell me the trouble with pictures—"

He scowled at her. "You always were a smart brat. You should have been a gag man."

"You give me enough laughs without that," she said, sliding from the desk.

"But seriously now, Nance," he said, and his voice was enthusiastic, "this looks like real money, and I'll cut you in. I've some preliminary work to do first; get her lined up, put a stop on her thinking for herself and leave that to me. Then when I'm ready you can write a swell gag on her. How about it?"

Nancy Hobbs laughed, not nastily, but nicely, with a suggestion of sympathetic pity.

"Poor old Bill," she said. "When this bum throws you down, come around and cry on mama's shoulder."

He swore at her as he watched her go, waited until she closed the door then picked up the phone.

2

THE GIRL WITH the big eyes was named Irene Schultz. Bill shrugged at the name, but that was easy. Hollywood was no respecter of names. He hung up the phone and went out through the main gate on to Sunset. For a moment he hesitated, then turned and walked west. At the corner he flagged a cab and gave the driver the address. The Schultz girl, according to the casting bureau, lived on North Windsor.

Lennox paid off the taxi and looked around. The address he had was the second door in a bungalow court. He rang the bell and waited. He waited a long time, then pushed the bell again. Steps clicked across wood and the door opened two inches, held in place by the night chain.

Through the aperture Lennox saw her, and his eyes quickened. Without makeup, she was prettier than she had been in the film. There was a troubled something in the depths of her eyes that made his smile widen. That appealing look was worth a million to General, if Lennox knew his box office, and there was no one in the colony that knew it better.

He said: "I'm Bill Lennox, from General-Consolidated. I want to talk to you a moment, Miss Schultz."

Recognition came into her eyes and Bill saw the pulse in the white throat quicken. "Oh—Mr. Lennox! I didn't recognize you."

Bill said: "That's all right, kid. Open the door. I never was good at talking through cracks."

She hesitated, then slowly the door closed, he heard the chain unlatched and it opened again. The girl was in a wrinkled wash dress. Her brown hair was mussed, and she wore no stockings. "I wasn't expecting visitors," she told him, and he thought she said it kind of shyly.

Bill said: "Never mind that. I've seen them in worse and next to nothing. Grab that chair over there and listen; but first, how much common sense have you?"

She said, uncertainly: "I don't get you."

He shrugged. "How long you been out here?"

"Nine months. I was in vaudeville for two seasons."

"So that's where you learned to pick them up and lay them down. Listen, bum! You've got something, see? You didn't look so bad in that *Footlights* piece, but you're no world-beater. If you'll listen to papa; you can go over. If you go getting ideas of your own, you'll be just another pretty girl, dealing them off the arm in a dairy lunch. What about it?"

She said: "Please, could you come back sometime, or could I see you in your office?"

Quick suspicion leaped into his eyes. "Who's been talking to you, kid? Has some other studio—"

She said hurriedly: "It isn't that; it's something—something else. Honest, Mr. Lennox, I won't talk to anyone else about pictures till I see you, but you gotta go now. You gotta."

She was going to cry. Tears were not far behind those big eyes.

Bill said, suddenly: "What's the matter, punk? Hungry?" He found a crumpled bill in his vest, but she shook her head violently.

"I worked four days last week. I've got plenty, but please go."

He rose with a shrug. "You're the doctor, kid. Come to see me when you're ready to talk."

He turned towards the door. Halfway across the room, he stopped and swore softly. The curtain which divided the room they were in from another room had blown aside slightly, exposing a man's foot. Lennox stared at it with narrowed eyes, then he took two quick steps forward.

The girl got in his way, trying to hold him back. There was fear in her eyes, more than fear, terror. "Please, oh please!"

Lennox pushed past, reached the curtains and parted them. The man lay on his back, his arms outstretched, his face distorted. Lennox knew that he was dead before he saw the knife wound in the side, just beneath the heart. The body was rigid and it was evident that the man had been dead some time.

Lennox straightened and swung on the girl. She wasn't looking at him, but at the body. Her shoulders drooped, and her head hung forward helplessly. "I didn't kill him, so help me—I didn't!" she babbled.

Lennox said; his voice brittle: "Who is he?"

She shook her head. "I don't know. I don't—"

He seized her wrist, drawing her towards him. "Stop lying. Who is he?"

She said: "Bert Rose, but I didn't kill him. I don't know who did, I found him, there."

Lennox dropped her wrist and stepped back. Suddenly he was tired, very tired. A burning sensation of anger crept through him, anger against the girl, against fate. He said:

"Let's have the story; not that it matters. The thing for you to do is call the cops if you haven't already. With a face like yours, and those legs, you're a cinch with any jury."

Desperation stopped her sobs. She moved forward and caught his arm. "But I didn't kill Bert. You've got to help me—

why should I kill him?"

Lennox shrugged. "Lots of reasons, sweetheart; but then, women don't need reasons for killing. Sometimes they just do it."

"But I didn't, I tell you. He was here, dead when I came in. I wasn't home last night, I spent the night at a girl's apartment."

She was crying again, not loudly, but hopelessly. In spite of himself Lennox studied her. Either she was a swell actress or this was on the level. Either way, it didn't matter. Again anger burned through him. A million-dollar bet, shot to hell because this Rose had gotten himself killed in her apartment. Lennox stared down at the man's body. The dead face seemed to grin up at him sardonically, adding to his anger.

He found a cigarette, loose in his coat pocket, and lit it. For two minutes he smoked furiously. The girl had turned away. He watched her back with thoughtful eyes, noted the way the hair curled away from her neck, the carriage, the—"Why not?" He was talking to himself, not her, yet she turned.

The man on the floor meant nothing to him. The fact that he was dead meant less. All Lennox saw was the girl, her appeal, not to his emotions but to the box office. He may have weighed the consequences of his act, but it did not stop him. It was a gamble—everything was a gamble, for that matter, if you wanted to do anything big; but he thought he could make it a safe gamble. He crossed the room and grabbed up the phone, dialing a number.

"Let me talk to Jake."

The girl was watching him now; hope struggling with fear in her eyes. Lennox's voice was harsh. "Jake, this is Bill. Listen, grab a truck, better make it a van, and an empty piano box. Get over here as soon as you can," he gave the street and apartment number. "Yeah, that's right. No, come alone and for gawd's sake, don't give your right name when you rent the truck."

He hung up and swung to the girl. All the lethargy had gone from his movements.

She said, wide eyed: "So you're going to help; but is it safe, having someone else know?"

He grinned without mirth. "Jake's okey. He'd do a stretch, if I said the word. But get this now: I'm not doing it to help you, I'm doing it because when I start something, I finish it. I started out to make you a star and by Judas Priest I'll make you one if I have to conceal evidence in a dozen killings. Get your things together. As soon as Jake comes, we're leaving and you're not coming back—here. First we'll go down to the studio and get your name on a contract, then we'll find a place for you to stay, but you've got to understand this: From now on, you don't have a thought of your own, you don't open your mouth until I give the okey. Is that a promise?"

3

SOME HOURS LATER, Bill Lennox turned in at *Sardi's*, found a table, and ordered, then opened the evening paper and looked at it casually. A quarter column item in the lower right-hand corner caught his eye. "Gambler's body found in San Fernando Valley."

He read it through with pursed lips. A dead man, identified as Bert Rose, dealer on one of the Long Beach gambling barges, had been picked up that afternoon on a side road a mile and a half from Sennett City. Rose, who, the paper stated, had served two years in San Quentin for attempted robbery, had been stabbed. The police surgeon stated that the man had been killed sometime during the night, and it was thought that he was the victim of a gang killing.

Lennox folded his paper and tasted his soup. From the paper, he judged that Jake had done his work well. Jake wouldn't talk, that much Lennox knew. It seemed that Bert Rose was a closed incident.

A group of younger film players came in noisily and passed Lennox's table. He nodded to them half-consciously, comparing them with the girl whom he had put under contract that afternoon. They didn't compare, and he smiled to himself. Irene Schultz was a thing of the past. Lennox grinned as he thought of her new name, Marian Delaine. The name sounded phoney, but then, most Hollywood names sounded phoney and most of them were.

He'd gotten her an apartment in a quiet house, just off Franklyn, and she had orders not to communicate with any of her former friends. Lennox wasn't taking chances. He rose, and moved towards the door. On the Boulevard he stood for a moment, his hat shoved well back, a cigarette dangling from the corner of his mouth. Lights were on, but he stood in a shaded spot.

"Lavender Lane, hell!" he muttered, "Just Main Street with mascara and rouge."

He moved to the curb. A taxi swerved in close to him, its rear door open. From behind, a hand between Bill's shoulders pushed him forward and he went to his knees on the cab floor. The door slammed and they moved away from the curb, fast.

Bill said, "What the hell?" and struggled to the seat. A man at his side pressed a round, hard circle against his ribs.

"Take it easy, Lennox."

Lennox took it easy. The cab went right at Highland, swung along the curved street past the entrance to the Bowl, and on over Cahuenga Pass. Beyond Universal City, the cab turned right on Tuluca Road.

Lennox said: "I like the country, but I wasn't planning on a ride tonight." The man at his side chuckled without mirth. "Getting sensible, are you? Rather thought that you would."

Lennox squinted into the darkness. "Maybe if you'd tell me what it's all about I'd get a general idea. Surely no one supposes that Sol would pay money to get *me* back?"

The man at his side laughed. "I never met Spurck, but from what I've heard, he isn't good at paying out dough. All we want is a little information." The voice hardened. "What did you do with that Schultz broad?"

Lennox's eyes narrowed into the darkness. He wished that he could see the other's face, wished that he had some idea who it was, but all he knew was that the gun was pressing harder into his side.

"Never heard of her."

The gun pressed harder. The husky voice said: "Don't lie, Lennox. You're not in such a good spot yourself. We know that she worked in that *Footlights Revue* that General is releasing next month."

Lennox said: "For —— sake, you don't expect me to know every extra that works on our lot? Hell, I can't even remember my girl's birthday."

The man said, softly: "But you know Schultz. You were at her house this morning. A man came with a truck and an empty piano box. I wonder what he took away?"

"You seem to know everything."

"Almost everything—except where the dame is and what happened to the twenty grand that Bert Rose had. It might interest you to know that the money belonged to me."

Lennox hid his surprise. "If Rose had twenty grand, the cops must have got it. Do you think that I'd roll a stiff?"

"What you'd do doesn't interest me." The voice had an edge now. "I want to know where that dame is. My men trailed her to the General gate this afternoon. She didn't come out."

Lennox grinned in spite of the gun against his side. Marian Delaine had gone to her new home in a town car, borrowed from Spurck for the occasion. The shadow hadn't expected that, had not looked closely at the car, evidently.

"I'll tell you," he said, with apparent candor. "I did go to Schultz' place this morning, but I didn't get a slant at anyone's twenty grand, and if the girl isn't around, she must have blown town. You can rod me, of course, but I can't see the percentage."

The man said: "Hell!" under his breath.

Lennox sensed that he was hesitating. The car swayed left into a side road, graveled and rough. They bumped across a wash and ground to a sliding stop. Lennox peered through the gloom and saw a shack, a crazy, tumbled down affair. The gun prodded him harder.

"Get out!"

He got the door open and obeyed. The driver was on the ground to receive him. The driver said: "In there," and pushed him towards the broken wooden porch. Lennox swung for the man's chin and missed. Something hard crashed into the side of his head, and he went down.

CONSCIOUSNESS CAME BACK slowly. He lay where he was for several minutes without moving, aware of the open door through which light came faintly, of the stale smoke-laden air, and the mussed, dirty bed. Then he swung his feet to the floor and started gingerly towards the door.

There was a man in the other room, seated in a chair, tilted against the opposite wall. A kerosene lamp burned smokily upon a rickety table. Lennox recognized the man as the cab-driver, not from his face, but from the semi-uniform that he wore. The man held a newspaper in his hands, but he wasn't reading it! He was staring at the door. "Awake, huh?"

Lennox stepped through into the other room, feeling the side of his head tenderly. The driver grinned, showing stained teeth. "Little boys shouldn't go round, striking at people."

Lennox said: "How long do I stay here?"

"That depends on you," the driver told him, tossing the newspaper to the floor. "When you get ready to talk, then we'll think about that. The boss is coming back at noon. You should have a swell story by that time."

Lennox shrugged and sat down. There was a whiskey bottle and a soiled glass on the table beside the lamp. He picked up the bottle, ignoring the glass, and took a long drink. It was lousy, but it sent warm fingers through his chilled body.

The driver said: "No use shoving over the lamp. We're four miles from the nearest place, and I'd find you in the dark. I'm like a cat."

Lennox didn't say anything. He returned the bottle to the table, found a cigarette, and lit it. The driver seemed to want to talk. "This is a hell of a hole to be stuck in," he said. "I had a date tonight."

Lennox said: "I'm sobbing for you," and stared moodily at his cigarette.

The driver grinned. "Better save your sobs for yourself. The boss likes to hear them squawk. He'll probably heat your feet if you don't spring the dope on that broad. He'd as soon lose twenty grand as his right eye."

Lennox looked at the man and started to say something, then he stopped, for the door at the driver's side had moved ever so slightly. The taxi man took no notice. "I don't see why you couldn't have kept out of this," he complained. "We had things coming our way when you stuck your schnozzle into the play. What the hell do you want with that broad, anyway? A guy with your job should be able to pick and choose."

"That's what you think," Lennox said, watching the door from the corner of his eye. "Besides, I haven't said that I know where she is." He was talking to cover any sound from the door, saying things at random. The crack was wider now. Air came through it, blowing against the lamp. The taxi man turned in his chair. The door came wide. He said: "What the—" and grabbed for his pocket; then stopped. There was a man in the doorway, a man with a gun.

"Go easy." The voice sounded excited, not certain. The newcomer stepped into the room.

Lennox called: "Keep back. Don't get too close to him."

The other's eyes wavered, went towards Bill. Lennox swore. He saw the taxi man move sidewise in his chair, his hand clawing at his coat pocket. Even as he saw—he sprang forward. His fingers closed on the man's wrist, forcing him backward, holding the hand. The chair went over sidewise with a splintering crash, and they went to the floor, Lennox on top. They rolled over twice, legs thrashing, fighting for control of the gun.

Lennox knew that it was only a matter of time. The other was too strong. His free hand was at Lennox's throat, forcing Bill's head back, slowly backwards. Then the newcomer moved. He had stood as one paralyzed for a minute, gaping at the twisted bodies. Now he stepped in and slammed the barrel of his gun against the taxi-man's head.

The fingers at Lennox's throat relaxed suddenly, the man went back on to the floor. Lennox rolled free and came slowly to his feet. For a moment he shook his head to clear it, then he got the gun from the unconscious man's pocket and dropped it into his own. His rescuer said:

"Don't try anything, Lennox."

Bill swung about to see the gun level with his belt. He said: "You too? What is this? Open season on me?"

The other had black hair and eyes. He was very young and

not too sure of himself. He said: "I want to know where Irene is?"

Lennox swore softly. Ignoring the gun, he walked to the table and took another drink. It burned his throat but cleared his head; then he looked at the black-haired one. "What's the idea, kid? Where do you come into this?"

The man with the gun said, hoarsely: "Where's Irene? Don't try to stall me, Mister, I mean to find out."

"Try guessing." There was an edge of contempt in Lennox's voice. He stared at the unmoving figure on the floor, then muttered: "I suppose I've got a long walk ahead—" Suddenly an idea hit him. He looked at the black-haired boy. "Say, punk. How'd you happen to blow in here?"

He said: "I followed you, Lennox. I was parked in a car half a block from the restaurant when you came out. I followed you there, then I followed your cab. My car's down the road a ways."

Lennox laughed softly. "Maybe you'll tell me why you're trailing me."

The boy said, angrily: "I have told you. I saw Irene leave her house this morning and go with you to the studio. She didn't come out. I asked the gateman, but he wouldn't tell me anything. Then I went looking for you. I saw you on the Boulevard, followed you until you went into *Sardi's*; then I went back and got the car and parked it where I wouldn't miss you when you came out. Lucky thing for me that I did, or I'd have lost you when you got into that cab."

"Lucky thing for me," Lennox told him, without humor. "Let's get your car and get out of here before Oswald's friends come back." He looked at the unconscious man on the floor.

The boy threatened: "I'm going to drive you straight to the

police station unless you tell me where Irene is. Don't think that I don't know how your type turns girls' heads." He sounded very young. Lennox shrugged, his brows drawing together in a frown.

"Listen, you! You've got the wrong angle, but I can't have you gumming things up. Gimme your name and telephone number and I'll have Irene call you as soon as I can get in touch with her."

They eyed each other in silence for a moment. The boy uncertain, Lennox impatient. "What's the name?"

"Rose, Wilbur Rose. Irene knows my number, but I don't—"

Lennox stared at him with lidded eyes. "Rose? Any relation to Bert Rose?"

Surprise showed in the boy's face. "I've a brother named Bert."

"Have you seen tonight's papers?"

"No—What are you talking about?" Lennox said, soberly: "He's dead. They found him in a ditch this morning"

The black-haired one seemed stunned. "Why—I— saw him last night. He—he was all right then."

Lennox's voice sharpened with interest. "Where'd you see him? What time?"

Rose's eyes were suspicion laden. "What's it to you?"

Lennox shrugged. "Nothing, except the cops are trying to learn who put him on the spot. I thought you might know something."

Rose said, hoarsely: "If I did, I wouldn't tell you. Bert and I weren't very close. He's done things that weren't so nice, but I'd like to find out who killed him."

Lennox looked at the quiet taxi-driver, started to say something, shrugged, and changed his mind. After all, he couldn't accuse anyone without having questions asked, questions which he did not care to answer. "Let's go to town," he grunted.

4

IT WAS FIFTEEN after twelve when they reached the corner of Hollywood Boulevard and Highland. Lennox unlatched the door on his side and stepped to the pavement.

"Go on home, kid, and stick by the phone. I'll have Schultz call you in a couple of hours and tell you that she hasn't been manhandled, but I'm warning you; try to see the kid and you'll gum things up for her plenty."

He slammed the door on the threat which Rose uttered, and strode across the intersection with the light. On the other corner he took a cab and gave the driver an address. They rode five minutes, then the taxi pulled to the curb and Lennox got out. He paid the driver and watched him pull away, then turned around and looked at the building. A large sign across the front said, "Boyton Tile Company." Lennox grinned.

The windows were dark, as was the front door, but he paid no attention to that. He went around the corner, stepped between the building and a signboard, crossed a parking lot half-filled with cars, and knocked twice at the side door. The door opened, held in place by a short chain. The door closed, the chain rattled. Then it opened again and a black-browed, one-eyed man said: "Hello, Bill! Long time, no see."

Lennox grinned. "Hello, One-eye. How's things?"

"Not good, not bad." The one-eyed man shut the door and refastened the chain. Lennox watched him with amusement. "What's the big idea of all the caution? The cops aren't bothering with liquor now, and the Feds are too busy clearing their dockets to make more arrests."

The one-eyed man grinned. "Gotta give the customers some thrills." He winked his single optic. "If we didn't, they'd go down to the nearest barbecue joint and buy beer."

Lennox nodded and went on into a large room. A long bar extended the full length of the far wall, five bartenders working busily. The room was crowded with the after-theatre gathering. Lennox swept the place with his eyes, nodded to Ham Robbins and Duke Smith, and then went into a phone booth. He dropped a nickel and called the number of the girl's apartment house. "Miss Delaine, eight-o-two," he told the switchboard operator.

A sleepy voice said, uncertainly: "Who is it, please?"

"Lennox," Bill told her. "Listen, kid! I just met a friend of yours, Wilbur Rose. Know him?"

He heard her draw her breath sharply, then: "Well?" She tried to make her voice sound normal and failed.

"He's hot and bothered," Lennox told her. "Got the idea that I'm a wolf and that your name is Red Riding Hood. I told him that I'd have you call him up and assure him that my intentions are honorable."

She said, uncertainly: "All right. Should I call him now?"

Lennox's tone sharpened. "Listen, kid! How well do you know this Rose?"

"Not so well."

"Stop lying." His voice was cold. "He knows you plenty."

"Well," her voice was stubborn, resentful, "we grew up in the same town."

Lennox swore under his breath. "What's the punk doing out here?"

"He isn't a punk."

"I didn't ask you what he was. What's he doing out here?"

"I don't know. Nothing, I guess. He's—he's just out here on a trip, or something."

"Or something—" Lennox repeated, in disgust. "So you lied to me this morning when you said that you didn't know Bert Rose very well."

"But I don't." Her voice had taken on a note of fear. "He was older. I don't know how he came to be—"

Lennox's voice rasped: "Shut up, you little fool! Someone may be listening. Now you get this: Call up Wilbur; tell him that you are okey. Tell him anything you like, but don't tell him where you are, what you're doing, or anything about his brother. Get me?"

She said: "Yes," in a very weak voice.

"And further. Get him to scram, to go back home, anywhere. We can't have him hanging about, recognizing Marion Delaine as Irene Schultz. Use your head, kid. You'll never get another break like this."

He hung up, giving her no time to answer, and walked towards the bar.

Duke Smith turned around and waved a glass at him. Lennox said: "What's new in the Fourth Estate?"

Duke shrugged, "I wouldn't know," he countered. "I'm only a leg-man."

Lennox said, idly: "Anything new on that killing up in the valley, Ross or something like that?"

"Bert Rose, you mean?"

"Yeah, that's the one. Did the cops get anything?"

Smith shrugged. "Not much, and Rose wasn't much loss, but there are funny rumors going around town."

"What kind of rumors?"

"Well—I don't know. Rose wasn't such a nice boy. He'd done a stretch, and then he'd been working on one of the gambling barges at Long Beach. I heard downtown tonight there was some movie extra in the picture, but we haven't got hold of her yet."

Lennox swore to himself. "Know which boat Rose was working on?"

Smith raised an eyebrow. "You're curious as the devil."

Lennox shrugged. "Thought maybe there might be a story in it. Which barge was he on?"

"The *Palace*. Speed boats leave from Seventh Street. I think I'll go with you."

Lennox stared at him; then he laughed suddenly and looked at his watch. "Almost one. We can drive it in an hour. Is that too late?"

The newspaper man said: "It's never too late until it's morning. My car's outside."

They went out and crawled into a Chevy coupé. Smith said, as he stepped on the starter: "Wouldn't want to tell me what it's all about?"

Lennox shrugged. "You wouldn't believe me if I told you."

He lit a cigarette and watched the speedometer climb past sixty. A cop swung in beside them and Smith brought the coupé to the side of the road. He listened in a bored fashion to the other's angry questions, found his press card, and passed it over. The cop looked at it, then went on with his lecture. "You newspaper guys think you own the world."

He passed back the card and climbed on to his machine. "The next time, I take you in," and he whirled away.

Lennox grunted: "The power of the press! Come on, fella. We're wasting time."

The coupé went on, cutting through the darkness. They came into Pedro, went through Wilmington, and along Harbor Boulevard. Ten minutes later they were cutting across the dark water in a speedboat.

Somewhere, muffled by intervening doors or distance, an orchestra still played as Lennox went up the swaying ladder to the deck above. Smith joined him a moment later, and they stood looking about.

"Nice layout," Bill commented.

The newspaper man said: "Swell. There's Harry Rossi. He runs the joint."

Lennox looked and saw a short, heavy-featured man standing beneath one of the deck lamps. He was talking to two women in white and they were laughing at something that the gambler had said. Smith grinned.

"Harry's quite a ladies' man. That's Madge Edmonds and Sally Barbeur. Wonder what they're doing this far south. Santa Barbara is their hangout."

As he spoke, two men in evening clothes appeared, their white shirts gleaming beneath the light. They nodded to Rossi and moved towards Lennox. Bill stepped back and waited while they descended into the bobbing speedboat. Rossi turned towards them, and Smith said: "Want you to meet a friend of mine, Harry. Bill Lennox, of General-Consolidated."

Bill felt the man's fingers close about his hand, heard Rossi say: "This is an honor, Mr. Lennox," in a voice that he knew. It was the voice that he had heard earlier in the cab. There was no surprise on Rossi's face, nothing. His heavy lips smiled faintly as he took Bill's arm, led him towards the companionway. "We've got a nice play here, Mr. Lennox. I've been hoping for some time that you'd pay us a visit."

Bill, conscious of Smith at his heels, smiled also. "That's swell, Rossi. I suppose that dealer of yours getting killed last night will hurt business. That kind of publicity won't help you."

The gambler smiled faintly. "I think you're wrong there, Lennox. Of course, we don't seek that type of publicity, but since it came—well, we have a bigger crowd here tonight than we've had in months."

He led the way into a crowded room. Three roulette wheels occupied the middle, while two crap layouts and blackjack tables were ranged about the sides. At one end, a spacious bar served beer.

Rossi said: "We don't serve anything but beer at the bar, but if you care to come into my private office—"

Smith said: "We sure do. I haven't had a good drink since the last time I was on this barge."

Rossi's white teeth flashed in his dark face. "Thanks, my friend. You are very kind."

He led the way down a short companionway and opened a white door, stepping aside for them to enter. The office was heavy with massive furniture. Smith and Lennox found seats on a cushioned locker at the right. Rossi opened a small barette and produced bottles and glasses. He looked inquiringly at his visitors.

Smith said: "The scotch is too good to spoil it with outside ingredients. I'll take mine straight, thanks."

Rossi looked inquiringly at Lennox, and Bill nodded. The gambler filled the short glasses, poured some water into tall tumblers, and carried the small metal tray to the locker; then he shot some soda into his own glass and raised it. "You'll pardon me, but I never drink during working hours."

Smith tossed off his drink. "With whiskey like that, I'd pardon you anything—even murder."

The full lids drooped slightly above the gambler's black eyes. His glance went to Lennox's face, but Bill gave no sign that he had heard. He raised his glass and drank it slowly. "You're spoiled," he told the reporter. "That's no way to drink good liquor."

The tension in the room lessened. Rossi said: "How's the picture business, Mr. Lennox? I hear that General has a good musical ready to release?"

Bill nodded. "As good as most," he said, indifferently. "Think I'll take a shot at your wheels."

Rossi smiled. "We expect that, of course. We hardly run this as a sightseeing station; yet I do not want you to feel obligated simply because I have given you a drink."

"And what a drink!" Smith's voice was hopeful. "Think I'll hang around down here a while if you don't mind, Harry. I want some dope on that dealer of yours that they found in the valley."

LENNOX WENT UP the passage to the gambling-room. He regretted having brought Smith. He wanted to see Rossi, to see him alone. For perhaps five minutes he watched one of the wheels, then put a dollar on seventeen and lost. Then Smith came up to him, stopped at his side and stared at the board. "Any luck?"

Lennox shook his head. "None. Think I'll try black-jack." He moved away and saw the reporter slide into the place which he had vacated. He paused at a black-jack table and lost five dollars, then moved around the room, keeping an eye on Smith. The reporter was winning and seemed engrossed in the game. Rossi was nowhere in sight.

Lennox went along the companionway and knocked at the office door. The gambler's voice bade him enter, and he pushed open the door. Rossi looked up from the desk, a faint trace of smile curving the thick lips. "Thought you'd be down."

Lennox closed the door and hunted for a cigarette. His hand touched the cold metal of the gun which he had taken from the taxi-driver. It gave him assurance. He found a cigarette and held his lighter to the tip, then put the lighter back into his pocket and looked at the gambler.

"Let's put our cards on the table, Rossi."

The other's only answer was a shrug and a gesture of his hands. Lennox took it for acceptance. "I know that you killed Rose," he stated, flatly. "Oh, I can't prove it," as the man at the desk started to speak, "but I can have some unpleasant questions asked."

Rossi said: "Has it occurred to you that you might have to answer some yourself? Some mouthpiece once told me that it wasn't strictly according to law to move a stiff before the cops got to look at it."

Lennox smiled thinly. "Okey, Rossi. You can't prove that I did that, either. You know it, but you can't prove it. So far we're even. Let's stay that way. I'll forget that I knew anything about a killing and you'll forget that a certain girl used to live at a certain number."

The man at the desk said: "But my twenty grand?"

Lennox shrugged. "I don't know anything about that dough and neither does the broad."

The gambler's eyes were very narrow. "How do you know that she doesn't?"

"Because she wasn't there when Rose was knifed. She spent the night with another girl. I checked that, and you can be sure that I know. She didn't find the body until a few minutes before I got there. Your men were watching the house. They can tell you that she hadn't been there long."

"What does that prove?" Lennox thought that Rossi sounded uncertain, but he couldn't be sure.

"It proves plenty," Lennox said, with disgust. "Didn't your hoods frisk Rose after they knifed him?"

"I haven't admitted," Rossi began, but Lennox cut him short.

"Leave that. You know that they did, that they didn't find the dough. How would the girl find it?"

Rossi said, stubbornly: "Maybe he hid it somewhere, somewhere where she would look."

"You're screwy. She went out with me. She didn't have it with her and she hasn't been back to that dump since. What's more, she's not going back. Get this, wop, and get it straight. Lay off that girl. Search the house all you please, but stay clear of her. I've written out a statement of what I know and planted it with a friend. If anything happens to me, you'll burn." He pushed out the cigarette in the metal ash-tray and, stepping forward, leaned across the desk. "I'm not trying to act tough, but better guys than you have tried to buck me in this town and they aren't here any more. Think it over."

Rossi said, slowly: "If I lay off the girl, what?"

Lennox shrugged. "I'm not a cop. As I see it, Rose wasn't such a swell citizen that I should waste tears on him. I never saw him alive and I'm not bowed down by grief, but so help me, if so much as a whisper about the Schultz broad gets out, you're going to move and move fast."

Hate looked at him from the dark eyes; hate, and a trace of fear. Rossi started to speak, stopped, took a long breath, then said: "It's a deal." He extended his long-fingered hand. Lennox ignored it, and looked at the gambler's face, which was darkening with gathered blood.

"I don't like you, Rossi. I'm not shaking hands."

The man at the desk managed a laugh, a choking sound, as he rose. "Okey, Lennox, if that's the way you want it."

"That's exactly—"

A white light winked on the corner of Rossi's desk. The gambler's oath was a startled sound. The blood drained from his face, leaving the skin sallow, almost yellow looking. Heavy feet came along the companionway. Lennox swung about as the door opened and men seemed to pour into the room. He saw Smith in the background, a sobered, curious Smith. The man in the lead swept Lennox with his eyes, then looked at Rossi.

"Hello, Harry!"

Rossi said, tonelessly: "Hello, Hampton. What's the idea?"

Hampton said: "This is a pinch; a rap that you won't beat, Harry. It's murder."

The man behind the desk did not move. He said, tonelessly: "You're screwy. Besides, you haven't any jurisdiction here."

The man laughed. "We thought of that, too. We've got a Federal man with us and a deputy from Orange. One of us has jurisdiction. We don't care which so long as we take you in."

Rossi smiled. "Who am I supposed to have killed?"

"Rose, Bert Rose. Get your hands out." He shook the cuffs so that they rattled.

Rossi's eyes flamed. "You rat," he stared across at Lennox. "You doublecrossing rat. So you'd make a deal with me you—"

Lennox said: "Shut up, you fool! I don't know what this is all about."

Hampton snapped the cuffs on Rossi and looked at Lennox. "Guess I'll take you along, too."

Lennox said: "Try it."

A man came up behind him and ran quick hands over his coat. "He's got a rod, Chief."

"And a permit." Bill's voice was unhurried, serene, but his mind was busy and he cursed silently. This was a tough break, a break he hadn't expected. Smith was at his elbow, grinning at the deputy from the sheriff's office.

"This is Bill Lennox of General films," he explained. "He isn't going to run anywhere."

The deputy looked at Lennox uncertainly, then at Rossi. "You'll have to come over to the sub-station and do some explaining," he said, finally.

Bill nodded, a trifle wearily. "Mind telling me how you happened to pick up Rossi?"

The man shrugged. "Sheriff's office got a call from someone who said that he was Rose's brother."

"Rose's brother?"

"Yeah. He told us to go out into the valley and pick up a taxi-driver; said that the driver knew something about his brother's death. We sent out the flash to the radio cars and they picked this guy up in a shack out there. Someone had bumped his head plenty, and he wasn't feeling so hot. The boys got him to talk and he named Rossi. That's all I know."

Bill said: "Thanks," and swore to himself.

If the cabman had talked, the chances were that he had spilled the whole works. Bill felt very tired, but he wasn't beaten yet. If he could get to the man in time— He stepped aside as they led Rossi past. The gambler's black eyes glowed like coals as he looked at Lennox. Bill thought for a moment that he was going to speak, then he went on.

They walked up the short companionway and through the gambling room. The place was already deserted. Lennox smiled. A lot of people in that crowd didn't want publicity. They were there with wives, but not with their own. The attendants were grouped forward on the deck, held back by two officers. Rossi's eyes swept the crowd; then, with a slight shrug, he moved towards the ladder.

The police boat was alongside the float, but at the far end was one of the water-taxis. Rossi went down first, using his manacled hands to steady himself. Suddenly, as if from a pre-arranged signal, the engine of the water-taxi raced. Rossi leaped across the float and jumped into the boat. It was already in motion, cutting away from the barge in a wide circle. Guns spat from the rail of the gambling ship. The police boat went forward and Lennox, standing beside Smith, saw Rossi stagger suddenly, then plunge headlong from the watertaxi into the dark sea.

5

SMITH SAID: "COME on, Bill. Gimme the story."

Lennox looked at him. "Honest, fella, I would if there was any to give. Rossi's dead. He was dead when he hit the water. The cops are going to ask questions that I can't answer, and I've got to make a phone call. It's up to you to help."

The reporter grinned. "Just a pal. You drag me all over Southern California and then don't spill the dope. Supposing I print that Bill Lennox was mixed up with Rossi in the killing. What do you think that would get me?"

"A swell libel suit," Lennox told him. "You know these guys. Get them to let me ride into town with you. I'll show up at the sheriff's office and spin them a yarn when we get in."

Smith said: "Do I get the real story?"

"Listen," Lennox's voice was harsh. "If you hadn't been with me, you'd have missed all this. See your friend the deputy; then call your paper."

Smith nodded. "Okey. But when I get washed up with the City Editor, you give me a job in the General publicity department."

Lennox said: "I'll give you the whole damn' studio. Come on! Snap it up!"

Ten minutes later he was in a telephone booth of an all-night drug-store. He called Sam Marx and waited impatiently until the lawyer answered.

Marx said: "This is a hell of an hour to get a man out of bed. What kind of jam are you in now?"

Lennox grinned without mirth. "Listen, Shyster! The sheriff's office is holding a cab-driver named Krouch, Ed Krouch. He's being held as a material witness on that Rose killing."

Marx's voice sharpened. "What about it?"

"He accused Harry Rossi, of the *Palace* gambling ship, of the killing. Rossi is dead, killed half an hour ago, trying to escape. Now get this: I want you to get to Krouch, find out how much he's talked and get him to keep quiet. Get him out on bail as soon as you can. Then tell him to jump it. With Rossi dead, the cops aren't going to care much."

Marx said: "What's the idea? Tell me what's up?"

"No time. Every minute counts. Krouch might spill something that would gum the works. You get him out and I'll stand the bail."

"Just a big-hearted boy." The lawyer's voice was mocking.

"Sure, but for —— sake, get the lead out of your pants and move. I'm in Long Beach now. As soon as I get back to town I'll go to your place and wait until you show up."

He replaced the receiver and left the booth. Smith was still talking on another phone. Lennox bought a coke and sat down at the fountain. The reporter came out of his booth and sat down at his side. He eyed the coke with disgust and ordered beer.

"What did Marx have to say?"

Lennox swore. "I've known nosey guys that got their schnozzles busted."

"You shouldn't talk so loud," the reporter told him. "Those booth walls aren't too thick."

He finished his beer and they went out to the car. The street looked pale, dirty in the uncertain light. In the east, a streak of crimson gave promise of a hot day. Lennox yawned as he climbed into the car.

"Sheriff's station, James."

Smith grunted and put the Chevy into gear. They went out Atlantic and swung towards town.

After his session with the sheriff they started on again.

At the corner of Broadway and Ninth Lennox got out of the coupé. There was a red-top in the cab rack. Lennox shook the driver awake and gave him Marx's address, then he climbed in. He was very tired, his head felt woozy and his mouth tasted of too many cigarettes. Half an hour later they pulled up before the lawyer's house. Lennox paid the man and, going up the walk, rang the bell.

Marx himself answered. He shut the door and led the way into his study. "You need sleep."

Lennox grinned wryly. "You're telling me. I thought I'd never get away from the sheriff's office. Did you see Krouch?"

"Yeah. He's over at Lincoln Heights. They haven't booked him yet, so I can't bail him out until after sunrise court. I've got a man over there, waiting. It'll be a couple of hours before they get here. Do you want to wait?"

"If you've got a spare bed."

For answer Marx led him upstairs and into a room with yellow bed covers. Lennox looked at the covers, grinned. "Shame to sleep in those alone." Marx went out without answering and, three minutes later, Lennox was asleep.

He was awakened by Marx's Chinese boy, who indicated a dressing-gown. "Boss, he say, you come."

Lennox shrugged himself awake, put on the gown, and followed the boy down the stairs. Three men were in Marx's study. Krouch, standing beside the window, looked around as Lennox entered. The taxi-man was hollow-eyed; his clothes were mussed, and a thick, dirty stubble covered his chin. He looked nervous, uncertain. Marx was talking to a big man who, Lennox judged, was the one that had attended to Krouch's bail.

The taxi-man said: "Marx told me you want to see me."

Lennox said: "Yeah! How much did you spill to the cops last night?"

The man said: "I told them that Harry Rossi did it. I hear he's dead."

Lennox said: "He is."

The man seemed relieved by the words. "I wouldn't have spilled that much, but they were sweating me."

"You didn't—say anything about where the body was—I mean at first?"

Krouch shook his head. "Why should I?"

Lennox's relief did not show in his face. He said: "How well do you like this town?"

The man shrugged. "I've seen ones that I liked as well."

"Then my advice is for you to scram."

"You mean for me to jump bail?"

"That shouldn't worry you. It isn't your dough."

Krouch's eyes got crafty. "Want tuh get rid of me pretty bad, don't you? Well, Mister, I'm not in any hurry. The cops haven't got a thing on me. I'll hang around until you make it worth my while. I didn't move any bodies—"

Lennox rasped: "Ever hear of a kidnaping rap? Think I've forgotten that you dragged me out into the valley? I figured you for sense." He swung about and looked at Marx. "You guys heard him try to blackmail me?"

Marx nodded, as did the big man at his side. Krouch looked at them uncertainly. "Trying to frame me, huh?"

Lennox said: "You framed yourself. Take him back and throw him in the can, Sam. I'm washed up. Then see the D.A. and tell him about the snatching and the little blackmail."

Krouch said, hurriedly: "I didn't mean anything. Honest, I didn't mean a thing. I'll scram, but I ain't got a dime. Gimme enough to eat on till I get located."

Marx looked at Lennox, who apparently had not heard. "Okey!" he said, suddenly. "Get a confession signed by him, Sam; then get him out of town. If he ever lands in this State again, give the confession to the D.A."

"Do I get dough to eat on?" Krouch's voice was a whine.

"Give him fifty," Lennox said. "I'll settle with you when I settle the bail. Now get him out of here."

He watched while the big man led the taxi-man into the next room, followed by Marx. In fifteen minutes, the lawyer returned to find Lennox asleep in the chair. He was about to tiptoe out when Bill suddenly opened his eyes. "Is Krouch gone?"

Marx nodded. "My man's riding him as far as San Berdoo. He'll get a rattler there."

Lennox yawned, stretched, and asked what time it was.

"Almost nine," Marx told him. "You want to sleep some more?"

Bill shook his head and reached for the phone. He called Nancy Hobbs' number and after a little wait, said:

"Hello, Nance! How's the brat this morning? Listen! Wantta do something for me? You don't?" He grinned. "Well do it anyway. I want you to interview a newcomer, and, boy! is she a comer?… Now, listen! She has a bit in *The Footlights Revue*—name, Marian Delaine. Yeah. I know you never heard of her, but I'll have that name in lights yet. Listen, kid! You're going up there with me, then you're going to get your boss to run it. I'll get you some pictures this afternoon. Where are you?… Swell! I'll pick you up there in three-quarters of an hour."

He hung up and looked at Marx. "Let me borrow your razor and a shirt," he said; "then call me a cab."

6

A COLD SHOWER drove the sleep from Lennox's eyes. As he rode across town in the cab, his active mind was already framing the interview which Marian Delaine was to give Nancy Hobbs. "A convent?" He considered the idea and discarded it as being trite, overdone. "I've got it," he said, so loudly that the driver turned to look at him. "She traveled with her father. He was—a—a mining engineer. Swell! He was killed—in China, by bandits. Yeah, that ought to go."

The cab swung towards the curb before Nancy's house, and he saw her smiling at him from the sidewalk.

"You look swell," he told her, as the cab started again.

"And you look like the devil," she said, frankly. "Give me the low-down, Bill. Tell me who this Delaine really is."

He grinned at her. "Wait until you see her, sweetheart." The cab went down Franklyn and turned right, stopping before the apartment house.

Nancy said: "Some class. Is she spending her own dough?"

Bill didn't bother to answer. He went in and asked at the desk for Miss Delaine. The switchboard operator rang her apartment, rang again. "Miss Delaine does not answer," she said.

Bill swore softly. "I told her not to leave the joint," he muttered to Nancy. "Come on up and we'll have a look."

They rode up in the automatic elevator and walked along the heavy rug of the corridor. Before the apartment door, Lennox paused and drew a key from his pocket. Nancy Hobbs watched him with amused eyes. He caught the look and flushed slightly. "Don't go getting ideas, brat. This is business."

He fitted the key into the lock and opened the door, then swore. The apartment was in disorder. Drawers were half open, doors swung ajar. Lennox went through the rooms rapidly, then returned to the front. Nancy Hobbs stood beside a small end table, fingering a large square envelope.

"This is for you, Bill."

He took it, read his name in a large, feminine hand, and tore it open. Looking across his shoulder, Nancy read:

Dear Mr. Lennox:

Sorry to run out on you this way, but Wilbur and I are going to be married; then we're going back to Topeka, Kansas. We have loved each other a long time, but did not have money to marry. Last night, Wilbur got a letter from his brother, one that Bert mailed before he was killed. There was twenty thousand dollars in it. Think of it—twenty thousand.

It was swell of you to want to help me, but Wilbur says that he does not want me to be an actress, as he thinks that actresses aren't very nice, so you just get another girl in my place. If you should ever come to Topeka, be sure and come to see us.

Your friend,

Irene Schultz (Rose pretty soon).

Bill dropped the letter and looked at Nancy. She was laughing, laughing so that her eyes were wet. He started to swear, stopped, and grinned a bit wryly. Slowly he drew an envelope from his pocket.

"Ever see anyone tear up a million-dollar bill, honey?"

She said, still laughing: "You're silly. They don't make them that large."

Solemnly he took from his billfold an oblong-folded paper and put it with letter and envelope, then put the halves together and tore them. The contract, signed by Marian Delaine, dropped to the carpet.

Positively the Best Liar

*A Count on the make finds Hollywood
pickings easy until Bill Lennox gets sore*

1

NANCY HOBBS LOOKED with widening eyes at Bill Lennox, troubleshooter for the General Studio. "My, I didn't know you could."

He said: "Hello, brat," and stared at his white shirt front with disfavor. "A fan writer should get a lot of dope here."

She smiled. "You should do it often, Bill. You look positively human when you're dressed up."

Noise welled up about them; noise, clamor and confusion, for Hollywood was celebrating—celebrating at Sol Spurck's expense.

"Do you dance, too?" She stepped towards him, and Lennox took her in his arms. They had progressed halfway about the floor when a youth with varnished hair and too black eyes, tapped Lennox's shoulder. He watched Nancy glide away, and then turned and sought his host.

Sol Spurck, head of the West Coast Studios of General-Consolidated, a benign Buddha with diamond rings, patted Bill's broadcloth shoulder with a short-fingered hand.

"Such a party did you ever see?"

Lennox said: "Yeah," somewhat absently, his eyes following Nancy Hobbs. "Must have cost you plenty."

Spurck spread his hands in a wide gesture. "Positively it did, y'understand, but Mommer's birthday, and I should consider expenses?"

Lennox said: "Sure. I was kidding, Sol." He moved away towards a large lady who was struggling valiantly in the arms of a character actor. "This is mine, Rose."

Rose Spurck smiled her relief. "Such a good boy you are, Bill." Her brown, rather prominent eyes were shining. "Ach! You don't want you should dance with an old lady like me."

"How you talk!" He smiled at her with genuine affection. "Like the party, Rose?"

The brown eyes were slightly misty. "Better it was just friends, yet, but Popper—look."

Lennox looked. Spurck was the center of a large group, the diamonds on his hands flashing as he waved them in conversation. "Yes-men," Lennox muttered.

Mrs. Spurck patted his shoulder. "Let Popper have his fun, yes. Then tomorrow you get the crazy ideas out from his head." The hand on his shoulder stiffened suddenly and Lennox, following the direction of her eyes, saw her daughter, Rachel, dancing with the black-haired youth who had cut in on Nancy Hobbs.

Lennox stole a look at Rose Spurck's face and did not like what he saw there. The kindly expression was gone from the brown eyes, replaced by worry, yes, by fear. She turned, meeting his gaze, trying to smile. The effort was hardly a success. Suddenly she seemed very tired.

"Do you mind, I go and lay down a while?"

Without speaking, he led her towards the door of the ladies' room and delivered her into the hands of the colored maid, then walked slowly back to the ballroom, lighting a cigarette as he went. He liked Rose Spurck; believed in her genuineness as he believed in few people in the movie capital. In the doorway, he met Nancy Hobbs.

Her face was flushed, her eyes shining; she caught his arm with both hands. "I thought that you'd run out on me."

"Nothing like that, pal." There was no answering smile on his lips. "Who's the black-haired rooster that cut in on us?"

She said: "Don't tell me that you're jealous, please don't tell me that. I couldn't stand the shock after all these years."

His eyes were on the colorful throng, probing, searching. Finally he picked out the black-haired one, still dancing with Rachel Spurck. "Who is he?"

She said: "No one you'd be interested in. He's a gentleman."

"Swell. What's the idea of stalling?"

"I'm not stalling." Her eyes were indignant. "He's a Count, a real one."

"First time I ever knew you to get enthusiastic over phony royalty."

"He's neither phony nor royal. He's an aristocrat, a Frenchman. Really, Bill, he's a good egg. You'll like him."

Lennox saw an associate producer tap the Count's shoulder, saw the Frenchman walk towards them. "Here he comes now. You might introduce us."

The Count paused before Nancy, and, clicking his heels together, bowed. "Mademoiselle is not dancing?" There was the barest trace of accent, but the English was flawless. For some reason, this annoyed Lennox.

Nancy said: "Bill, I want you to know Count de Lidney. Monsieur le Count, this is Bill Lennox." Their hands met. The Count's teeth were a white flash as he smiled. "So this is the so great Lennox?"

Bill's ears were slightly red. He sensed the mockery beneath the other's tone, and his eyes narrowed slowly. If Nancy Hobbs noticed, she gave no sign. She tucked a small hand under the Count's arm. "Raoul finds our parties amusing."

Bill said, rudely: "I'm glad someone does," and turned away. As he turned, he noticed that Spurck was watching him. The producer's face had lost its expression of enjoyment, and held a worried frown. One fat hand rose and motioned to Lennox. Bill crossed to his employer's side.

"What's the matter, Sol?"

Spurck said: "That loafer is making up to Rachel. Positively I tell you. Bill, he is no good."

Lennox's eyes followed the swaying figure of the Frenchman. Certainly he was handsome. Certainly he had poise, assurance. Nancy Hobbs was laughing as they danced. Her face seemed alive, eager; then Bill's eyes shifted to Rachel Spurck, who stood talking to a famous novelist. It was obvious that she was giving scant attention to the writer's words. Her black eyes were gazing across the dance-floor, following the Count.

"Have you told her so?"

"Have I told her?" Spurck's voice rose with excitement until it almost eclipsed the music. "She laughs at me; at me, her Popper." His fat shoulders sagged with sudden weariness. "I tell you positively, Bill, she'll marry that *schlemiel.*"

Lennox said, grimly: "Keep out of it, Sol. You'll only gum things up. Let me handle this punk."

Short fingers caught his arm. "Do that, Bill, and I cancel what you owe me."

2

LENNOX GOT A taxi at the side of the hotel and rode out Wilshire to Vine, then across Vine to Hollywood. Four men were eating in one of the leather booths when he entered the *Brown Derby*. They greeted him loudly, and Lennox nodded to them. He stopped for a moment and put his hand on Hugh White's shoulder. "Just the bum I wanted to see. Come over here a minute, will you?"

White stared at him in surprise, rose, and followed Lennox to another booth "What's on your mind, Bill?"

Lennox said: "You used to be Paris correspondent for the *World* before you degenerated into a scenario writer. Ever hear of a guy named de Lidney, supposed to be a Count?"

White's eyes were narrow. "I know him," he said, somewhat shortly. "He *is* a Count."

Surprise made Lennox's eyes wide, "So the title isn't phony. Gimme the low-down, will you, Hugh?"

White shrugged. "There isn't much. He's in rather bad odor at home. No money, too good at cards, barred from Monte Carlo. Women are his specialty."

"Just a nice boy?"

White said: "The kind Hollywood will fall for. He should go big here, Bill."

"Anything else?" Lennox waved away the approaching waiter.

White took his time to answer. "Something about a duel," he said. "Italian officer. They went over the line at Biarritz, and the wop died. Made rather a stink, but it's mostly gossip."

Lennox said: "Thanks," and rose. "Bring your next lousy story out and I'll see what I can do."

He left the restaurant and stood for a moment, staring at the almost deserted Boulevard, then walked to the corner, entered a drug-store, and dropped a nickel into the phone. An irritable voice answered. Lennox said: "Is Sidney Blanchard there?" Blanchard was movie critic on the *Post*.

A heavy voice with blurred accent reached him. Lennox said: "This is Bill Lennox, Sid. Listen. There's a French Count around the village. I want to know where he's staying?"

Blanchard said: "This is one swell party. You'd better come up."

"Maybe later. This guy's name is de Lidney. Where is he when he's home?"

Blanchard's voice cleared. "What's up, Bill? Does he rate a contract?"

Lennox grinned sourly. "This is private. He owes me two dollars, and I'm trying to collect it."

Blanchard coughed, breathed deeply, and said to someone at his end of the wire: "Thanks, sweetheart, I needed that." Into the phone: "He's at the *Greyton*, on Franklyn. If there's a story, don't forget that I work for a living."

Lennox said: "Since when?" and hung up.

He went outside and walked to the cab-rack. "*Greyton*," he told the driver, as he climbed in.

It was an imposing building, with a palm-crowded patio opening into an imitation marble foyer. The night-man looked up from the switchboard and smiled when he saw Bill. "Hello, Mr. Lennox."

Bill pulled his top-coat together so that it concealed as much of his shirtfront as possible. He felt almost undressed in these clothes. "Hello, bigfella. Got a guy named de Lidney here?"

"You mean the Count? He's in 422, but he's not in."

"I know it," Lennox said. "Slip me the key and I'll go up and wait. He'll be along pretty quick."

The night-man's face got worried. "Gee, I can't do that, Mr. Lennox. I'd lose my job, sure."

Bill said: "No, you won't. There won't be any kick-back on this, and, if you do, I'll see that you get a better one. His hand, with a five-dollar bill folded in the palm, went across the desk. The boy at the telephone shook his head.

"I'll take a chance, but I don't want your dough." He found the key and passed it across. "Don't get me in Dutch."

Bill grinned, took the key, and walked towards the automatic elevator. Once in the car, he pressed the fourth-floor button, then felt in his overcoat pocket, found a stub pencil, and wrote on his starched cuff: "Find job for Sam, a good one." He underlined it, dropped the pencil into his pocket and, as the car stopped, slid back the door and stepped out into the thickly carpeted corridor.

He paused before the door of 422, slid the key into the lock, pushed the door open, and stepped through into a lighted entry hall. The rest of the apartment was in darkness. He closed the door, shoved the black, soft felt that he wore, far back on his head, and walked through, switching on lights as he went.

There was no kitchen, but there was a small butler's pantry with an electric refrigerator and a built-in barette. Lennox opened the barette, found a bottle of UDL, searched until he located a corkscrew, and helped himself. That done, he continued his explorations. There was a large bedroom and a larger sitting-room. Lennox looked about with narrow eyes.

White had said that the Count was broke, yet apartments at the *Greyton* did not come cheap. Bill guessed that this one would draw three hundred, even in the depression; perhaps more. He opened the closet door and stared at the suits hung in an orderly row; at least twelve pairs of shoes were in the rack below them. "Looks like a leading man's wardrobe," he muttered, closing the door and turning his attention to the bureau. There was nothing in the drawers except clothing. Lennox looked them over and closed the drawers in disappointment. He'd rather hoped to find something, what, he was not quite sure.

There was a desk in the sitting-room. He tried that next, without success. Finally he closed the drawers and straightened. "Someone is putting up dough for him," he muttered, "a lot of dough. Now I wonder who it is, and why they're so big-hearted?" Since he could think of no answer, he went back to the barette and took another drink, then lit a cigarette and started back to the sitting-room. In the doorway stood the Count, a gun held loosely in his hand.

His eyes widened as he saw Lennox. His body, which had been poised forward on the balls of his feet, relaxed slightly. Lennox said: "How are yuh?" He ignored the gun.

The Count's black, almost beady eyes were fixed on the other's face. "This is a surprise, a pleasant one, Monsieur." He made no move to return the gun to his pocket. "How did you find me, so soon?"

Lennox said, easily: "I know things, de Lidney, if that's your name."

The Count's face darkened; then with a shrug, he dropped

the gun into his pocket. "Perhaps you will be kind enough to explain why I am being honored by this call, at, ah, such a strange hour?"

Lennox grinned. For the first time that night he was beginning to enjoy himself. "Thought I'd come up and talk to you," he said, easily, his eyes on the other's face. "Like to talk about things: Monte Carlo, for instance, and duels. Hear you're good at duels—when you're fighting wops."

The color went slowly from the Count's face, leaving it the shade of a dirty lemon. "You learn fast." It was a dry whisper, hardly carrying to Bill's ears.

Lennox smiled. "You'd be surprised, de Lidney. I not only learn fast, I also hand out good advice. You're going back to France. You find you don't like the California climate, that you're afraid you won't keep healthy if you stay here."

"Meaning?"

Lennox shrugged. "Do I have to draw you pictures? We can get along swell without you."

De Lidney laughed, not a pleasant sound. "You are droll, my friend. I like it here. Here I remain. What is your interest in my movements? Ah, I have it. The so beautiful Rachel, is it not?" He snapped his fingers. "For you, and your warnings, I care nothing."

"Care for this then," Lennox took two steps forward. His left hand caught the Frenchman's wrist, as the other's hand darted towards his pocket. Lennox's right came up in a half swing, crashing into de Lidney's jaw. The man sat down, suddenly. His eyes were blurred for a moment. He stared up at Lennox with a startled, half stupid expression. Then his eyes cleared, darkened with hate.

"You will fight me for that." It was a statement.

Lennox laughed. "I'll fight," he told the man on the floor, "but not the kind of fighting you mean. Get up. We'll finish it now."

De Lidney stayed where he was, prudently. He rubbed his jaw slowly, staring up at Lennox. "There is a time and place for everything, my friend."

3

SOL SPURCK WALKED up and down his heavily carpeted office in the administration building at the General Studio. "All-ll right. All-ll right." He threw his hands in the air as if appealing to heaven. "Do me a favor once. Go home, home, and stay there."

The black-haired girl who was his daughter slid from her seat on the corner of the massive desk and moved towards the door, her long jade eardrops swinging as she turned her head to stare at Lennox, intense dislike firing her eyes; then she went out, slamming the door. Spurck dropped into his chair and cut the end from an enormous cigar.

"Y'understand, Bill, I ain't saying positively that you wasn't right, hitting that loafer, but, yet, women is funny."

Lennox nodded gloomily, and stared from the window at a distant street scene which was supposed to represent New York in the nineties. "I didn't figure that he'd tell her, Sol."

"You didn't figure—?" Spurck had his cigar lighted. He laid it carefully in the beaten bronze ash-tray out of harm's way. "You didn't figure? Must I do everything around here? I tell you, Bill, women is funny. My Rachel, now, is a nice girl, y'understand, even if she does fool with paints and a brush, instead of staying home by her mommer; but positively, she would not look at that loafer de Lidney, only she thinks that I don't want her to."

Lennox understood. His private opinion of Rachel Spurck was not a high one, but he could not forget the look of pain he had seen in the eyes of the girl's mother. "Someone is putting up dough for that guy," he said, half to himself. "I'd like to know why?"

Spurck said: "Detectives." He said it with gestures.

Lennox said: "I've tried that. I've tried everything, even the immigration authorities. This de Lidney's papers are okey. We'll just have to wait for a break."

"Wait for a break?" Spurck's voice rose almost to a squeak. "Do you think I want that *schlemiel* for a relative yet? I tell you, Bill, my Rachel is strong-minded. To Yuma she is liable to go."

Lennox shrugged and turned towards the door. In his mind was the thought that de Lidney might be an improvement on some of Spurck's relatives, but he did not voice the idea.

In the long corridor outside the office he encountered Rachel. The girl faced him wrathfully, her full red lips fixed in a pout of anger. "Why don't you mind your own business, Bill Lennox?"

Bill's right eyebrow lifted, quizzically. It seemed to infuriate the girl. "You run father, you run the studio, and now you're trying to run our family affairs. I won't have it." She stamped one foot. "I tell you, I won't have it." The foot came up again, then down. This time it did not land squarely and the high, almost pointed heel, was pulled from its moorings.

Bill left her there, standing on one foot, glaring after him. Outside, it was already dusk. Lennox shivered against the cold fall wind, blowing from the ocean. He turned up the collar of his coat and looked up and down for a cab. A small coupé with shining nickel pulled to the curb before him, and Nancy Hobbs waved a slim gloved hand.

"What do you think of the jaloppy?"

Lennox said: "Swell. Things seem to be looking up?"

She said: "The old one had halitosis. At least, there was something the matter with the carburetor, and the darlingest sales-man took me for a ride—"

"I'll say he did." Lennox found a cigarette and lit it. "You might be useful and run me over to my place."

She said: "We might go places, Bill. Let's drive down to Venice and have dinner at the *Ship Café*."

He said: "Sorry, but I'm busy."

"Still after my Count?"

"I wish he was yours."

She made her eyes very wide. "Why, Bill Lennox? And here I've thought all these years that you and I would walk up the center aisle sometime and say, 'I do,' in concert."

He growled at her as she stepped on the starter: "Why do women always fall for birds like de Lidney?"

She said: "After all, I've managed to restrain my girlish enthusiasm. When did you set yourself up as a protector of Hollywood womanhood?"

He said: "To hell with Hollywood womanhood. I'm think-ing of Rachel Spurck."

Nancy's mouth was a red cherry. "Oooh, so that's it. Well, if you ask me, it's the Count that needs protection, not Rachel."

Bill said: "You and me both, sweetheart, but Rachel happens to have a pretty swell lady for a mommer. I'm thinking of Rose. She's not going to get hurt if I can help it."

The girl was silent. She also liked Rose Spurck. "Can I help?" she asked, in a small voice.

He patted her shoulder. "You're not such a bad mugg at heart, Nance. Keep those long ears open. You might hear something about his nibs."

The coupé pulled up before the apartment hotel which

Lennox called home, and Bill moved his long legs to the side-walk. "When I get this washed up, I'll buy you all the turkey you can eat. Now scram." He turned and walked towards the double plate-glass doors. The girl watched him go, then, thoughtfully, she put the car in gear, and slid into the stream of passing traffic.

The day man said: "Cold evening, Mr. Lennox," and slid four letters across the desk. Bill nodded, glanced at the letters, and, seeing that they were bills, stuffed them into his pocket. Then he rode up to the sixth floor in the automatic elevator, and hunted for his key.

A man was seated on the divan, facing the doorway, as Lennox entered. The first thing that Bill noticed was the gun, which lay close to the other's side. "An honor." He shoved his sun-stained hat far back on his head, and stared at his visitor.

Another man came through the door from the bedroom. He stopped when he saw Lennox, and grinned. The man on the divan said: "This is just a friendly call."

Lennox stared at the gun. The man saw his eyes, and smiled. "That's to show you that we mean business."

Bill walked slowly towards the table, careful not to make a sudden move. He took a cigarette from the carved wood box, lit it slowly. "Let's hear the story."

The man in the door said: "No story, just some swell advice. Try minding your own business for a while."

Lennox's eyes were narrow, his face expressionless, but his mind was racing. "Whose toes have I been standing on?"

The man in the door said: "de Lidney's a nice guy. Lay off."

"So that's what it is?"

"That's exactly what it is." The man lounged slowly into the room. He was black-haired, with a streak of gray at the temples. The lips were thin and the eyes very cold. "You're supposed to be a smart boy. Try keeping your nose clean."

Lennox said, slowly: "You can tell the frog to lay off Rachel Spurck and I'll lay off him."

The seated man laughed unpleasantly. "You'll lay off, mugg." He rose slowly, picking up his gun as he came, and moved towards Lennox. Without warning, his free hand shot out towards Bill's jaw. Lennox ducked instinctively, and the heavy gold ring which the man wore cut into his cheek "That's a warning." The man stepped back, his gun ready. "You'll get worse than that if you don't play nice. Come on, Joe." They moved towards the door.

Lennox went into the bathroom and looked at himself in the glass. His cheek was bleeding and there was a white circle about his lips, put there by rage. He soaked a towel in hot water and applied it to his cheek. The towel was hot, and he swore softly, but pressed it to the cut. Finally he stopped and went into the other room. The phone was ringing sharply. Lennox stared at it with distaste as it rang again. He picked up the receiver and said: "Yeah?"

Frank Aarons said: "Bob Haines is giving a party for Mona Lea. Did you forget about it?" Aarons was publicity director for General. Mona was their newest foreign importation.

Lennox said: "Yeah, and I'm going to keep right on forgetting."

Aarons' voice was sharp. "Spurck can't go. He expects you to be there."

Bill shrugged. "Okey; but listen, mugg. Don't make a habit of this."

He hung up, then rang the desk and told the clerk to send out for two cheese sandwiches and a piece of apple pie. He went into the bedroom, stripped, and stepped under the shower, then put on a flannel robe, just as his door buzzer sounded. It was the boy with the sandwiches. Lennox paid him, shut the door, found a half-empty bottle of Scotch, and carried it into the bedroom. He put his burden on the night stand, lay down, and ate slowly; then he set the alarm for eight-thirty and switched off the light.

4

IT WAS STILL cold when he left the apartment and climbed into a cab. The cab went over Franklyn to Western, left up the hill to Los Feliz. Bill got out in front of Haines' house, paid the driver and walked through the paved patio.

Haines was big, with bushy hair. To Lennox, he always looked something like an ape, but there was no denying that he was one of the best directors in the business. He came forward now, his arm about a blonde's shoulders, his other hand occupied with a glass. "Hi there, Bill."

Lennox said: "Hi there," without enthusiasm. He accepted a drink from a white-coated Filipino, and looked around.

It was a small party, perhaps twenty people scattered about the long, low-ceilinged room. The foreign importation in whose honor the party was given sat alone at the far end of the room beside the stone fireplace. She looked unhappy, puzzled, and a little weary of the noise which eddied about her.

Lennox eyed her critically. Spurck's brother, head of the New York office, had brought her back on his last trip to Europe. She was Hungarian, Polish, something, Lennox couldn't be sure. In fact, no one was sure from the maze of publicity which Aarons had issued about her. Lennox started across to pay his respects, then he stopped, for two figures had come through the French doors at the girl's left and stopped to speak to her. One was Rachel Spurck, the other was Count de Lidney.

Lennox set his glass down on the polished table, ignoring the fact that it would probably mar the finish. For an instant his fingers strayed to his cut cheek, touching it carefully; then he turned to speak to his host.

The party went on. Other people drifted in, some left. Lennox was beginning to wonder how soon it would be convenient for him to drift, unnoticed, through the door. The foreign importation was dancing with the Count. As they passed him, Lennox heard them talking, in French. Rachel Spurck stood beside the fireplace, looking across the room; then she turned and came towards Lennox.

He said: "I see you have a new heel, on your shoe, I mean."

Color welled up beneath her dark skin. "Listen, Bill, there's no use for us to fight."

He stared at her, surprise making him dumb. They had never been friends, not since his first day at the studio. Something was wrong. A tiny bell seemed to sound warning in his brain. "What is it, Rachel?"

She was close to him now. The heavy scent which she used hung about them. "Bill, I need—" She stopped, staring across his shoulder, her eyes widening. He turned, and saw the Count approaching, his teeth flashing with his usual smile.

"My so good friend, the great Lennox." There was no doubt about the sarcasm in the words. His long-fingered hand, slender as a woman's, was extended. Bill ignored it. He said, evenly, "I don't like you, de Lidney, and I never was good at pretending." Then to the girl: "I'm taking you home."

It seemed to him that she wanted to come, feared not to, yet did not dare—the Count's soft voice was silky. "It's your choice, *cherie*."

She shook her head slowly. "I came with Raoul."

Lennox shrugged and turned towards the door. Halfway

across the room, he stopped. Everyone stopped. The noise died suddenly. Two men had come through the door. A glance across his shoulder showed Lennox that two others had entered from the patio. There were masks across their faces, guns in their hands. One of them posted himself as guard. Lennox saw that he clutched a sub-machine-gun.

A harsh voice said: "Everyone take it easy." No one moved. "Hands in the air." The hands went up slowly, Lennox's rising level with his shoulders, staying there, his mind working. This was probably the gang that had been terrorizing Hollywood parties for months.

He said: "You can't get away with this."

The man beside the door laughed and shifted the Lewis. "We're doing it," he said flatly. At command, the guests lined up against the wall. Lennox was beside a blonde in a green dress. He saw the string of square-cut diamonds at her throat, heard her sobbing breath.

He said, heartlessly: "If you'd left those things in the safe, you wouldn't be losing them now."

She gave him a look of pure hate. One of the bandits appeared from the dining-room, a tablecloth in his hand. He spread it, then held it by the four corners. "Come on, shell out." They did so, protestingly, as he came down the line. The glittering pile in the center of the white cloth grew. The bandit paused before Lennox, ran quick fingers over him, made sure that there was no gun, "Contribute, fella."

Lennox produced six one-dollar bills, a handful of change and a watch he had won in a crap game, eight years before. The bandit looked at the collection with mocking eyes. "I oughta crack your skull, you cheap heel."

Lennox did not answer. He was staring at the heavy ring on the other's hand. He'd seen that ring before, felt it. The bandit moved on to the blonde. He made sounds of satisfaction at sight of her diamonds. She was moaning now, with fear and grief. A moment later, the diamonds had been added to the pile of loot. Two minutes later, the gang was gone. Everything clicked like clock-work. The man with the machine-gun lingered in the doorway.

"Don't no one move for five minutes." His eyes swept their faces. "I'll be outside, waiting." He was gone also, fading into the darkness. A car's engine raced, then all was still.

Frank Aarons leaped towards the phone in the hall. He rattled the hook loudly, without success. The line was dead. Haines said: "Try the one in my study. It's a private wire. Maybe they missed it."

Aarons charged through the door. Lennox heard his eager voice, but he wasn't calling the police; he was calling the papers.

"Listen," Aarons' words were almost tumbling over each other. "Mona Lea, General's new foreign star, was held up this evening, yeah, at a party at Bob Haines', yeah; same gang that's been working parties all year, four men, masked. Got it right? Mona Lea. Yeah, she lost plenty. How the hell do I know how much? Say fifty grand. That's close enough; beautiful jewels."

The blonde in the green dress brushed by Lennox, and, crossing the room swiftly, caught Aarons' arm. "Listen, Frank. Don't forget me. I was here. My rocks were worth twice what that dago's string were."

Aarons pushed her away, for she wasn't under contract to General; she worked for a rival studio. Lennox turned from the door. As he did so, he saw de Lidney draw a jeweled cigarette case from his pocket, select a long white cylinder, and light it. Lennox's eyes were narrow as he watched. He saw again in his mind's eye, the gold ring on the bandit's hand; then he touched the cut on his cheek. That cut had been made by that ring, he would take his oath on that. Which meant what?

Aarons was calling the police now, his calm voice giving the details of the robbery graphically. Haines was attempting to comfort the green-clad blonde. Lennox met Rachel Spurck's eyes across the width of the room, read fear there, panic. He realized that she knew what he had just learned, that de Lidney had some connection with the bandits.

5

THE TELEPHONE RANG sharply, jerking Lennox awake, rolling back the clouds of sleep which blurred his mind. It rang again, accusingly. A woman's voice said: "Bill! for —— sake, Bill!" It was Rachel Spurck.

"What is it?" His mind was still drugged, slow moving.

"I'm in trouble, bad trouble. I've got to see you."

"Come up here."

"I can't. Have you seen the papers?" Lennox hadn't.

"It's terrible, Bill. You've got to help me."

He said: "Where are you?"

There was a whispered conversation at the other end of the phone. Lennox couldn't make out the words, but someone seemed to be arguing.

"Don't bring anyone with you." Her voice was insistent, fearful. She gave him an East Side address. "It's room four twelve."

He frowned as she hung up, climbed from bed, then picked up the phone and called a number. A heavy voice answered. Lennox said: "Listen, Jake. Grab a cab and get over to my place as soon as you can. I'll be out in front."

He hung up and stepped under the shower. While he was dressing, the phone rang again. It was Spurck, a very much excited Spurck.

"Bill, Bill, I tell you, Rachel did not come home last night. Her bed has positively not been slept in, y'understand."

Lennox said: "Have you mentioned it to anyone? Do the servants know?"

"But why—"

Lennox cut him short. "Do they?"

"Mommer, she is worried y'understand. Maybe she—"

"Listen to me," Lennox's voice cracked like a rifle. "Don't say anything to anyone. If any of the servants know, muzzle them. Don't let them out and don't let them telephone. If the papers get this—"

Spurck made a moaning sound. "Bill, what is it? My Rachel!"

Lennox said: "She's all right. I know where she is, but I can't stop to explain now. Keep quiet until you hear from me."

A Red-Top was at the curb when he reached the sidewalk. The door swung open and Lennox saw Jake's big shoulders and massive head. He stepped into the cab, slammed the door, and told the driver to take them to Sixth and Maple. Then he looked at his companion.

Jake was ugly, with a broken nose and thickened ear. He played heavy parts at the studio and operated a small gym in Hollywood. Lennox had gotten him his first engagement, and found backing for his gym.

He said: "Swell morning?"

"Got a gun?" Lennox's voice was sharp. "I forgot to tell you."

Jake grinned slowly. "Every time you send for me, boss, I bring my gun." He tapped his coat, just above his heart.

The cab stopped for a signal, and Lennox leaned forward and waved at a newsboy. As the cab went on, he spread the paper across his knees. Two-inch type stared up at him. "Police Catch Party Bandits. Two Men Seized with Loot."

Lennox grunted and read the accompanying article. "Two men, giving their names as Pete Cronin and Joe Larkiski, were arrested at their apartment on Fountain Avenue, early this morning, by Detective Lieutenant Floyd Louman and Detective Sam Berger. Acting on a mysterious telephone tip, the officers gained entrance to the apartment through a ruse. Cronin fired as the officers entered, his shot striking Berger in the arm. Louman fired twice, both bullets striking Cronin in the chest. The wounded bandit was rushed to the hospital, where it is reported that he may die. Larkiski, surprised in the bathtub, had no chance to escape. Jewelry of unestimated value was found concealed in the apartment. Some of it was identified as belonging to Mona Lea, Hungarian actress, who is under contract to General Studios. It is thought by police that this gang has ——." Lennox swore softly.

Jake said: "That was quick work. Wonder who gave the cops that tip?"

Lennox shrugged. He was wondering that himself, but there was nothing in the paper about Rachel Spurck, nothing about de Lidney, and he breathed a sigh of relief. The cab pulled up to the curb and they got out. Lennox paid the driver, watched him pull away, then turned to Jake.

"I'm going over to the *Trovers Hotel*. It's a couple of blocks, but I am supposed to come alone, and I didn't want anyone to spot you. Trail me there and hang around outside. If I don't show in half an hour, come in. The room number is 412."

A sleepy-eyed youth with a scar on his right cheek-bone looked up from the high desk at one side of the dark, narrow lobby. His eyes went over Lennox slowly, suspicion in their depths.

Bill said: "I've some friends in 412. They're expecting me."

Suspicion went out of the other's eyes. He said, with a shrug: "Stairway to the left. There's no elevator."

Lennox went up the narrow-treaded stairs to 412. He knocked with his left hand, keeping his right in his coat pocket.

Steps sounded on the squeaky boards within. Someone turned the key and pulled the rickety door open two inches. Lennox gave it a shove and it went wide, exposing de Lidney. The Frenchman's usual smile was missing. There was a gun in his hand, held level with Lennox's stomach. He motioned the other in, stepped aside for him to pass, then peered into the dark, empty hall. Satisfied, he closed the door and turned the key in the lock. Then he put the pistol into his pocket.

Rachel Spurck sat on a kitchen chair beside a white bed from which pieces of enamel had been chipped. The girl's eyes were puffed, her nose was red. It was evident that she had been crying, but there was no sign of tears now. De Lidney said: "My friend, the so great Lennox," and managed a smile.

Bill said harshly: "Smile now, fella. You won't be smiling long."

The other's eyes flecked. The smile went away, leaving his mouth a thin, hard line. "You are wrong. You're the man that is going to help me out of my so-called difficulties."

Lennox laughed, but not with mirth. "You've been hitting the pipe," he said brittlely. "I'd pour water on you if you were drowning."

De Lidney bowed. "But of course. That I understand. It is not me that you help, but the so beautiful Rachel. Consider her." He waved a hand towards the girl in the chair.

Lennox took a step forward. With his free hand he caught the front of the man's coat, yanking de Lidney towards him until their faces were separated by inches only. "You'll leave her out of this," he gritted, "or, so help me, I'll work your face over until the cops themselves won't know you."

He gave de Lidney a sudden shove which sent him stumbling backwards until he went over on to the bed. It creaked, groaned beneath his weight, but held.

The girl said, in a frightened voice: "You've got to help me, Bill. You've got to. Think of Mommer."

He said, harshly: "You should have thought of her before. Maybe if you'd listened, you wouldn't be in this jam, For all of me, you could take the rap, but Rose is different. This guy hasn't a thing on you but some nasty publicity. We'll tell him to go to hell."

De Lidney straightened. His face was grim, a whitish blue. "You're a fool, Lennox." The tone was vicious. "How do you think we got our information about the parties we robbed? Fool! We got it from her." His voice rose. "I have the notes she wrote me. When the judge sees them, try to make him believe she was innocent." He pulled his gun from his pocket with one hand. With the other he drew a package of bluish gray envelopes from his inside pocket, and waved them in the air.

"These are my protection, but I was a fool to listen to her. A fool! She said that you would help us, but no. I will call Spurck." He was on his feet, backing towards the door. Lennox watched him with narrow eyes.

"Spurck can't help you. I can, but it will take time."

The other hesitated, his hand already on the knob. "Well?"

Lennox said: "I'll have to call Sam Marx, the lawyer. He'll know what to do."

He stepped forward. De Lidney looked at him uncertainly, stepped aside. For an instant, his gun was down. Lennox's left hand shot out, grabbed the man's wrist, forced the gun down. His right crossed, smashing against the Frenchman's teeth. De

Lidney sat down suddenly, his eyes blurred, almost crossed. Lennox was on top of him in an instant. He had the other's gun, dropped it into his pocket, then he pulled forth the packet of letters, and added that to the gun. That done, he straightened.

The girl was on her feet, staring at them, wide-eyed. He snapped at her: "I wouldn't lift a finger to keep you out of San Quentin, but your mother is one grand lady. Promise me that if I get you clear, you're going to stop acting like a half-baked Indian with a lot of oil-money. Do you get it?"

She nodded in silence.

"All right," he told her, drawing the letters from his pocket and thrusting them into her hands. "Jake Fergus is at the corner of Sixth and Los Angeles. You know him. Get down there fast and send Jake up here. Tell him to have a cab out front, ready. You wait in the cab."

She was gone, almost before he finished.

De Lidney said, uncertainly: "What are you going to do?"

Lennox rose to his feet, shrugged, and found a loose cigarette in his pocket. "Don't know yet, Frenchie, but I'm going to walk you out of here and ride you to some place where the cops won't find you until I'm ready."

The door behind him creaked suddenly. He swung about, but he was too late. There was a man in the doorway, a man with a gun. Lennox guessed that it was the machine-gun bandit he had seen the night before.

The man swore. "Look what we got here, Blackie." He stepped forward and another man followed him in and stared at Lennox. "Who's this guy, Frenchie?"

De Lidney rose slowly. "It's Lennox." His voice choked with rage. "He's trying to double-cross us."

"Where's the girl?" The man with the gun never took his eyes from Lennox. "Take it easy, punk. You might get his rod, Blackie, then he won't have funny ideas."

Blackie stepped forward and removed the two guns. De Lidney said: "There's another guy coming up. The girl went after him. Funny you didn't meet her on the stairs."

The man with the gun said: "We was in our room. Better get outside, Blackie, and lay for this other punk." The black-haired one disappeared.

"Where are the letters?"

"The girl has them," de Lidney said, bitterly. "She'll be waiting in a cab downstairs. I'll get them as soon as this other man shows up." He fell silent as footsteps sounded in the hall.

6

THE DOOR STARTED to swing inward, then it stopped; there was a muffled curse, and Blackie's voice said: "Hands in the air." The door came open, exposing Jake, his hands level with his shoulders. He stepped into the room and stared about, his small eyes wrathful.

"Sorry, Boss."

Bill said: "My fault." He said it bitterly, bitter at himself for being careless, then he looked at de Lidney. "This isn't going to buy you a thing," he warned. "When the cops get through with Larkiski, he'll talk, talk plenty. There'll be a dragnet out for all of you. You can put us away, of course, but a murder rap is tougher to beat than a robbery one."

De Lidney said suddenly: "The girl, the letters!" and started hurriedly for the door. Jake's foot got in the way, and the Frenchman went headlong, clutching the ex-fighter as he passed, pushing him, with the force of his fall, into the arms of the surprised Blackie.

The bandit swore and tried to free his gun arm. Jake hit him in the mouth, a short stab without much force, then wrapped his massive arms about the other, carrying him to the floor. The third bandit leaped in, his gun up, ready to clip Jake's head. Lennox pivoted on his heel; his fist crashing against the man's face as he went past, sending him spinning sidewise across the room. The bandit went over on to the bed, bringing it down with a sharp, explosive bang. His gun flew from his grasp and landed against the wall. Lennox dived for the gun, across the broken bed. He rolled free, came to one knee, the gun in his hand, just as de Lidney straightened, his gun leaping from his coat pocket.

Lennox fired twice. The Frenchman spun about, then sat down, slowly. The man in Jake's arms relaxed, the fighter's fingers digging ridges into his throat. Jake stared at him, then rose warily, scooping the gun from the floor as he came. He backed away and threw a glance towards Lennox. Bill was frisking the man on the bed. He found his own gun in the man's pocket, transferred it to his coat, and tossed the gangster's weapon to Jake.

"Listen, Jake. The cops will be here in a minute. You'll have to stick here till they come. Probably they'll give you a ride, but don't tell them anything except this is the holdup mob."

He was gone, running towards the stairs. Below him, heavy feet, loud voices, sounded in the lobby. He raced down to the second floor, to the rear. There was a fire-escape outside the window. He went down it to the ground.

Dodging through a littered alley, he came out on Los Angeles Street, and walked rapidly to the corner. There was a crowd before the hotel as he came forward, shoving his way until a traffic policeman barred his path. Bill said: "What's the trouble, sergeant?"

The officer shook his head. "Keep moving, keep moving." There was a taxi at the curb, its engine running. Lennox saw Rachel Spurck inside. He opened the door and got in. The girl turned a scared face towards him.

"Don't say anything now," he warned her; then to the driver: "Go out Wilshire to Beverly. I'll give you the address then."

He settled back in his seat and stared at the passing traffic.

The girl said: "What happened, Bill?"

"Plenty," he told her, shortly, his brows drawn together, his eyes narrow, thoughtful. "You still got those notes?"

She handed them to him, silently. He took the package, glanced through them. As he read, the frown grew. There was nothing on the face of them, just informal notes, inviting de Lidney to certain parties, telling him who would be there, but a clever District Attorney might twist them to mean many things. Bill drew matches from his pocket and lit their corners, one at a time. He held each until the fire almost scorched his fingers, then let it sail through the cab window. The driver looked around sharply. Lennox said: "Keep your eyes in the road. I'll pay for the heap if it burns. This is my morning exercise."

The man shrugged. He'd been driving a cab too long to be surprised at anything. When the last note had disappeared, Lennox found a cigarette, lit it, and inhaled deeply. "That's that. I wish whoever tipped the cops last night had waited until I could get organized. Wonder who it was?"

She stared at him. "Don't you know? I did."

"You did." He looked at her. "For —— sake, why?"

She said: "Don't you understand? I suspected something before last night. I wasn't sure what, but Raoul was always asking about different women, about their jewels; then last night I recognized one of the men in spite of his mask. I'd seen Raoul talking to him the day before. When we left Haines, I was sick, scared, angry. I accused Raoul. He was angry at first, then he laughed. He said that I wouldn't dare tell anyone, because I had been furnishing the information for the robberies, and I would never be able to make anyone believe that I wasn't a member of the gang.

"I told him that that was absurd. Then he showed me some of my notes, which he had kept. I realized then that I was in danger, but, well, he took me up to that apartment on Fountain. I suppose his idea was to implicate me further. He tried to give me a diamond ring," she shuddered. "It was one that Mary Turner lost in the robbery last month. When we left the apartment we went to *Martin's Restaurant*. Raoul was hungry; I wasn't. I excused myself and went to the ladies' room. I don't think he would have allowed me to go, except that there is only one exit, and he was seated where he could watch the door. There's a phone there, and I called the police. I don't know why. Impulse, I guess. I was almost crazy."

His eyes approved her. He had never liked Rachel Spurck, didn't yet, but he recognized nerve. "Where have you been since then?"

She said: "Raoul wouldn't let me go home. We drove to Ventura and had breakfast there. When we got back, the papers were on the street with the story of the raid. Raoul was scared. He took me to that horrible hotel and got a room; then he was going to call my father and threaten that unless he protected them, I would be implicated. I persuaded him to call you instead. That's about all."

Lennox nodded abstractedly. The cab came to a stop; the driver turned and peered at him. "Where now, chief?" Lennox apparently did not hear the question, and the man repeated it. Bill gave him Sol Spurck's address, and the taxi swung right, towards the hills.

The girl said, "Poor Mommer. This will about finish her."

7

LENNOX NODDED WITHOUT answering. They rode for ten minutes; then the cab pulled to a stop before the Spurck house. There was a police car in the driveway, a uniformed chauffeur its only occupant.

Lennox said, sharply: "I'm doing the talking, kid. Whatever you do, don't open your mouth."

She nodded, a tight-lipped smile flashing at him. They went up the long, curving walk, skirting the massed shrubbery which screened the front of the house, and stepped into the small entryway. Lennox had hardly touched the bell when the door came open, the butler was pushed aside, and Rose Spurck gathered her daughter to her bosom.

"Rachel, *Mein Liebchen.*"

They were crying together, Rachel quietly, Rose with emphatic abandonment. Lennox watched them for a moment, then the hall seemed to fill with people. He saw Spurck, a worried figure; saw the servants in the background. A square-built man with jutting jaw crowded forward. Lennox recognized Detective Lieutenant Louman, of the Hollywood Station. Louman put a blunt-fingered hand on Rose Spurck's shoulder and drew her back. She clung to her daughter as if fearful that if once Rachel escaped the protection of her encircling arms, she might vanish forever.

Louman hesitated. It was very evident that he was at a loss as to how to proceed. "Please, Mrs. Spurck. We've got to question her."

Rose Spurck made a moaning sound. Lennox grinned. The

reason for Louman's hesitation was clear enough to him. He knew that the detective did not care to antagonize one as politically powerful as Spurck; yet realized that this case, interwoven as it was with prominent names, could make him.

Lennox said: "Let's go into the library and talk this over."

Louman's hesitation gave him an assurance which he had not theretofore had. Gently he disengaged Rose Spurck's arms and half coaxed, half shoved them across the hall into the big paneled room.

The detective said: "You seem to be taking things pretty much upon yourself, Lennox."

Bill shut the door and looked at the other coolly. "Think so? Well, someone has to do the cops' work in this man's town."

Louman's face got red. "This isn't going to help," he snapped. "I've seen wise guys before. I know what you're trying to put over, Lennox, but you can't talk the girl out of this jam."

Lennox's eyebrows seemed to climb. "Is she in a jam?"

The detective growled, then he swung on Rachel Spurck. "Where were you last night after you left the Haines party?"

She stared at him, wide-eyed, then looked appealingly at Bill. Louman thundered at her: "Where were you? Answer me."

Lennox said, mildly: "She's not under arrest, you know, Louman."

"She soon will be," the detective snapped.

Bill laughed with more gaiety than he felt. "For what?"

The detective almost struck a pose. He said, triumphantly: "As an accessory in those jewel robberies. Everyone knows that she's been playing around with that Count. We've got him dead to rights. Larkiski talked, talked plenty. The girl was at that apartment on Fountain last night."

Bill said, with apparent relief: "Is that all? I thought maybe she'd been speeding." Rose Spurck put up her hands silently. Sol bit his cigar until a white circle showed about his lips.

"Don't speak, Rachel. Mine attorney will speak with this loafer yet."

Louman grunted. He took no notice of the girl's parents, but said to Lennox: "It's no use, Bill. I've got her dead to rights. We'll be as easy as we can."

Lennox laughed unpleasantly. "If you'd stop thinking with your lungs for a minute, and listen, you might not make such a fool of yourself. If we waited on the cops to get things done around here, someone would steal the man-hole covers in the streets. Miss Spurck got suspicious of this Frenchman as soon as he showed up. She didn't know what his racket was, but there have been so many fakes here that she came to me and I suggested that she play around with him a bit and see what she could find out."

There was a broad, self-satisfied smile on Louman's lips. "It's a swell story, Bill, even if no one believes it."

Lennox ignored the interruption. "Last night at the Haines', she recognized one of the bandits as a man she had seen de Lidney talking to the night before. She told me, and I suggested that she accuse the Count and see what he did. We had no real evidence against him, and that seemed the best way. She did so as soon as they left the party. At first he was very angry, then he laughed and told her that she wouldn't dare accuse him, because if she did, he would implicate her. He took her to that Fountain apartment—"

Louman said: "This is better than one of your pictures. Go on."

"After that, they went to a restaurant. Rachel went into the ladies' room and called the police. She was the one that gave you the tip for your raid."

"What?" The detective lost a trifle of his assurance; then he laughed. "You're stalling, Bill."

"Am I?" Lennox's grin was feline.

"Sure." Louman was himself again.

"You read about that tip in the papers."

"You traced that call, didn't you?" Bill shot at him.

"Yes-s-s."

"All right. You know where it came from. I have no way of knowing unless it was Rachel who made it. I say that it came from the pay-station in the ladies' room of *Martin's Restaurant* on Hollywood Boulevard. You can check up with the waiters. One of them, at least, should remember what hour Miss Spurck was in there last night. She's rather well known in the late spots, you know."

The smile had gone from Louman's face. He stared hard at Lennox. "That call did come from *Martin's*. Is this on the level?"

"Check for yourself."

"Okey! Go on."

"Then Rachel was afraid that de Lidney might do something that would queer the raid, so she decided that the safest thing was to get him out of town, and persuaded him to drive to Ventura for breakfast. Where'd you eat?" he asked, turning towards the girl.

She told him in a colorless voice.

"While you're checking up," Lennox said, pleasantly, "you might check on that."

"Where's de Lidney now?" Louman's voice had lost some of its force.

"Probably headed for Lincoln Heights, along with his other two pals."

"What?"

"I was coming to that. When they got back to town, de Lidney saw the papers and got scared. He took Rachel to the *Trovers Hotel.* He was going to call Sol—Mr. Spurck, and try for protection by threatening to expose his daughter. She persuaded him to call me instead. I took Jake Fergus and went down there. There was a little trouble, and I dropped de Lidney. I don't think he was hit bad, but I didn't stay to find out. I left Jake to guard them until the cops arrived, and came out here."

Louman tried to sneer: "A swell story." The attempt was weak.

Lennox said: "Call Lincoln Heights Station," and, as the detective moved towards the phone: "Tell them to go easy with Jake; he should have a medal."

They waited in silence while Louman telephoned. Finally he turned away from the instrument. Lennox read the expression of his face, lacked the heart to jeer.

"Listen, Floyd," he said. "Miss Spurck doesn't want publicity, neither do I. If the gang tries to implicate her, you say she was working with *you* all the time."

A slow smile spread Across Louman's lips. "Say—do you mean that, Bill?" He was already headed for the door.

Rose Spurck put an arm about her daughter and said, coaxingly: "Come up and lie down"; then, as the girl nodded, she looked at Lennox. "You're a good boy, Bill, but to get my daughter mixed with such goings on—" She shook her head, and they left the room.

Sol Spurck dropped into a chair, found a fresh cigar in his

pocket, and lit it with slow care. "I don't want you should get insulted, y'understand, Bill, but you are positively the best liar I ever saw."

They grinned at each other.

Trouble-Hunted

Bill Lennox is paid to keep trouble away from General-Consolidated, but this time the tables are turned and trouble hunts him

1

THE BAIL BONDSMAN was short with a thick neck and thicker shoulders. His hair was wiry, black, and smallpox had been unkind to the broad, flat face. Bill Lennox, trouble-shooter for the General-Consolidated Studio, stared at him and decided that he was a Pole.

The steam radiator in the stuffy frame office sputtered as it sent out waves of heat into the tobacco-laden air. The bondsman grinned. "I tell you, sport, I been out here two years. I left Youngstown when the mills closed. Used to run liquor from Detroit for Big Ed Marsetta; a hundred bucks a trip, and the sheriffs fixed all the way. Not bad, huh, a century for a night's drive."

Lennox looked at the watch on his wrist. It was twenty after two, and he yawned heavily. "How soon will the wagon from Wilshire be here?"

A squad car whirled up the street from the direction of Pasadena Avenue and slid to a stop at the opposite curb. The bondsman rose and peered from the dusty window, then shook his head. "That's not Wilshire." He returned to his desk and picked up the phone, gave a number, and waited. "What'd they get your friend for?"

Lennox said, viciously: "He's no friend of mine. They picked him up in a gambling raid on Pico. He's an actor, Robert Macy, and he's got an eight o'clock call. He phoned the studio and they called me. It looks as if I don't get my sleep tonight."

The bondsman said into the phone: "Wilshire? Listen, Sarge.

Got a guy named Macy, Robert Macy? Gambling. Yeah. When's he coming over?—Oh, they left fifteen minutes ago, huh? Thanks." He hung up and lit a cigarette. "It won't be long now."

Lennox said: "Let's go outside. The air in here is crummy." He shoved open the glass door and they stepped out on to the stone block which served as a porch. Wind whipped Lennox's coat about his long legs driving through him, making him shiver. The bondsman did not seem to mind. He was without hat or overcoat. Three men walked past.

The bondsman said: "That's Sarano, the big one in the middle."

Lennox looked. He'd heard of Sarano. Lots of people had heard of him, few ever saw him. Rumor said that he had five swank places in Hollywood alone. The bondsman muttered: "They must of nabbed some of his girls, he—" He stopped speaking as a patrol wagon whirled beneath the bridge and came to a stop in front of the station. "Here's Wilshire now."

They crossed the road and stopped beside the car. The uniformed guard nodded to the bondsman. "Big load," he grinned.

Lennox watched the girls as they unloaded. Some were laughing, others were silent. None of them seemed scared. The bondsman said: "Sure they must be some of Sarano's."

Lennox was silent. He had been watching them idly, suddenly he stiffened. The last girl out of the car seemed different from the others. She seemed scared, almost terrified. For a moment, she stood on the sidewalk, then the policeman pushed her towards the steps roughly. But in that moment, Lennox had recognized her and, as she turned, her eyes widened suddenly and her lips formed a whispered: "Bill Lennox." Then the cop shoved her up the steps, the wagon pulled on down to discharge the men passengers, and the bondsman said to Lennox: "Come on," but Lennox grasped his arm.

"That last girl, the one just going through the door. What's she in for?"

The bondsman shrugged. It was an old story to him. "The usual thing, probably."

Lennox shook his head. "Not her, she's straight. I know her. Find out what she's in for."

The bondsman went up the steps. In five minutes he returned. "Offering," he said, shortly. "Want to take her out?"

Lennox nodded and the other said: "Come on, then," and led the way down to the other entrance.

2

THE ACTOR SAID, angrily: "This is an outrage. Think of me—of me in jail. You should have gotten me out sooner. How can I work tomorrow when I haven't had sleep?"

Lennox looked at him coldly. They were in the bail bond office, filling out the blanks. He said: "For all of me, you could have stayed in. They needed you on the *'Right of Way'* set in the morning. If you hadn't taken that swing at the cop, they wouldn't have given you a ride. Weren't you ever in a raid before?"

The actor signed the blank and threw down the pen. "I'll see Spurck about this impertinence," he threatened.

Lennox grinned mirthlessly. "Better not. There's a morality clause in your contract. Sol might tie the can to you."

Macy jammed on his hat and slammed his way from the room. The bondsman grinned. "Nice people," he said. Lennox looked at the girl on the couch. "Well, Mary?"

She said, nervously: "It's lucky for me that you are here. I'd have died if I'd have had to stay in that awful place. I'll try and square—"

"Nerts! Come and sign this and let's get out of here. I've seen enough of this hole for one night."

She answered the bondsman's questions steadily, signed her name, and watched while Lennox laid the money on the desk. Then he took her arm and they stepped out into the cold wind.

The taxi-driver was asleep and Lennox shook him into wakefulness.

"Glad the studio is paying for this hack," he muttered, as they climbed in. "Hope they stick Macy for it. That ham gets under my skin." The cab jerked into motion.

The girl breathed deeply. "I can't thank you—"

Lennox said: "Forget it, kid. When I came out here from New York, green to the game, you were nice to me. You were about the only one that was. I haven't forgotten. In the morning, I'll see if I can get your case dismissed. Here." He fumbled in his pocket, found some loose bills. "You can pay me when the breaks come." His voice was rough, masking feeling.

She drew her breath sharply. "No, Bill, not that. I've got plenty."

He stared at her uncertainly as the cab passed under an arc-lamp. She said, quickly: "You didn't think that I was guilty—I was framed, I tell you, framed." She made it vehement.

"I believe you, Mary."

She seemed to search his face, not satisfied. "If I thought that you didn't—"

"But I do. Let's not talk about it."

She said, desperately: "But I want to talk about it, Bill. You're a swell guy. I always thought so, even when I was script girl at General. Tonight, I was just going into my apartment when I met a fellow I knew. I didn't know him so well, but we hadn't seen each other for some time, so we stopped to talk. My door was already open, and the natural thing was to invite him in. He sat down in the living-room and I went into the kitchen to get a drink. When I came back, he had his shirt off and his hair mussed. Then the cops broke in."

Lennox stared at her through the darkness. "That straight?"

"Straight," she told him, gravely.

"Who's the fellow? What's the point in framing you?"

She took a long time to answer. "I don't think that I'll tell you, Bill. You've been swell, but there's no sense in your mixing up in this further. It's dirty, and it's going to be dirtier."

He said: "What's dirty?"

She shook her head. "I'm not going to tell you. I was scared tonight. I'd been warned, but I wouldn't listen. I think I will now. I've got my feet on the ground again, and I'll use some sense. I'm not going to get you—"

The cab lurched suddenly; the driver swore and jammed on his brakes. They squealed protestingly, and it seemed to Lennox that for no reason at all, the driver was attempting to climb the curb. Then he saw the reason and swore his surprise. A black touring car was swinging in from a side street, crowding over.

The taxi-man cried out. Lennox never knew whether it was from fear or rage. He saw the man wrench open the door at his side, swing on to the running-board and then leap into the street. But his eyes were no longer on the man, they were on the other car. It veered sideways, missed the cab driver by inches, and bore in again. Lennox caught the glint of light on metal, and pushed the girl forward and down, on to the cab's floor, half falling, half sprawling over her.

Glass rained about them suddenly, and the spiteful coughing of a tommy-gun bit through the night. Then the cab leaped the curb and crashed into the brick building, coming to a sudden grinding, groaning halt. The engine of the other car raced, the machine-gun was still. The cab engine died with a smothered cough. Everything was quiet except for the other car, as it hurled away through the foggy night.

For a moment Lennox lay where he was, then he felt the girl stir beneath him and struggled to his knees. He cut his hand on the shattered glass as he forced the jammed door open, and half crawled into the street. The cabman was nowhere in sight as Lennox came to his feet. He turned, and stepped back to the wrecked car.

"Hurt, Mary?" He grasped her beneath the arms, lifting her out. Another moment and she was standing at his side, clutching at him with terrified fingers. He fumbled in his pocket, found a match, and struck it on his fingernail. The flaring yellow light showed him her white face, her staring eyes.

She wasn't crying, but there were tears in her voice. "Bill, I'm sorry."

The match burnt his fingers and he let it drop. "For what, kid?"

She said: "For dragging you into this mess. You should have left me in jail. There's no use both of us taking this rap."

A siren sounded in the distance. Lennox looked up, startled. He had forgotten for an instant the noise which the shooting and the crash had made, the possibility that the police would arrive at any moment.

He said: "Let's get out of here, fast."

She did not argue. The hand on his arm tightened as they went along an alley and came out on the next street. He stopped beneath an arc-lamp and did things to her face with his handkerchief, then they walked on rapidly. "Got any place to go, kid?"

She looked up at him uncertainly. "I've got an apartment on Kenmore."

"Same place the cops got you?" She nodded, and he shook his head. "That won't do."

They walked on in silence towards the lights of an all-night drug-store. Lennox went into the phone booth and called a number. A heavy voice inquired profanely what he wanted.

Lennox said: "Listen, Jake. Get a car and hop over here. I'm in a jam and I don't want to call a cab." He gave his location and hung up, then called another number. "Hello, Nance. Didn't know whether or no you'd be in." Nancy Hobbs, writer for Hollywood fan magazines, said, sleepily: "It must be love. You wouldn't call me up at this hour otherwise."

He swore softly. "Listen, brat, this is serious. You remember Mary Renner. Used to be Hamilton's script girl when I first came out to General. Well, she's in a jam. Can't go home, so I'm bringing her over to your place for the night."

Nancy yawned loudly. "What are you doing, Bill? Crusading again?"

He said: "I'll explain when I get there. I've called Jake and we ought to be at your place in forty minutes. Have the front door open." He hung up and went back to the girl he had left waiting in the dark doorway.

3

NANCY HOBBS CAME back into the living-room of her apartment with a drink in either hand. She gave one to Bill and settled herself at his side on the divan. "I got her quiet finally. Had to give her a sleeping powder. What happened?"

He explained. "Someone framed her. Whoever it was didn't like the idea of my taking her out, and turned those choppers loose on us. I haven't the least idea what it's about. She wouldn't tell me."

Nancy looked at him with eyes that were hard to read. "Why do you always manage to land in trouble? Don't you have grief enough with Sol Spurck without going out and mixing in something like this?"

He said, defensively: "But I couldn't leave her there, could I? Jeeze, Nance! When I first came out here, that kid was the only one at the Studio that had a decent word for me. Now she needs a friend, and I'd feel like a yellow dog if I didn't shoulder in. You would, too."

The girl studied the glass in her hand reflectively. "You're right, I guess. I'll keep her under cover here until I hear from you. Call Sam Marx in the morning and tell him to get her case dismissed if he can. Then we'd better get her out of town. Whoever is behind this plays rough."

He said, as he rose: "You're not mixing in this further, brat. I didn't have any other place to park her tonight; but after tonight, you're not in it."

She was on her feet, facing him. "Listen, Sir Galahad. My

shoulders are as broad as yours. Let a gal have some fun in life, can't you?"

He put his thumb against her nose and pressed gently. "Nix, pal. Now get yourself some shut-eye. I'll ring you in the morning."

She followed him to the door. "Some time," she warned, "I'm going to have some fun, and I won't cut you in on it."

"Is that a threat?" He grinned at her, and shut the door before she could answer, then he went down the stairs and out through the dark, deserted lobby to the car. Jake was asleep beneath the wheel. Lennox punched him awake and climbed in at his side. The big man stepped on the starter and grinned.

"This night life is killing me." He swung the car towards the apartment hotel which Lennox called home. In the east, a widening streak of light showed that morning was near.

The lobby was empty as Lennox came through the door and walked towards the automatic elevator. He rode up to his floor and went along the thick carpet of the hall to his door. He fitted the key into the lock, shoved the door open, closed it behind him, and felt his way along the inner hall towards the living-room door. His fingers found the switch, pressed it, and he stood blinking in the sudden radiance from the center lamp. A man rose slowly from his easy chair, another from the divan.

"Takes you a hell of a while to get home," the first complained.

Lennox looked from one to the other. "I didn't expect company," he told them, his eyes narrow.

"Frisk him, Whitey." The man from the divan moved forward and ran quick fingers over Lennox. Bill offered no objection, said nothing until the other stepped back. Then he took off his hat and tossed it into a chair.

"You guys won't find much in this dump."

The one called Whitey shrugged. "What did you do with the broad?"

Lennox made his eyes wide. "What broad?"

"The one that you took out of Lincoln Heights?"

"She's home, I suppose."

"She wasn't, twenty minutes ago."

Lennox shrugged his way out of his topcoat. "Then I wouldn't know. I sprung her and sent her home in a cab."

"You're a liar." Whitey took two steps forward and slapped Lennox across the mouth. "That's for lying. Try it again and you'll get worse. You rode out with her in a cab. An accident happened, and listen, smart guy, unless you unbutton that lip, fast, another accident is going to happen, right now."

"Like that." Lennox dropped into a chair, one hand against his bruised lip, his eyes on the other's face.

"Just like that." Whitey's voice was ugly.

The other man said:

"Take it easy, Whitey." Then to Lennox: "You've got the reputation around this burg of being a pretty smart onion. What's this Renner dame to you?"

Lennox shrugged. "Not a thing. I used to know her, recognized her tonight, and took her out for old times' sake. That's all."

The man's eyes were on him, studying, penetrating. "That straight?"

"Yeah." Lennox caressed his bruised lips with the back of his hand. "That's plenty straight."

The other hesitated. Whitey said, hoarsely: "Let's give him the works." The phone rang, sharply, and the gangsters looked at each other. It rang again, and the big man lifted the receiver that was close beside Lennox.

"Yeah?" he said, in a voice that he tried to make sound like Lennox's, and didn't.

Lennox heard Nancy Hobbs say: "Bill, Bill, is that you? Are you all— Say, this isn't Bill— Who is it?"

The gangster swore under his breath. The girl's voice was strident. "Operator—operator, are you listening? There's something wrong in Mr. Lennox's apartment. There's something—" The big man slammed the receiver and swung about.

"Let's scram. They're calling the cops."

Whitey said: "What about him?" jerking his thumb towards Lennox.

The other hesitated. "Listen, Lennox. Get that broad out of town, and keep her out. If she shows in the next two weeks, both of you get it, plenty." He was already at the door. A moment later, they disappeared. Lennox rose swiftly, followed them to the hall door, shot the bolt, then went rapidly to the phone.

The switchboard operator's voice was excited. "I just called the cops, Mr. Lennox. Miss Hobbs told me to listen in on her call."

Bill said: "Mistake, John. Call back and tell them so, then get me Miss Hobbs at Hillcrest 8-9650." He waited until he heard her voice. "That you, brat? Yeah, thanks. I'll tell you about it tomorrow. Everything is swell now." He rang off, mixed himself a drink, and went to bed.

4

BILL LENNOX READ the papers as he rode towards the Studio in a cab. There was an account of the accident, but no names were mentioned. Lennox whistled, folded the *Times,* and tried the *Examiner.* Nothing about him in this paper, either, and he was about to throw it aside when his eye caught an item on the first page of the second section.

"*Sensation Expected At Weller Murder Trial. Defense Hints At Mysterious Witness. Political Expose Promised.*"

Lennox snorted and dropped the paper to the seat. Weller was an ex-county supervisor, being tried for the murder of Tom Barrows, former politician and insurance man, who had been shot to death in his Hollywood Boulevard office four months before. Lennox neither knew nor cared about Weller. Investigations were old stuff, at best. He lit a cigarette and swung the door open as the cab pulled up before the Studio gate. At the shine stand, he paused for a moment and rubbed his fingers in the kinky wool on the boy's head. "For luck," he grunted.

The boy grinned, flashing white molars. "When's you all gwan to star me, Mister Lennox?"

Lennox said: "Pretty soon, Sam." He'd been saying it for two years.

He walked across the lot towards the executive building, entered, went past the information desk with its long benches of waiting hopefuls, and through into the office of Spurck's secretary. "Sol here?"

The secretary nodded a marcelled head. "And in a swell

humor. He must have lost at his hearts game last night." She grinned. They were old friends, trusting each other as they trusted very few people on the great lot.

Bill went through to find Spurck pacing up and down behind his enormous desk. The General Manager of General's West Coast Studio waved both hands in the air at him. "Is it that I haven't trouble enough yet, but that you must cause me more?"

Lennox seated himself on a corner of the large flat-topped desk. "What now?"

"He asks me, what now?" Spurck appealed to the ceiling. "Positively, sometimes, Bill, I wonder why I don't fire you. That Macy, in my office he is, complaining, when I get here. For why must you insult him, before that picture is finished?"

Lennox said: "No one insulted that ham. No one could. He was shaking dice in a Pico gambling joint when the cops walked in. If he'd have kept quiet he wouldn't even have gotten a ride. As it was, he took a swing at the sergeant, and I spent half the night at Lincoln Heights, springing him. If that's an insult, I'll throw him back in and let him do thirty days."

Spurck seated himself at the desk and drew meditatively on his cigar. "It isn't that, Bill, but you know, actors have temperament. Macy's feelings was hurt, y'understand, because you pay more attention to some bad girl, which is riding in the same wagon, than you do to him."

Lennox grinned widely and, after a moment, Spurck's lips twitched. "I think," he said, "we do not renew Macy's option."

Lennox rose. "Good boy, Sol. A million years more with me around and you'll get some brains." He left Spurck's office and walked towards the cubbyhole which was his own. Nancy

Hobbs was seated in the chair beside the desk, examining her nails. He stared at her, his eyebrows climbing.

"Thought you were playing nursemaid, brat."

She said: "My patient's gone; flew the coop."

He swore at her. "I thought I told you—"

"I know," her voice was contrite. "But we needed some stuff for breakfast. I never thought that she might walk out. If I had, I'd have hidden her stepins. When I got back, she was gone, and there was a note on the table." She pulled forward a white leather pocketbook, opened it, and handed him a folded sheet of paper.

He read:

Dear Nance:

Thanks a million for all you and Bill did, but I've been thinking it over, and the best thing for me to do, is to go. Don't try to find me. I'll be okey. I'm leaving a check to cover the bond. Tell Bill to send it to the bonding company.

Mary.

He crumpled the sheet and tossed it into the waste-basket. Then he sank into the desk chair and looked through the stack of mail, absently. "I guess it was the smart thing for her to do at that," he muttered. "Wonder what the kid did to get those rough boys on her trail?"

Nancy shrugged.

"I'm sorry for her, of course," she said, "but in a way, I'm glad she's gone. You're always getting yourself into a jam over something that is none of your darn' business."

He grinned at her.

"Trouble hunts me," he said. "The heck of it is, I like trouble. I'm bad folks for your to know, child."

She said: "I know, but the hell of it is, I like you. Now that I've put aside maidenly discretion, you might at least buy me lunch."

He started for the door, said over his shoulder: "Keep that chair warm for twenty minutes and I'll do that very thing."

5

NANCY HOBBS PARKED her coupé on Vine Street and they walked slowly through the noonday crowd towards the *Brown Derby*. A clock at the corner registered one-thirty as they passed, and Lennox yawned. "I'm getting too old to stay up all night," he complained.

The girl caught his arm. "Bill, look!"

Lennox said: "What?—Oh!" He was staring down at a pile of papers on the sidewalk before the cigar store. A picture of a girl faced him from the front page, a picture of Mary Renner. The black headline above the picture read:

"Mystery Witness Slain. Barrow's Secretary Found Dead on East Side."

Lennox found three pennies and tossed them into the small box. He picked up the paper, still so damp that the type blurred slightly, and walked mechanically towards the restaurant. Nancy Hobbs said, in a choked voice: "If I only hadn't gone out after that bacon."

He patted her shoulder. "Forget it, brat. This was in the cards."

They found seats and Lennox, spreading the paper, continued to read.

"The body of Mary Renner, pretty, dark-haired mystery witness in the Weller murder trial, was found this morning on Wall Street between Eighth and Ninth. The girl, who had been shot twice in the abdomen and evidently pushed from a speeding car, was the former secretary of Tom Barrows, Los Angeles politician who was shot to death in his Hollywood office four months ago—"

There was almost a column more, but Lennox quit reading and turned to give his order.

Nancy Hobbs said: "I can't eat, Bill, I can't."

He nodded and folded the paper. "Buck up, kid! Things like this happen all the time. The only difference is that we don't know the people." He broke off as a director stopped at the table to invite them for a week end at Santa Barbara. When he had gone, the girl said: "But they'll trace her and drag you in, Bill."

Lennox shrugged. "It won't be the first time I've been dragged in. Come on. I'm not hungry either. Run me back to the studio for a minute, then we'll go down and take a look at the ocean." They rose and walked out to her car.

FLOYD LOUMAN, WITH a new badge and added authority said: "How are you, Lennox?" without offering to shake hands.

Bill nodded. "Congratulations, Captain."

He crossed his office and sat down.

Louman said: "About this Renner girl, Lennox?"

"What about her?"

"She was picked up on an offering charge last night. You took her out on bail. So far as we can learn, you were the last one to see her."

Lennox nodded slowly. "No use my denying that, Floyd. The bondsman would identify me. So would the ham actor I was out there to spring. I took her out, so what?"

Louman said: "She's dead. Maybe that isn't news to you?"

"It isn't. I read it in the papers."

"Just like Will Rogers," Louman sneered. "All you know is what you read in the papers."

"Just that. I recognized the girl. She used to work here at the Studio. I took her out and sent her home."

"She didn't go home."

Lennox shrugged. "That wasn't my business."

Louman's voice got hard. "Listen, Bill. There was a cab found this morning on Pasadena Avenue. Choppers had worked on the hack, and it was plenty wrecked. The cab company's records show that it was called from your apartment hotel at eleven fifty-five last night. The hotel switchboard man did not want to talk, but he decided to. You called that cab. You rode away in it."

Lennox nodded. "So what? Someone blasted the cab. The driver lit in the street, running. I don't know where he is, and that's only half of it. I don't care. It wasn't my fault and I don't like headlines. Going to run me in for not reporting it?"

Louman said, speculatively: "I might run you in for murder. Where'd you take that girl last night?"

"I've told you—" Lennox's voice was weary, but Louman stopped him with a gesture of his hand.

"Save it," the detective advised. He drew a crumpled ball of paper from his pocket and smoothed it out upon the desk. "I found this in your wastebasket," he pointed to the end of the desk. Lennox's eyes got narrow as he saw that it was the letter which Mary Renner had left at Nancy's apartment. "I think," Louman said, slowly, "that I'll have to talk to Miss Hobbs." He turned to the plain-clothesman who lounged just inside the door. "Send that Hobbs woman in."

Lennox said: "Listen, flat-foot. I've got you out of a couple of jams when you were too bullheaded to listen, but you never learn. Leave Nance out of this, I'm telling you. Renner's body was found about ten-thirty this morning. It couldn't have been there long. They'll tell you at my apartment what time I left this morning. They'll tell you here, what time I got to the Studio. If you think I had anything to do with that killing, go ahead and try to prove it, but leave Nance out of the picture."

Nancy said, from the doorway: "Thanks, Bill, but you should learn that I can fight my own battles." She gave Louman a dazzling smile. "Anyway, I like to see old friends."

Lennox grinned sourly. "I wouldn't call him a friend. He'd turn up his mother to keep that gold badge."

"You're too rough on him, Bill." She made her smile wider. "Not his mother, surely not his mother. Maybe his grand-mother, but not—"

The detective captain growled. "Have your fun now. You may not later. Come on, you two. Tell me what you know about Mary Renner."

Nancy Hobbs told him. She told it in short, crisp sentences. She pointed to the note on the desk. "That's the best alibi we could have, you poor lug. Do you think we wrote it ourselves?"

Louman said, angrily: "I wouldn't be surprised. I wouldn't be surprised at anything you'd do."

"That," Nancy told him, "is one swell compliment, coming from you."

6

LENNOX SAID: "THAT'S what I hire a smart shyster like you for, Sam. Louman can't do much to me outside of some unpleasant publicity, but he's trying to make things nasty for Nance."

Sam Marx nodded. "I'm trying to locate that punk that was in Renner's apartment when the cops broke in. If we get him, we may be able to learn who's behind the play. I've also sent for Weller's lawyer. He may know something."

As if in answer to his words, the door from the outer office opened and Marx's secretary appeared. "Mr. Gilman to see you."

Marx nodded, and a minute later Gilman came into the room. He was short, inclined towards flesh, with a red face and very thin hair. He shook hands with Bill and sank into a chair. "I wanted to see you, Mr. Lennox. I thought perhaps Miss Renner had told you something which I could use to help my case."

Lennox's eyes narrowed. "She didn't tell me a thing," he said, flatly. "I didn't even know that she was mixed up in that murder trial until I read it in the papers."

Gilman sighed. "That's the breaks," he said.

"But surely you've got a statement, something?" Marx's voice was stringent.

The other lawyer shook his head. "I haven't. She wouldn't give one. I'll tell you exactly what happened. Miss Renner was Barrow's secretary. At the time of his murder, the police questioned her and she said that she knew nothing, that she was out to lunch when it happened. The evidence against my client is purely circumstantial, but very convincing. There's no doubt but that Weller hated Barrows. There's no doubt that Weller was within a block of Barrows' office a short time before the murder. Three witnesses saw him there, and he does not deny it. The defense seemed hopeless. Then a week ago Miss Renner called at my office. She said that her conscience was hurting her, that she had evidence that would clear Weller. I tried to get a statement, but she refused. I think she feared a leak from my office. However, she offered to testify."

Lennox said: "But why did they frame her on that vice charge?"

Gilman shrugged. "I'm guessing," he admitted, "but I think that they wanted to discredit her testimony. If it could be shown that she had been arrested, the jury might not have believed her. Also, they may have intended to offer her a trade; to have her case dismissed if she did not testify. Your taking her out, spoiled that, of course."

Lennox nodded. "And who are they?"

Gilman ran a hand through his thin hair. "The men that murdered Tom Barrows, the men that are trying to send Weller to the chair in their place. I wish I knew who they are."

"Well—" The phone rang sharply. Marx picked it up, listened for a moment, then handed it to Lennox. "For you," he said.

Lennox said: "Hello!" The voice of Sol Spurck's secretary was excited.

"Listen, Bill! A man just called up. He said it was a matter of life and death that he get hold of you, so they switched the call to me. At first he wouldn't give the message; then he told me to tell you that they've got Nancy Hobbs, and that they're holding her. If you don't talk, she won't be hurt. If you do—" her voice broke off suggestively.

Lennox said, hoarsely: "Talk about what?"

The secretary said: "I don't know. Whoever the man was, said that you would understand, then he hung up. I'm having the call traced, but if it came from a dial phone, we're out of luck."

Lennox said: "Thanks," dully. "If you find out anything, call me here. If I'm gone, give Sam the message."

She said: "Can I help? What's it all about?" but he hung up.

Sam Marx said: "What is it, Bill? Here!"

He pulled a bottle of whiskey from his desk. Lennox waved it away. "They've got Nance," he said, slowly making his hands into fists. "They think that Renner spilled her guts to me. They think that I'll testify for Weller. If I knew where they are, who they are—"

Marx swore softly, then he said, suddenly: "Go to Malone, Bill. He knows who's behind this. There's damn' little in this town that he doesn't know, and he likes you. Maybe he'll help."

Lennox's breath seemed short. "It's worth a try, Sam. I'll see him, then I'll call you back. Whatever happens, don't let the papers get this. If the gang thought that I had talked—"

He went out, slamming the door. In the cab, riding across town, he tried to think things out, couldn't, and gave it up.

Ham Malone's office was on the sixth floor of a Broadway office building. There was no name on the door and Ham had no official business, but he had more power in political circles than any other one man in Southern California. The girl at the reception desk looked at Lennox uncertainly, then at her watch. "He never sees anyone, this late in the day."

Bill said, grimly: "He'll see me. Tell him that Lennox of General-Consolidated is here, and in a hell of a hurry."

The girl disappeared, to reappear a moment later. Bill went in. Malone was at his desk; a small, shriveled man with a booming voice that startled people who did not know him.

"How are you, Bill? What's the matter? Want a traffic ticket fixed or a license for a beer garden?"

Lennox said: "Neither. You read about that Renner kid getting bumped on the East Side, this morning. Well, I'm tied into that."

The little man nodded, "Good looking kid, from the picture."

Lennox nodded, and went on to explain what had happened. "And now they've got Nance," he ended. "I want to know what rat's behind this. If you don't know, you can find out. I'm asking it as a pal, and I don't ask favors often."

The politician said: "Why come to me?"

"Because you're the one man that can help. You hear things, Ham, things that don't get around."

Malone said, slowly: "Yeah, I hear things. What do you want me to do?"

"Tell me who's behind the Barrows killing. That's the rat that has Nance, the rat I'm going to get."

"Better lay off. He's tough."

Lennox's laugh had an edge. "So you do know. Swell. He may be tough, but I'll handle him."

Malone was silent a long time. It was evident that he was coming to some decision. Lennox waited impatiently. "Ever hear the term, 'Keep your nose clean'?" the little man asked, finally.

Bill said, harshly: "For —— sake, Ham, don't you get it? They've grabbed Nance, my pal, and you sit there talking. I'd be the last one to ask you to rat, but hell! There are certain things that don't go down. That isn't fighting fair, grabbing a woman."

The little man shrugged. It was evident that the plea left him unmoved. "Okey! But I'm not doing it because of your spiel, I'm doing it for you. I like you and, if I have to take sides, I'll take yours. Sarano put Barrows out. He didn't do the job himself, but he paid the bill. I can't prove it, but that's straight."

Lennox's mouth was a white line. "Thanks, Ham. I'll be seeing you." He swung towards the door. Malone stopped him with a sharp word.

"Fool! I'd be doing you one swell favor to tell you that and then send you up against that wop's guns, alone." He reached for the phone and barked a number.

Lennox said, from the door: "Never mind." He said it grimly. "This is my job. I kill my own rats."

Malone glared at him. "And I thought that you had brains. You'd spend hours hunting that wop's hangout. Sit down."

Lennox sat down unwillingly. The big man said into the phone. "Is Louman there?"

Lennox was on his feet. "Keep that ape out of this."

Malone paid no attention. "Floyd, this is Malone. Yeah. Well, Bill Lennox is in my office. Yeah. A girl named Hobbs has been snatched. That's right. We think Sarano has her. Yeah. It's tied in with that Renner killing on the East Side. That's right, and if there's anything happened to the girl, you know what to do." He hung up, and looked at Bill. "You stay here. Louman will call me as soon as they crash the joint."

Lennox said: "Like hell I will. Come on, Ham. You're my

pal. Where is this joint? Come on—don't you get it? Something might happen to her while the cops are busting in. I've got to be there."

Malone breathed quickly. "All right." He wrote the address on a slip of paper. "Here you are, lug, and I'll send flowers to your funeral."

Lennox did not answer. He seized the paper and dashed across the office. An elevator door was just closing. He caught it, pulled it open, and jumped into the moving car. Three girls gasped. The operator said, angrily: "That's a swell way to get killed."

Lennox paid no attention. As soon as the car stopped, he was out, crossing the foyer at a half run. As he reached the street, he saw a cab at the opposite curb, just discharging a passenger. He dived across, through traffic, wrenched the door open, and threw himself in.

THE HOUSE WAS large, set well back from the palm-lined street. Lennox saw with satisfaction that he had beaten the squad car. He shoved a bill to the driver and went up the walk, fast. As he went, he loosened the gun in his shoulder-holster. His lips were thin, his dark eyebrows a straight line above his narrowed eyes as he jabbed at the bell.

A heavy-set man opened the door. Lennox gave him no time for thought. He put his free hand in the other's chest and shoved. The man was forced to step back to keep himself from falling. Lennox went in after him, slammed the door. "Where's Sarano?" Another man appeared from the right. Lennox recognized Whitey.

Whitey eyed him without excitement. "Hello, Lennox!" The

heavy-shouldered man looked startled.

"What the hell do you want here?" He moved his hand towards his pocket, then stopped. Lennox's gun was in his hand.

"This is my party. Where's Sarano?" Whitey said: "You might as well take it easy. Playing tough won't buy you a thing."

Lennox advanced slowly. The heavy man stepped back, leaving Whitey standing alone. Lennox hit the gangster in the mouth with his free hand. "That's for that crack you took at me," he said. "Where's Sarano?"

A voice from behind said: "Drop that rod, Lennox, and turn around."

Lennox obeyed slowly. Sarano was standing behind him in the wide hall. Lennox did not know where he had come from. He said: "I want Miss Hobbs."

The man's eyebrows climbed. Whitey laughed unpleasantly. "So you want Miss Hobbs? Well—you shouldn't crowd into things. People that do, get hurt."

Lennox said, steadily: "I'm not crowding in. I took that Renner kid out on bail because I thought that she was in trouble. She didn't tell me a thing. I never knew that she was tied into the Weller trial until I read it in the paper this morning."

Sarano moved his head from side to side like some great dog examining an enemy. "We'll wait until after the trial," he decided. "Maybe we'll wait until Weller burns. I've got a good thing in this town. I'm keeping it."

Whitey laughed. "Let me tend to him, boss. Let me tend to him." The voice was eager.

Lennox said, desperately: "You fool! Why do you think I broke my neck to beat the cops out here?"

"The cops?" Sarano's head stopped moving, and his deep-set eyes fastened themselves on Lennox; then he laughed. "The cops aren't bothering us. There isn't one in this burg that would—"

"Listen!" Lennox's voice cut at him. "You've been tossed over. The sign's out for you. You're through, washed up. Louman will be here with the squad in five minutes. You'd better scram."

The other narrowed his eyes. "Why the warning? You'll be telling me next that you're my pal."

"I'll see you burn." Lennox's voice was hoarse. "I hate your guts. There's nothing I hate worse, but I knew what might happen to Hobbs while the cops were shoving you around. I got here first to stop that, to give you a chance to get out. I want Nance. Don't you savvy that, you thick-headed—"

Sarano's lips still smiled, but his eyes were cold. "That straight, Lennox?"

Bill said: "So help me." He said it earnestly.

"So-oo? Listen. Whitey. Get the broad. We'll take her along. She might be useful. Al, you get the boys and the cars. Move, you lug."

Lennox took a half step forward, his hands working. The gun came up. He could see the hairy-finger tighten on the trigger. "I've an idea to blast you." The man's voice was passion ridden. If it hadn't been for you—"

Whitey moved towards the stairs. Al moved also. There was noise in the house now, loud voices, hurrying feet. Lennox said between his teeth: "You'll never take the girl out of here. Alone, you might stand a chance. You—"

Brakes squealed somewhere, noise from without filtered in. Someone fired from the corner of the house. Half-way up the stairs, Whitey paused. Sarano screamed at him.

"Go on, you fool! There's still time to get the girl out the back way."

His eyes, for the barest moment, were on the man on the stairs. In that moment, Lennox leaped forward. He caught the man's wrist with one hand, forcing the gun away from him, crashing his other fist into Sarano's thick neck. The powerful arms closed about his shoulders, forcing him backwards. The gun was coming up slowly. Sarano panted: "Go on, Whitey, I'll handle this punk."

Noise came from beyond the front door. An axe crashed against the panels, but they held. Lennox brought his knee up suddenly. It caught Sarano in the groin. Pain twisted the other's face. He clung desperately. Lennox forced himself away and hit the other's face with a short right jab. He jabbed again and yet again. Blood from the man's nose sprayed over them, then Lennox tore himself free. The force carried him to his hands and knees. Over his shoulder, he saw the gun come up steadily and kicked out with both feet. They caught Sarano in the chest, driving him backwards to the floor. His head hit wood with a dull thump, and he lay quiet.

Lennox looked only once, then he threw himself towards the stairs, catching at the rail. Whitey was bending before a door halfway down the hall. It seemed stuck and he was swearing in his haste. He heard Lennox coming, turned too late, and snapped two hurried shots. They both missed, and Lennox was on top of him. Whitey brought up his gun and raked it across the side of Lennox's skull. It staggered him for an instant, then he leaped in, beating down the other's guard, pounding his head with both hands.

A voice from the stairhead said: "My ——!"

Heavy feet pounded toward him, big hands pulled him back, and he was staring into the broad, flat countenance of Floyd Louman.

The detective captain's mouth sagged. "Bill Lennox!"

Lennox wiped his battered nose with the back of his hand. "Hello, copper! Did you get Sarano?"

Louman said: "What are you doing here?" He said it angrily.

"Hobbs, Nance Hobbs. She's here. I came to get her before you boys started pushing Sarano's mob about." He dragged himself towards the door and pounded on the panel. "Nance! Hey, Nance! It's Bill." There was no answer from within.

A cop in uniform appeared at the head of the stairs, carrying an axe. Lennox waved to him. The cop looked towards Louman. Louman nodded. A minute later, the door was down, and Bill was diving through, then he stopped. The room was empty. For a moment he stood staring around, then with a little cry he stooped in the center of the rug and caught up Nancy's white leather pocketbook.

They crowded in after him, but it was Louman who found the passage through the closet to the next room. "They took her out this way," he said.

Lennox stared at him. "Did some of them get away?"

"Two carloads. The boys will get them before they get clear. The dragnet is out."

Lennox leaned against him heavily. "They'd better," he said. It was a hoarse whisper.

7

LOUMAN CAME OUT of the hospital at Lennox's side. His big hand was under the other's arm, supporting him. "You ought to stay in for a couple of days at least," he growled.

Bill shook himself free. "When I need a nurse, I'll get someone besides a big-footed lug like you. Why aren't you out after that gang?"

Louman said: "Steady, Bill! You did everything that you could. We'll do our part."

"Then do it, Nance, my—"

Louman piloted him towards the squad car at the curb, put him in, and told the driver to take him to his home.

Lennox leaned back wearily. "If you hear anything, Floyd—"

Louman said: "Sure, sure!" He watched the car pull away. At the apartment Lennox got out heavily. He scorned the driver's offer of assistance, and walked slowly through the double doors. Inside, he stopped, steadying himself with one hand on the door jamb. Nancy Hobbs was seated in a deep leather chair in one corner of the lobby. It was very evident that she was asleep, her rather full lips parted in a tiny smile. For a moment, he stood there, staring at her, then he crossed the lobby slowly and put one hand on her shoulder.

"Hey, brat, wake up!"

Her eyes came open and she looked at him for a moment without comprehension; then sleep went out of her eyes and she smiled. "Hello, Bill! I thought that you'd never come."

He said: "Yeah?"

"Yeah," her voice mimicked him. "I had to see you. Every time you get into trouble, I have to get you out. Well, I got into trouble, and I got myself out."

"Swell!"

"You don't believe me. Well, I was kidnaped, actually kidnaped. I always thought that only important people got kidnaped."

He managed to make his eyes wide. "No?"

"It's a fact. Sarano had me kidnaped. He asked me a lot of questions about Mary Renner. Then he locked me in an upstairs room. There was a passage through the closet. It wasn't a secret or anything, just a door, a double closet. I guess they forgot to lock it, or maybe thought it was locked. Anyhow, I simply walked through into the other room, raised the window, got out on the porch roof, and dropped to the ground. Aren't I the smart girl?"

"Very smart."

"I'm going to tell Louman about it, but I wanted to see you first." She rose, then she stopped. "Why, Bill, where'd you get that bruise on your cheek?"

He said: "What bruise?" and fingered it without thinking.

Her eyes narrowed and suddenly she reached forward and pulled off his hat, exposing the long strip of adhesive tape that covered the groove made by Whitey's gun. "Bill—what happened? Can't I even be kidnaped without you sneaking off and getting into trouble? What happened to you?"

He grinned at her sourly, and patted the hand which still held his hat. "Nothing important, honey. I just ran into a door."

Tears Don't Help

*Bill Lennox picks a nice bunch of trouble
with more than a headache in it*

1

BILL LENNOX, TROUBLE-SHOOTER for the General-Consolidated Studio, sat beside Moyer, the director, and watched Mary Grier. The set was a beer hall, patterned after the nineties. A pianist, on a small raised platform, played steadily to a crowd of extras. Alone, at a small table at the side of the platform, Mary cried into her beer.

Lennox grinned. She was good, plenty good; sixty-five, and the best box-office attraction since Valentino. He remembered the first time that he had seen her. Almost twenty years ago he, a bare-legged kid, sat high in the gallery of a mid-Western theater; sat and watched, yes, and worshiped. They had said that she was slipping then, past her peak, on the way downhill, and now here she was, twenty years later, queen of Hollywood and a grand old trouper.

He watched as the cameras were cut, the lights rearranged; watched Mary rise and walk to the edge of the sound stage, watched the dress extras gather in little groups, saw the director talking to the head cameraman, and then he saw Mary's negro maid hand her mistress a gray envelope.

He watched idly as Mary tore it open and unfolded the single sheet. He was too far away to see her expression, but he did see her sway. Even as he came to his feet, she fell, crumpled, rather, into a little heap. Lennox vaulted the empty chair at his side, crossed the set and pushed through the extras. An assistant director was bending above Mary, his thin face white beneath its Malibu tan. Lennox shoved him aside and gathered her into his arms. As he did so, the piece of gray note-paper fluttered to the floor. He scooped it up and stuffed it into his pocket; then he lifted the unconscious actress and carried her across the lot to her dressing-room.

Sol Spurck, head of the West Coast Studios of General-Consolidated, came panting into the room, a worried frown on his benign, fat face.

"Always trouble," he moaned. "If it ain't one thing, it's the same. First the story is not right and I get a new writer, but for a thousand dollars I should take a chance. And now Grier collapses when we are half done shooting."

Lennox said, tensely: "She's sick, Sol. The doctors don't seem to know what's the matter with her."

"Phooey, doctors! For a hundred dollars they can't tell what's wrong, but then, they ain't been in this business for twenty-three years, like me. Positively, I'm telling you, Bill, it is temperament, nothing but temperament."

Lennox shook his head. "I wish it were, but Mary is too good a trouper for that, Sol."

Spurck found a chair and sat down heavily. "Maybe," his voice was doubtful, "but we gotta do something. The picture, it is two weeks behind schedule already, and the New York office—I wish those *schlemiels* was out here once."

The door from the other room opened and the doctor appeared.

Lennox said: "How is she, Doctor?"

The other hesitated, then shrugged slightly. "To tell you the exact truth, I don't know. She's had some kind of shock, she won't tell us what. She's resting quietly now, but her general condition is puzzling, I—"

Lennox said: "It's okey to see her, isn't it?"

Again the man hesitated. "Well, don't excite her if you can help it."

Spurck rose quickly for one of his weight, but Lennox stopped him with a motion of his hand. He walked across the room and knocked on the connecting door. A white-capped nurse opened it and looked at him uncertainly.

Lennox said: "The doctor told me that I could see Miss Grier."

The nurse studied him with disapproving eyes, hesitated, then stepped reluctantly aside. Lennox went in. He saw Mary Grier on a wide studio couch, her eyes closed. They opened languidly as he came towards her. "Bill!"

He took one thin, blue-veined hand in both of his. "Hello, trouper!"

She said, weakly: "Thanks for coming, pal. I need you."

He pulled a stool over beside the couch and sat down. "What do you want done?"

She said: "Tell that fool doctor that I'm not sick. That I've got to get up."

He tried to soothe her. "Remember that you're a trouper, not some beauty contest winner, fresh from Ohio. The doc is running this show and your lines call for a bedroom scene for a couple of days."

Two tears, put there by weakness, forced their way from beneath her lids and trickled down the grease paint that was still on her cheeks. "I can't be sick today. I've got things to do."

He said: "The picture can wait. It will have to wait, or maybe they can shoot around you."

She roused herself, tried to sit up, but he restrained her. She said, weakly: "To hell with the picture! This is personal, important. I've got to get up."

"You can't." His voice was finality itself. "Stop acting screwy and get yourself well. Let me handle things."

Her eyes were on his, probing, studying, then worry again showed in their depths. "That letter—I've lost that letter."

Lennox drew the gray sheet from his pocket and folded her old fingers about it. "No you haven't, honey."

She stared at it, relief replacing the worry in her eyes; then they went to the silent nurse. "Tell her to leave."

The nurse hesitated; Lennox jerked his head towards the door. After a moment she went, and Mary Grier settled back with a little sigh. "You've got to help me, Bill. I can't go myself, and I haven't anyone else to trust."

2

NANCY HOBBS, STAFF writer for one of the better fan magazines, sat on the corner of Lennox's desk and looked at him as he pushed open the door of his own office. She said: "What's this I hear about Grier's collapsing on the set? They wouldn't say a thing in the front office."

He patted her shoulder and walked around the desk to the chair.

"There's nothing in it, brat. At least, nothing for publication."

Her voice was defensive. "Remember, we girls have to eat."

He said: "Pick on the blondes, they love it, but lay off Grier."

She stared at his serious face. "What is it, Bill? What's the matter?"

He hesitated. "It's Grier's grandson," he said, finally.

The girl said: "I didn't know she had one."

"There's lots of things that you don't know," he told her. "Grier took damned good care that no one knew it. Her daughter married some no-good hoofer with an eye for blondes. She died when the baby came, and the hoofer walked out of the picture. Mary had the kid educated in England and France; but he's here now, here in Hollywood. Ever hear of Frank Blair?"

Nancy said: "Oh, not *the* Frank Blair, not the one who came here recently and has been burning up the night-clubs?"

Lennox nodded shortly. "That heel," he said. "Grier's idea of giving the kid a break was to shovel out the dough, and he's been spending it. That worried her, but although she talked to him, it didn't buy her a thing. Then she got this, today." He drew the sheet of gray note-paper from his pocket and handed it to the girl. Nancy read:

Dear Miss Grier:

Maybe you don't know me, but there are plenty of people in this town who can tell you who I am. Your grandson is in trouble, bad trouble. I'd come to see you, but I'm afraid. If you could come to my apartment between three and four today or tomorrow, it would be best. Wear old clothes and get off at the above address, and take elevator to fifth floor, but don't ask for me. Whatever you do, don't show this note to Frank Blair.

Tiny Armstrong.

Nancy Hobbs' brows drew together. "What has Tiny—"

Lennox said: "You're right, honey. What has a two-timing little tramp like Armstrong to do with Frank Blair? Well, I mean to find out. I'm going over there now."

"It looks like blackmail," the girl told him.

He grinned mirthlessly. "If it is, I'll make Tiny sorry that she picked Mary Grier." He walked around his desk and, pulling out the top drawer, slipped a gun from it and into his pocket. Nancy watched him with widened eyes.

"You're headed for trouble again, Bill."

He said: "For Mary Grier I'd take all the trouble there is, and like it. She's swell people."

The girl swung off the desk. "My coupé is out front. I'll drive you over."

He said: "Want to be in at the kill, huh?"

She said, steadily: "Someone has to look after you. It seems to be my job."

The apartment in which Armstrong lived was big, imposing, with an imitation marble lobby and potted palms. When Nancy Hobbs pulled to the curb she said: "I'm coming in with you."

Lennox shook his head. "No you're not, brat. You've got a kind face. Seeing you, Armstrong might not believe when I threaten to heat her toes if she doesn't talk."

He climbed out of the coupé and went through the lobby to the elevator. The colored boy eyed him, but said nothing as he got out at the fourth floor. Lennox waited until the car dropped from sight, then walked rapidly to the stairway and up to the floor above. He paused before the door marked five-o-two, looked both ways, then knocked. No sound reached him from within. He knocked again, louder this time, and stood, chewing his lower lip thoughtfully.

Still no sound, and his hand dropped to the knob. To his surprise, it turned beneath his hand. He pushed the door open, went through into the square entryway, and shut the door behind him. There was no sound from the apartment beyond. He crossed the littered hall and pushed open another door, then stopped. A girl lay on her side in the middle of the rug, one arm outstretched beneath her head, her dark hair tumbled about the small, pert face. Fear and anger made ugly lines about her mouth, which even death had not erased.

Lennox stepped in cautiously, his hand on the cool metal of his gun, his eyes shifting quickly about the room. A door to the right stood open, exposing a bedroom with an unmade bed and scattered clothing. Nothing stirred in the apartment. Noise came through the open window from the street below, making him look that way, sharply; then he looked back at the crumpled figure.

Tiny Armstrong lay quiet upon the rug. Never again would her name figure in a divorce action; never again would her slim slippers tap madly on some hotel dance-floor. He bent above the body, noting the crimson patch where blood had stained the multi-colored dress. Her skirt was torn at the side, exposing a white thigh and the top of a silk stocking. Runs threaded their way from the stocking top down over the round of her calf to the trim ankle. Lennox stared at the runs, his eyes very narrow. Even in the privacy of her apartment Tiny would never have worn such stockings; rather, far rather, no stockings at all.

He straightened slowly. There had been something concealed in that stocking top, something which the murderer had wanted; something which had been taken hurriedly, violently; so violently that the runs had been left as mute evidence.

There was a high desk against the farther wall, a period desk. Lennox took his hand from the gun in his pocket, crossed the room, opened the desk, and went through the collection of bills which it contained. He did not know what he was looking for. He only knew that Armstrong had had information for Mary Grier, information which she had not lived to give.

There was nothing in the desk and he turned away, stared at the silent girl as if she might rise and give the answer; then his eyes came up and narrowed as a man stepped into the doorway. Lennox had never met Frank Blair, but he recognized him from newspaper pictures. Tall, light-haired, with pale blue eyes which seemed to lack both feeling and depth, he stood there in the doorway, staring into the room, at Lennox, beyond Lennox to the littered desk. His hand slid into his coat pocket and appeared a moment later, a small, stub-nosed gun catching the glint of the late afternoon sun. "Up!"

Slowly Lennox raised his hands. He wanted to laugh, in fact, a half-mocking smile twisted at the corner of his thin lips. He had come here to rescue Blair and now— He said: "You don't know me, but I'm Bill Lennox of General." The blue eyes did not change. "Your grandmother sent me to see Armstrong, about you."

Surprise showed in Blair's voice. "You know who I am?"

Lennox said: "I've seen pictures."

For a moment Blair was silent. "Why'd you kill her?" His free hand indicated the girl on the floor. The gun was still steady, on the second top button of Lennox's vest.

Bill said: "She was that way when I came in."

"And the desk?" Blair's voice did not change.

Lennox started to say something, stopped. He remembered suddenly that Armstrong's note had warned Mary Grier against showing its contents to her grandson. "It was that way when I came in, but Blair, let's get away from here. The last thing you want is this kind of publicity. We—" He stopped. Someone was knocking sharply on the outer door. In silence the two looked at each other as the knocking continued. Lennox saw the blue eyes deepen, gain fear. He ignored the gun in Blair's hand and stepped towards the entry.

Zorman, the apartment manager, stood in the hall as Lennox opened the door. He said: "Why, Mr. Lennox!" His voice was heavy with surprise.

Bill said: "Hello, Zorman! What's the matter?"

Zorman said: "I've got to see Miss Armstrong at once. It's very important." He was small, with dark, oily hair, and too prominent eyes.

Lennox hesitated, then shrugged and stepped aside. Zorman

went past him to stop in the inner door. Lennox heard him swear softly. Then he stepped forward into the room and bent above the body. When he straightened, his face, usually so cold, so expressionless, held a sick look. "Bad business, Mr. Lennox, very bad."

Lennox said, without interest: "This won't help your house."

The manager moaned. "Fifty thousand we just spent, redecorating and new furniture. A nice, quiet, respectable house."

"A cesspool," Lennox corrected him. "If there's one house in town with a lousy reputation, it's this one." He looked across the room at the silent, white-faced boy. "Take it easy, Frank." His tone was calm, reassuring, but his mind was racing. Zorman made it tough, plenty tough. He'd hoped to get the boy away before the cops arrived. Having her grandson mixed up in a murder case wasn't the kind of medicine that Mary Grier needed, but now— He crossed the room and picked up the phone. When he reached the Homicide Bureau, he asked for Spellman. He told the detective captain what had happened and hung up; then he turned around to find Zorman moving towards the door. He said: "Not until the cops come." Zorman hesitated, then sat down. They waited fifteen minutes. Someone pounded on the door and Lennox rose and opened it. Spellman came in, followed by two men. He grunted when he saw Lennox. If he was pleased, he concealed the pleasure without difficulty. His penetrating eyes, screened by heavy lids, went to Zorman. "What have we here?"

The apartment manager said: "A killing," and wrung his hands in the air. "But honest, Captain, it ain't the fault of the house. Swell references, she had."

Spellman cut him short. "Who did it?" He stared at Lennox.

Bill said: "She was that way when I came in." He found a cigarette and rolled it between his fingers, so that loose tobacco spilled at both ends.

Spellman's eyes went to the boy. "All right, you!"

Lennox cut across the words. "He's with me, Floyd."

"He could be in better company," the detective said, without humor. He stepped around Lennox and caught the boy's shoulder. "Come on! Why did you kill her?"

Blair's white face seemed to whiten further. His pale eyes lost color until they hardly showed. With a gesture of contempt he freed himself and stepped back. "Some day, you'll get in trouble, doing that."

3

LENNOX SAID: "IT'S a mess, honey; a swell mess."

Nancy Hobbs did not look at him as she twisted the coupé through traffic. "What do you think?" she asked.

He said, in a tired voice: "I wish I knew what to think. Blair's clear, as far as the killing goes, but he's a nasty kid if I ever saw one, and Spellman thinks the same. The cops will ride him if they can."

She said, musingly: "I wonder what she wanted to tell Grier?"

He shrugged. "I guess she was just pulling a little quiet blackmail on the side. The chances are we won't hear a thing more about it, but that kid is going to cause plenty of grief."

The coupé pulled up before the apartment hotel which Lennox called home, and he got out.

"Thanks for the ride, punk." He mussed her hair affectionately. "I'll be seeing you." He watched the coupé pull away, then turned and went into the building.

An hour later, as he was knotting his tie, someone knocked on the outer door. With an expression of disgust he crossed the sitting-room and pulled it open. Two men came in with the door. A gun jammed its way into Lennox's side, just above the hip bone, jammed hard. The other man closed the door and said: "In there."

They went into the sitting-room and Lennox watched his visitors with narrowed eyes. "What's the idea?"

The man with the gun said: "Don't be funny, fellow! We want the stuff you grabbed in Armstrong's apartment."

"You're screwy." Lennox backed away from the gun. "I didn't take a thing."

The man with the gun said: "Might as well search the joint, Phil. Sit down, you, and keep your hands on the chair arms."

Lennox sat down. The anger which had flowed through him was cooling and he watched with detached interest while Phil proceeded with his search. Certainly it was systematic. Pillows were ripped apart and thrown to the floor. The rug was rolled back, the walls searched. Then he went into the bedroom. Half an hour later the gunman came back into the room. "Nothing here. Guess we'll have to make him talk."

Lennox said, through thinned lips: "You're screwy— I tell you that I didn't—" The man with the gun hit him sharply across the mouth.

"That's just a sample," he said, pleasantly. "Come on, talk!"

Lennox heaved himself from the chair and dived for the other's legs. They went down on to the floor together, struggling for the gun, rolled against the table, upsetting it on top of them. The other man sprang in, his gun clubbed, trying to reach Lennox. Bill's fingers were clawing at the man's throat. The other managed to break loose, came to his knees and shoved the table across Lennox. He panted: "The noise, let's scram." Lennox caught his leg and hung on, then he saw the clubbed gun coming, tried to duck, and failed. The gun came down twice, striking him above the ear. His grip on the leg relaxed, and he lost interest.

4

THE ROOM SEEMED full of men when he managed to
get his eyes open. For a moment he stared about uncertainly,
saw the broken table, the scattered furniture; then he looked
up and recognized Spellman. "Hello, copper! Imagine seeing
you here." He tried a grin, but only partly succeeded. "How
long was I out?"

Spellman said: "About five minutes. I was downstairs, just
coming up, when we heard the racket. Who were they?"

"Your guess is as good as mine." Lennox managed to sit up
and look around. He saw the house manager, the night clerk,
and the elevator boy. "We seem to be giving a party."

Spellman looked about. "You can go," he told them. "You can
clean up this mess later." They went, reluctantly. When the
door was closed, the detective turned back to Lennox. "Come
on! Who were they?"

Lennox touched the side of his head gingerly with an inquiring finger. "You won't believe me, but I haven't the slightest
idea." His finger came away, sticky, and he stared at the blood
as if puzzled.

Spellman barked: "Of course I don't believe you. You lied to
me about Armstrong this afternoon. You're lying now."

Lennox struggled to his feet and went swayingly towards the
bathroom. Spellman called after him: "Better have a doctor
look at that head. It's pretty messy."

Lennox soaked a towel and held it lightly to the spot.
"Thanks, no. He might decide to amputate. I've got some

medicine, in a flat bottle, four years old. At least the bottle is." He went towards the barette and drew it forth. Spellman said:

"We're wasting time. Come on! Who were they?"

Lennox poured himself a drink and looked inquiringly at the detective, drank, and replaced the bottle. "I needed that."

Spellman's voice was harsh. "Come on, Bill! Gimme the low-down. Who worked you over? What were you doing in Armstrong's apartment this afternoon? I've got a hunch that you know who killed her."

Lennox said: "Which makes it a hundred per cent. Your hunches are always wrong. I don't know who killed her, or why, but I do know that the gentlemen who were just here thought that I lifted something from that apartment, something they wanted, bad."

Spellman said: "Did you?"

"I did not. By the way, you didn't come over here to buy me a dinner, did you?"

Spellman grinned heavily. "You know better than that."

"Then just what did you come for?"

The detective's brows drew down heavily above his eyes. "I want some dope on this Blair," he said. "You claimed that he was with you. I know now that you're lying."

"Just a pal." Lennox carried the towel back into the bathroom and held it under the hot water tap. "Why should I lie?"

"That's what I'm asking you? Why should you lie—" The phone rang sharply. Both Lennox and the detective stared at it as it rang again; then, with a groan, Lennox crossed the room and picked it up. "Yeah— What?— When?" He listened for a minute, then said: "I'll be right over," and hung up.

Spellman saw his white face, came half out of his chair. "For gawd's sake, Bill! What's the matter?"

Lennox said, stupidly, slowly, as if only half awake: "Mary Grier died ten minutes ago."

5

THE HOUSE WAS blazing with light when the squad car swung to the curb. Lennox, closely followed by Spellman, pushed open the gate, went across the tile-paved court, and into the house. The scared negro maid caught his arm with fingers that clung. "I'se glad yo'ah here."

He unfastened her fingers gently, went down the wide hall, and into the paneled study. Sol Spurck turned around as he came in. For a moment neither spoke; then Lennox said: "What happened?"

Spurck shook his head. "I was still at the studio, y'understand, when the call came. Right away I send for you; then I came here."

Lennox said: "Is the doctor here?"

Spurck jerked his thumb towards the bedroom. "In there."

Lennox went in. The doctor stood at one side of the room, talking to the white-capped nurse. The woman's face was red, angry. He turned around as Bill came into the room. Lennox said: "What was it? Her heart?"

The doctor shook his head. "I'm not sure, but I think—" He stopped a moment as if to choose his words. "You'd better call the coroner."

Lennox said, sharply: "Just what do you mean?"

"I mean," the doctor told him, "that I can't sign the death certificate. Unless I'm mistaken, she died from an overdose of sleeping powder."

There was a groan from the door behind. Sol Spurck said: "Oi! A murder yet!"

Spellman shoved his way into the room. "What's this, what's this?" Both the doctor and nurse stared at him.

Lennox said: "This is Detective Captain Spellman. You'd better tell him exactly what you told me."

Lennox went out while they were talking.

The Negro maid was crying quietly in the corner of the kitchen. Lennox put a hand on her shoulder and said: "Take it easy, Maud. Tears don't help."

She looked up, wiping her eyes on a corner of her white apron. "Mary"—she'd always called her mistress Mary—"knew she was gwan to die."

He said, sharply: "Nonsense! Your imagination is running loose."

The girl shook her head, stubbornly. "That's why she rit yuh dat letter."

"What letter?"

The girl rose, crossed the room, and took a white envelope from one corner of the cupboard. Lennox was beside her. He took it and turned it over in his hand. "When did she write this?"

The maid said: "This afternoon. She give it tuh me. Made me promise what eber happened tuh give it tuh yuh."

The letter was unsealed. Lennox pulled it forth and opened it. Suddenly he said: "So you read it?"

The maid's face was sullen. He could see the denial form on her thick lips, then she nodded. "I read it."

He unfolded the note. The writing was a weak scrawl, not the precise script that he remembered.

Dear Bill:

I have a hunch that I'm washed up. I always have played my hunches, so I'm playing this one. If something happens to me, I want you to look out for Frank. He's wild. Maybe it's my fault. I suppose that it is, but I did the best I could.

Mary.

He folded the note slowly and slipped it into his pocket as Spellman came into the room.

"The doc was right," he said, shortly. "We don't know yet whether the nurse made a mistake or whether—" His voice trailed off suggestively.

Lennox said: "Any use in my sticking around?"

The detective shook his head. "Guess not. You might as well shove off home. Grier's secretary just came in. She was away, Santa Barbara. She'll handle things."

Lennox nodded and walked into the hall. He called a cab, found his overcoat, and slipped into it. His head was throbbing dully as he crossed the patio and climbed into the cab. The driver said: "Where to?" as he threw his flag. Lennox stared at him. He remembered suddenly that he did not know where Frank Blair lived. He started to tell the man to take him home, then changed his mind, and gave the address of Armstrong's apartment, which they reached in short order.

Lennox went into the manager's office and asked his question.

Zorman said: "But Mr. Lennox, I don't even know him."

Bill shrugged. "I just took a chance. He's been playing around with Miss Armstrong for six weeks. Thought maybe you'd know his address."

The apartment manager spread his hands. "I'd like to help, but I don't know. People come, people go. I see them, but I don't know them."

Lennox nodded and rose. He left the manager's office and walked towards the door. Halfway across the lobby he had another idea, and changed his course towards the desk. "Are the cops still in Armstrong's apartment?"

The clerk shook his head. "They left a while ago. Guess there wasn't any reason to hang around."

Lennox said: "Let me have the key. Spellman forgot something."

The clerk hesitated. "I'd like to, Mr. Lennox, but I'll have to ask"—a folded five-dollar bill was slipped into his palm.

Bill said: "The key," and the clerk shoved it towards him.

The elevator wasn't in sight, and Lennox went up the stairs. He saw no one in the upper halls; not a sound reached him save a radio playing loudly on the third floor. He stopped in front of the apartment door, slid the key into the lock, and threw the bolt. It made no sound, and he pushed the door open and went in. Then he stopped.

Light showed from the front room, drifting through a crack in the connecting door. He stared at it a moment in silence, then he went across the little hall, his hand buried in his coat pocket. Gently he shoved the door open, then he swore. Frank Blair stood in the middle of the room, looking around. His eyes came about, fastened themselves on Lennox's face. His shoulders gave a convulsive jerk of surprise. His hand dropped towards his coat pocket, then it stopped. For perhaps thirty seconds there was no movement in the room. They stared at each other. Suddenly Lennox laughed, not from amusement, but in self-mockery.

Blair said: "What's the matter?" His voice sounded uneasy, strained.

Lennox said: "I've been looking for you, and I find you, here."

The boy's blue eyes seemed to flatten, lose depth. His hand, which had been hovering above the edge of his pocket, moved slowly. Lennox's voice was brittle. "Keep that hand in sight."

Blair wet his lips with the tip of his tongue. "What's the matter with you? Did you come to tell me that my grand-mother is—"

"Is what?" Lennox's voice seemed to crack.

"Why, I—"

Lennox said: "You knew that Mary was worth a million. Is that why you killed her?"

"Damn you!"

Blair seemed to uncoil suddenly as he leaped forward. Lennox had no chance to get his gun clear, and he did not want to shoot. After all, this boy was Grier's grandson; he might be her murderer, but the law could take care of that. Lennox stepped quickly to the left. His right hand came up in a short, quick jab which sent Blair back on his heels, crossed his eyes for the moment, but did not put him down. For an instant he stood there, shaking his head so that the fair hair tumbled about his face; then he leaped forward again, his hands like claws, reaching for Lennox's throat.

Bill hit him over the heart, felt the hands close on his shoulders, and realized the other's surprising strength. They went over together on to the stained rug, Blair on top, his fingers digging into the flesh above Lennox's collar, pressing, shutting off his wind. Lennox caught one wrist with one hand, twisted it suddenly, heaved himself three inches from the floor, and managed to roll over. He had the man's hand over his shoulder, came to his knees, threw him across his head, rolled on to him. A moment later he had an arm lock and Blair was writhing on the carpet.

Lennox leaped clear and the next moment had his gun out. "All right, you rat! On your feet."

Blair rose slowly, sullenly. He turned his back at Lennox's command, and Bill got his gun. "What's the idea?" he panted.

Lennox said: "The idea is that I don't like killers." His voice was choked with anger. "You lousy bum! Mary sacrificed her life for you, and you kill her for money."

Blair straightened his coat. "You haven't a thing on me," he said, with returning confidence. "I didn't kill the old lady. I didn't even know that she was dead."

Lennox said: "We'll let Spellman handle that. After he works on you, you'll talk and love it. I'd do the job myself, but I can't be trusted. I might kill you. Come on."

"Where?"

Lennox did not dare to turn, but he knew that voice, knew that Zorman stood behind him. He said, harshly: "I'm taking this punk downtown, down for murder. Keep out of this, Zorman."

The apartment manager's voice seemed velvet. "You should have kept out of this, Bill." Something round, hard, pressed between Lennox's shoulders. "How much does he know?"

Blair said, savagely: "Not much, I think, but he's a swell guesser."

The gun in Lennox's back jabbed harder. "Drop that rod!"

Lennox let it slip through his fingers to the carpet and slowly raised his hands. He felt Zorman's fingers go into his coat pocket and remove Blair's gun, then he turned around. The apartment manager was regarding him thoughtfully. "The desk clerk knows that you're here," he said, as if speaking to himself, "therefore he's got to see you leave." He looked past Lennox at Blair, his eyes seeming to be asking a question. The other said, sullenly: "I didn't find it. She must have taken it out somewhere."

Zorman swore. "She couldn't have. Dick and Phil watched her, I tell you. It's got to be here."

Lennox watched him with narrow eyes, gauging his chances. He decided that they weren't good when Blair pressed close to his side and he could feel the gun through the other's pocket. The fair-haired one said: "I hope you give me an excuse to shoot, fellow. I don't like you."

Zorman's voice was sharp. "Cut that! There ain't going to be no trouble, understand. We're walking out of here nice, quiet like; then we're going to take a ride."

The short hairs at the back of Lennox's neck crawled. "Like that?" he asked, tonelessly.

Zorman laughed, not a pleasant sound. "You mistake. Nothing so crude as that, if you are sensible. We are not looking for trouble. No, no!"

Lennox said: "I understand. You figure that if my body turned up, Spellman might ask questions. Well, you're right; he would. He doesn't like this punk here now."

Blair made a noise in his throat. Zorman said: "We waste time," and, opening the hall door, peered out. "Come on."

6

THEY WALKED THROUGH the deserted lobby, went through the doors and out on to the sidewalk, where there was no one close by. There was a closed car at the curb, a black Cad with curtains. Zorman got in first, Lennox in the middle, with Blair at his other side. The door was closed and the car moved away. Evidently the driver already had his instructions. They drove around the block and into the alley behind the building. Lennox said: "Nice long trip."

"Long enough," Zorman told him. "The clerk thinks that we've gone miles."

They got out of the car and went into the back door of the apartment. There were stairs to the right, leading downward. Zorman jerked his head and Lennox went down. He knew that Blair was behind him, his gun in his hand. They went along a concrete paved passage, past the furnace room and laundry, turned to the right, and stopped before a closed door. Zorman fitted a key into the lock, threw the door open, and punched a switch. Lennox saw another stairway, leading upwards.

He said: "What is this? A treasure hunt?"

Zorman said: "You're seeing things that not one person in a hundred thousand knows anything about."

Lennox's tone was dry. "Thanks a lot, but I'll pass up the honor if you hand me the chance."

Zorman laughed. "This is one time that I have to insist." He went ahead up the stairway, opened a door at the top, and disappeared.

Blair said: "Get going, cull," and pushed his gun between Lennox's shoulders. Bill went up the stairs, along the short hall and through the door. It opened into a closet lined with woman's clothes—a long closet and there were lots of clothes; there were also a number of bottles still in their paper wrappings. Then he stepped through into a bedroom to find Zorman waiting for him.

Lennox nodded, looked around the room, then walked to the connecting door and looked out. There was a desk in the other room, a desk with filing cases.

It wasn't hard to figure. The basement for bringing in the liquor; the closet from which to feed it out, and the files indicating the proportions of the prerepeal business. Lennox whistled.

He said: "I've heard of lots of blinds, but this is the first time a whole apartment house has been used. Go on, Zorman. You can make it interesting."

The other shrugged and sat down at the desk. "It's your turn to talk. What did you do with that paper you took from Armstrong's apartment this afternoon?"

Lennox stared at him. "I've said that I didn't take anything. Will it do any good if I repeat it?"

The apartment manager shook his head. As he did so, he turned so that the light struck his profile. Lennox stared at him. "Say—I know you."

Zorman's eyes narrowed. He said: "Certainly you know me. You've known me three years."

Lennox shook his head. "I knew you before that," he said. "I never thought about it before, but the way the light caught your face reminded me of one night backstage at the old Gilpin

Theater. Your name wasn't Zorman then, but you were Mary Grier's manager."

The man at the desk half rose, then he settled back in his seat. "I congratulate you, Lennox. You're the only one who has recognized me."

Lennox's face was grim. "You always were a rat, Zorman. I remember now, Mary fired you, didn't she? There was an argument about some contract. You waited a long time, but you got even finally, you and the rat for whom she spent her life. Well, you won't cash in on it. You'll never see any of her money."

Zorman's face was a maze of conflicting emotions. "So you found it?" he gasped. "You've got it? Where is it? I'll—"

Lennox watched him through narrow eyes. "Well, say that I did find it, say that it's in a safe place. What are you going to do? Do we trade?" He had no idea what the apartment manager was talking about, but he was playing for time.

Zorman settled back in his chair. The anger which had clouded his face a moment before was gone. "What's it worth, Lennox, to play with us?"

Bill said: "It's worth plenty. Make an offer."

Zorman said, slowly: "Is it worth your life?"

"What do you mean?"

"Just that. Give us the envelope you took from Armstrong's apartment and we'll see that you live, otherwise—"

Lennox's brain was racing. "Okey!" he said, suddenly. "But how do I know that you won't cross me when you have the—envelope?"

"A nice question." Zorman was silent for a moment. Suddenly he said: "You wouldn't want Mary Grier's grandson to hang. Come here, Frank."

The gun still in his hand, Blair stepped around Lennox to the end of the desk. Zorman said: "Look at him, Lennox. He does look like Grier, doesn't he?"

Bill said: "He may look like Mary, but he must take after his father. I won't pretend that I like him, Zorman. I don't. I hate his guts."

"But—well, he's her grandson."

"Which makes it worse, worse than if he were a stranger."

Zorman's voice changed suddenly. "You haven't got that envelope, Lennox. You lied."

Bill stared at him. Zorman said to Blair: "Call Phil and we'll lock this guy up until we decide what to do with him." They waited five minutes, then Phil and another man came into the room. He grinned when he saw Lennox. "Hello, sweetheart! I'll finish that job now."

"Nix," Zorman said, sharply. "No rough stuff. Take him up to the fourth floor and tie him up. We'll handle him tomorrow."

7

THE GAG IN Lennox's mouth hurt, his wrists burned from the tightly drawn rope, and his ankles were numb. How long he had lain on that couch he could not be sure, but the room had grown steadily colder. The chill which precedes daylight crept through his clothes, adding to his discomfort. A slight noise at the apartment door drew his eyes in that direction, a tiny scratching sound as if someone was feeling for a keyhole. He could not be sure, but he thought that the bolt had been thrown back gently, that the door was being pushed open; then light drifted through from the hall, outlining for a moment the dark figure which slipped through, then the door closed and everything was quiet.

Lennox lay there, straining his ears in an effort to hear. Someone was in the apartment, someone who evidently did not belong there. There was a slight sound as a foot struck a chair leg, then a louder noise and a muffled curse. Lennox tried to make a sound around the gag, but failed.

He could hear the other's breathing now, sense the presence in the room; then movement came again. A hand touched Lennox's cheek and was quickly withdrawn. For what seemed like minutes nothing happened, then the hand came again, inquiring fingers which ran over his cheek and felt along the gag. The hand was withdrawn. Silence, and then the click of lights. Lennox blinked in the sudden radiance, twisted on his side in an effort to see across the room.

A boy was staring at him with widened eyes, uncertain eyes,

which seemed to ask questions. Lennox tried to work his jaws about the gag without success. The other took an uncertain step towards the couch, then another, his eyes always on Lennox. Suddenly he seemed to make up his mind and, coming forward, went to work on the gag. The knot proved difficult. The fingers seemed bungling, and it was five minutes before the handkerchief, with its wad of gauze, fell away. Lennox tried to speak, found that his tongue was so thick that he could only make sounds. He managed to lift his bound ankles, and in another moment, the boy was on his knees before the couch.

Lennox said: "Glub—culm—tonks." He worked his tongue back and forth, said hoarsely: "Thanks."

The boy looked up quickly. For an instant a fleeting smile touched his lips, and was gone. "Who are you?"

"Bill Lennox." The name seemed to mean nothing to the boy. "And you?"

"Frank Blair."

Lennox said under his breath, sharply: "Fool!" The other looked up with surprise and Lennox grinned. "I'm talking to myself," he said, as the rope about his ankles came free. "Try the wrists."

The boy tried and succeeded after a time. Lennox flexed his hands to restore circulation. The skin below his cuffs was red, almost raw. He stood up and stamped gently, trying to drive the needles from his legs. Then he put one hand to his aching jaws. "I've been looking for you, but I didn't know it."

Surprise lighted the other's eyes. "Looking for me? Oh, my grandmother! How is she?" There was an eager note in the voice. "Then Tiny succeeded in getting word to her?"

Lennox said: "Sorry, Blair, but your grandmother is—"

The boy's fists clenched. "I knew it, those devils. They killed Armstrong, too." He was silent for several moments. "I found her this afternoon."

Lennox said: "Hadn't you better start at the beginning and tell me about it?"

The boy said: "I don't understand it all myself. Zorman met me in New York. I knew him. He used to be grandmother's manager. He said that Mary couldn't come East, so she had sent him. He cautioned me not to tell anyone who I was, said that it would hurt Mary if anyone found out that she had a grown grandson. We came West and he put me in an apartment here. I didn't suspect anything at first; then I began to feel sleepy all the time."

Lennox said: "So they doped you?"

The boy nodded. "I didn't know that, but Tiny told me. She was with Zorman in New York, and came out here with me on the train. I think she liked me." There was a wistful note in his voice. "Anyhow, she warned me not to eat the food they brought me. She used to sneak me things that weren't doped. Then she took my passport and said she was going to see Mary and tell her the truth."

Lennox said: "But why didn't you walk out?"

The boy shrugged. "The gang lived on this floor and the next. There used to be someone guarding the stairway down on the third floor, but they didn't pay much attention to me. I'd sneak out and go to Tiny's apartment. I did that this afternoon and found her dead." He stopped, shuddered. "I knew then that they had suspected Tiny. I was afraid that they had found my passport. It was the only thing that I had to prove who I am."

Lennox said, suddenly: "So you took it from the top of her stocking?"

The boy nodded. "I knew she carried it there. I was scared and in a hurry. I tore her dress, getting it."

Lennox said: "It's a wonder that they didn't kill you."

The boy nodded. "I wondered that myself, but Tiny used to say they were afraid to. They thought that something might happen and they couldn't get her money by using an impostor, so they kept me alive. They thought that I was drugged. That's why they didn't watch me closely."

Lennox was rubbing his wrists. "We've got to get out of here." He rose and walked about the room, looking for a phone. There wasn't one. Then he thought of Armstrong's apartment upstairs. "You must have a passkey to the rooms upstairs."

The boy nodded: "Tiny got me one." He extended it, and Lennox slipped it into his pocket. He opened the outer door cautiously and peered out. The hall beyond was deserted and, motioning Blair to follow, he led the way towards the stairs. A man's figure cast a dim shadow on the wall below as Lennox looked over the rail. Evidently Zorman had posted his guard. Lennox turned and mounted the stairs to the fifth floor. No one was in sight and he led the way towards the door of Armstrong's apartment. Once inside, he crossed the room rapidly and picked up the phone.

The boy said, quickly: "Don't do that. The switchboard." Even as he spoke a voice came over the wire, a voice that Lennox recognized as Zorman's.

"Say, who's up there? That you, Phil—"

Lennox slipped the receiver back into place and turned around.

"Sorry, kid. That was a dumb play. Where do we go from here?"

"The roof." Blair's voice shook for a moment, then steadied. "The stairs are at the end of the hall. There's a trap door—"

Lennox was already in the hall, Blair at his heels. Below them, feet pounded on uncarpeted steps. They ran along the hall and went up the ladder-like stairs. Lennox shoved the trap open and stepped out on the flat roof. He replaced the trap as soon as Blair was through and looked about for something to weight it. There was nothing.

Two chimneys loomed to the right. A three-foot parapet of brick surrounded the roof. There was nothing else. Lennox led the way to the chimneys. At least they would offer shelter for the moment. They crouched behind their shelter, their hands against the rough, cold bricks. The lights of the city made a dull crimson glow against the fog. The roof was moist, chill, as was the air. In the east a streak of dirty gray told that in an hour it would be light. Lennox wondered vaguely if they would live that hour.

Time dragged slowly, seconds seemed minutes; then there was noise from the trap. A hoarse voice said: "I don't see them." A fainter voice said: "They gotta be up there. Maybe they're hiding behind the chimneys."

More noise from the trap, heavy shoes crunched across the gravel of the roof. Other shoes made noise, following the first. Lennox tensed, his left hand against the chimney, his right hanging loosely at his side. He did not know what Blair was doing, did not dare look.

The steps came on, cautiously now. A voice said: "Come out from there. Come on, or I'll blow you out." Silence. Lennox could hear the man breathe, then there was a cautious step forward. He saw the man, too far away for an effective blow, the gun held ready. "Come out!"

Lennox stepped sidewise, his hands shoulder high, palms foremost. The man was Phil. He said: "Got 'em, Chief." Satisfaction dripped from his voice. "I—"

He went over suddenly, as Frank Blair leaped at him from the other side of the chimney, in a beautiful flying tackle. Lennox jumped forward, seized the man's wrist and wrenched the gun from his grasp. Someone was running towards them across the roof, light hair flying. Lennox snapped a shot at him, saw the man stop suddenly, then go to his knees. Another head appeared suddenly in the trap, outlined in the light from below. Lennox fired and saw the head disappear. Blair and the gunman were rolling over and over upon the roof. Lennox stepped in and brought the barrel of the gun down upon Phil's head. The man's arms relaxed, and Blair rolled clear and came quickly to his feet.

Lennox said: "Swell work, kid!"

A gun flashed from the open trap, the bullet chipping brick from the chimney at their back. Lennox dragged the boy to shelter, withholding his fire. "As long as we have the gun," he growled, "they won't be in a hurry to come after us, and even a deaf cop ought to hear this shooting."

As if in answer to his words, brakes squealed before the apartment, hoarse voices reached them from below. Lennox said: "Sounds swell. Must be the cops." They squatted behind the chimney and waited. Sound reached them from below, muffled voices, dull splintering blows. Lennox rose cautiously. Nothing happened, and they moved across the roof.

A burly cop in a mussed uniform met them halfway down the steps and shoved a gun into Lennox's face. "Here's a couple more, Cap."

Spellman appeared through a shattered door. "For gawd's sake, Bill!"

Lennox said: "Hello, Floyd! you're the answer to a prayer. How'd you happen to show up?"

Spellman stared up at them. "You ain't going to like this, Bill, but I've got a warrant for Grier's grandson. After you left, the maid talked. Seems like she promised Mary that she wouldn't tell, but that rat of a grandson was there this afternoon. Sneaked in while the nurse was in the kitchen. The maid saw him sneaking out. She told Mary, and Grier made her promise not to spill it. I've a hunch that the old lady suspected what had happened, but she didn't want the kid to take a rap, even then. Women are funny."

Lennox said: "You've got the wrong dope, Floyd. You don't want Grier's grandson."

Spellman cut him short. "I know how you feel, Bill. You figure that Mary would want him to get off, but the law doesn't see things that way."

Lennox said: "The guy you want is out on the roof. I had to plug him. Come here, Floyd, and meet Frank Blair, the real Frank Blair. He's even got a passport to prove it."

That's Hollywood

Bill Lennox finds one too honest to live

1

THE GIRL WAS small, a tiny figure in a red coat. She came up the slanting concrete runway which led from the stage door to the street along the edge of the parking lot. Bill Lennox, troubleshooter for General-Consolidated, stood beside the coupé, working his fingers into gloves. She said: "Hello, Mr. Lennox." Her voice was uncertain, as if not sure that she would be recognized.

Lennox raised his eyes, said: "Hello, there," and stared at her. The thin face with its border of reddish yellow hair was familiar yet— "Oh, hello, Miss Sterns."

She smiled like a pleased child. "I wasn't sure that you would remember me."

He grinned. "I didn't for a minute. How are they breaking?"

The little shoulders moved in a tiny shrug. "Not good, not bad. I'm dancing in the prologue. It'll last two more weeks." She took another step up the runway. "Good-by."

Lennox was opening the door of the coupé. "Can't I drop you somewhere?"

She hesitated, moved another step, then suddenly turned and came towards him. "Would it be a lot of trouble?"

He shook his head and helped her in, realizing as he did so how small she was, how starved. He slipped beneath the wheel and started the motor. He knew her only as a dancer who had doubled for Deborah Day in the latter's picture, *Dance Team*. He swung the coupé from the parking lot into the side street, and stopped at the corner of the boulevard. "Where do you want to go, Miss Sterns?"

The girl did not answer and he glanced towards her. She was looking back through the rear window, unconscious of the fact that he had spoken. He touched her shoulder with his gloved hand and she looked around, her dark eyes meeting his. Lennox was startled to see that they were very wide, staring almost, and that there was fear in their depths.

"Anywhere." Her voice had a breathless quality which spoke of a rapidly beating heart and nervous strain. Lennox stole a look in the rear-view mirror. He saw that a black car which had been parked across the street from the runway was turning around. Aside from the car, the street for the moment was empty.

The girl said: "Hurry please." She had turned again towards

the window, her eyes on the black car. Lennox put the car into gear and turned into the traffic of the boulevard. At the corner of Highland he turned left with the light, left again at Sunset, and drove to Glower. There was no sign of the pursuing car when he pulled up at the curb.

"And now where do you want to go?"

She turned from the window, settling back into the seat. "It doesn't matter. This will do," and she started to open the door. Lennox's hand closed over hers.

"What's the matter, kid? What are you running away from?"

She said: "Nothing; nothing at all." Her tone made it a lie. For a moment Lennox hesitated, then he shrugged, watched her open the door and step out on to the pavement. "Thank you." The door closed, and she was gone. For a moment, he sat and watched, then lit a cigarette and swung the car away from the curb.

2

SOMEONE KNOCKED SHARPLY at the door of Lennox's apartment. Knocked again, impatiently. Bill hoisted himself out of his chair and crossed the room. The door came open and a man came in. He was small, dark-haired, with a thin, beak-like nose. His eyes were jet and too close to his nose. His right hand was in the pocket of his dark coat; he put his left against Lennox's chest and pushed with surprising strength. The door, he slammed behind him.

Lennox swore under his breath. "What's the big idea?"

The visitor grinned mirthlessly, his thin lips pulling away from teeth which were very white. "You aren't at the studio now, Lennox. I'm giving the orders here."

Lennox said: "Swell! Suppose you order yourself out of here. It's funny, but I don't like you."

"Wise guy. I heard that you were a smart egg, but that's not going to help. Where's Laura Sterns?"

Lennox shrugged and raised his eyebrows. "Laura Sterns?"

The man's voice grated. "Stop it. You were recognized tonight when you picked her up in your coupé outside the theater. Where is she?"

Lennox said truthfully. "I haven't the slightest idea." His voice was impatient, irritable. "What's more, I don't care."

The man's gun came out of his pocket. Lennox saw the hood-like silencer, saw the other's eyes glint. "You've made rather a name for yourself around this village, butting your nose into things. You aren't going to gum up this game. Neither you nor

Sterns. Do you get it?"

Lennox stared at the gun, knew that the man would shoot, that his finger was already tightening on the trigger. His mouth felt suddenly dry, his lips stiff. "Hold it a minute."

The man said: "Ready to talk, huh?" deep satisfaction in the voice. "Where's Sterns?"

"At her home."

"You're a liar." The gun, which had lowered slightly, came up again. "She hasn't been there since this morning. Do you think that we didn't check up?"

Lennox said: "I let her out at the corner of Glower and Sunset. She didn't say a thing to me, merely asked for a lift. I don't even know what you're talking about."

The man's face expressed his disbelief. "It's no use, Lennox. She threatened her sister this morning, threatened to come to you. Do you think that we're dumb? As long as you're around, we won't be safe, but you're not going to be around long." The gun was steady, the man's eyes fixed. "Last chance. Where's—?" There was a knock at the door, sharp, short, then another. The man stared at Lennox, then his eyes went quickly about the room. Bill said:

"Sorry, but there's only one way out of here, through that door." The knock came again; a voice called, faintly: "Hey, Bill!"

Lennox said to the gunman: "They know downstairs that I'm in. There's no use waiting for them to go." His answer was a muffled curse.

"I'm going to put this rod into my pocket," the other told him. "Make a move and I'll splatter you across that wall and take my chances." He slid his gun into his pocket and stepped back. "Now open that door, and be careful."

Lennox obeyed silently. He pulled open the door and stared his surprise. "Hello, Sol!"

Sol Spurck, head of the West Coast Studios of General-Consolidated Films, moved his short legs into the room with the monotony of an animated cartoon. A tall man followed him, tall, thin, with a gleaming head and heavy eyebrows. Lennox nodded to him and closed the door. Spurck said: "For why didn't you answer?" Then he saw the gunman in the corner and stopped.

The man was standing quietly in his place, the dark eyes boring, yet uncertain. Lennox smiled slightly. "I was having a little argument. My friend is just leaving." He looked directly towards the other, his eyes mocking. The man hesitated, moved towards the door.

"I'll see you later." He said it as if he meant it. "Talking hurts people at times." The door closed and Lennox jumped towards the phone; then he stopped and turned slowly back to his visitors.

Spurck was staring at him. "Positively, Bill, sometimes I think that you are crazy."

Lennox gave him a thin smile. "Sometimes I agree with you," he said, finding a cigarette. "What's on your mind?"

The tall man cleared his throat noisily. Spurck said: "You know Goldfinch, Allied Pictures."

Lennox shook the bony hand of the president of Allied Pictures. "Glad to see you."

Goldfinch cleared his throat again. Spurck said: "Jake is in trouble. He has been telling me about it, y'understand, and right away, I think of you."

Lennox said: "Strange. Well, what is it?"

Spurck prodded the other with a stubby finger. "Tell him, Jake."

Goldfinch hesitated. It was evident that he either did not share Spurck's confidence in Lennox, or he was too nervous to stand still. He paced slowly back and forth across the little room until Spurck said sharply: "Sit down once, will you?"

Goldfinch dropped into a chair. "Maybe you know my son-in-law, Sam Biermann?"

Lennox nodded. He probably knew Biermann better than did Goldfinch. "What about him?"

The other worked nervously with his long fingers. Spurck said, with impatience: "I want you should help Jake. I ain't saying that we haven't had our troubles in a business way, y'understand, like when he pulled that raid last year and signed up two of our best stars, even though they was washed up and about through—"

"Who was through?" Goldfinch was on his feet, his nervousness forgotten. "Why if I was to show you the box office report on Tryson's latest picture, you wouldn't hardly believe—"

Lennox said, sharply: "Come on. Kiss and then tell me what's the trouble with Biermann."

They both looked at him uncertainly, then Goldfinch said: "Oh, Biermann! Well, you see, Mr. Lennox, my daughter who has been in New York all winter is coming back Wednesday, and I don't want that she should find him worried, y'understand."

Spurck said: "Girl trouble. That low-life is a looker."

"He is not." Goldfinch's voice rose with anger. "You don't understand the boy, Spurck. It is just that he has a kind heart. But I got to admit that he has me worried. Something is wrong, I can tell, but he didn't say anything to me, and I can't ask him."

"We thought," Spurck cut in, "that you hear things, Bill. Maybe you hear somewhere that Sam Biermann is in trouble, yes?"

Lennox shook his head and Goldfinch sighed deeply. "If it isn't one thing, it's the same. Trouble—trouble, if Edith's mommer, *olav hasholom,* was alive, I wouldn't worry, y'understand. Such a wonderful woman, Irma was, but I can't bear that a *schnorrer* like Sam Biermann, should cause my Edith worry."

Spurck patted his bony shoulder. "Don't worry, Jake. Bill will fix things, won't you, Bill?" Lennox did not answer, but Spurck continued:

"Biermann is at the *Brass Rail.* Half an hour ago we see him go in, y'understand. Be a good boy, Bill. Put on your coat and see him once. Jake ain't slept for three nights yet, and at his age, sleep is one thing which he has to have."

3

LENNOX DUG HIS chin deeper into the upturned collar of his coat, paid the cab-driver, and turned towards the beer-hall. A hurrying figure in a fur collared coat and sailor hat had almost collided with him. A voice said: "Why Bill. I thought that you'd gone home to bed?"

He said: "Hello, sweetheart," and stared down at Nancy Hobbs, staff writer for one of the fan magazines. "I was in bed, almost, but Sol handed out another job."

She stared at him, the corners of her full-lipped mouth twitching slightly. "What is it this time? Has one of the lions for that jungle picture gotten loose?"

He shook his head. "Jake Goldfinch is worried about his son-in-law. Edith is due in from New York, and Jake is afraid she'll find out things."

The girl said: "What things?"

Lennox shrugged. "That's what Jake doesn't know, what he wants me to find out. It's bad enough wet-nursing Spurck's family, but when he starts to farm me out—"

Nancy said: "Edith Biermann is one sweet kid."

Lennox nodded. "They don't make them better. Have you heard anything about Biermann recently?"

She shook her head. "He keeps looking, but I don't think that it means anything. As far as I know, he hasn't been seen with the same girl twice."

Lennox shrugged. "Okey, pal! I'll go in and talk to the boy friend. Sleep an hour for me, will you." He opened the door and walked into the crowded room.

Pushing his way through the mob, he went towards the rear of the room. To the right, a piano played noisily. Two waiters with reddened noses and false mustaches sang nasally. Lennox peered around and finally saw Sam Biermann at one of the wall tables with another man. He fought his way forward through the crowd until he reached Biermann's side. "Hello, Sam!"

Biermann looked up. He was small, with large features, black eyes, and hair that waved. Part artist, part business man, at thirty he was one of the best production executives in Hollywood. Lennox knew his story. Hester Street, push-carts, a father who had come to America for opportunity and failed, Biermann had fought his way up through the industry until he had almost reached the peak. "Hello, Bill! Sit down."

Lennox wedged his way into a chair and nodded to Biermann's companion. Tom Bardee returned the nod. Heavy set, with powerful shoulders, and a face that smiled, Bardee was well known to everyone in the film colony. His money, provided by an eastern uncle who made good washing-machines, left him a genial idler who asked nothing from life except to be included in all Hollywood social functions. Rumor had married him to a dozen stars, rumor and nothing more. He remained single, a lavish host, a good friend to the denizens of the Boulevard. He reached across the table and shook Lennox's hand, waved to a waiter, ordered beer, and settled back. Biermann, after his first greeting, said nothing. Elbow on table, chin in palm, he seemed to be staring at nothing in particular.

Bardee put a large hand on his shoulder and shook him playfully. "Come on, Sam! Snap out of it. You act like a morgue keeper."

Biermann managed a nervous smile. "It's the noise that gets me. Come on! Let's get away from this joint."

Bardee laughed. "That's an idea! I've had so much beer that I'm waterlogged. Let's go up to your place and get a real drink. Come on, Bill!"

Ordinarily, Lennox would have refused, but now he rose and followed them out to Bardee's car. The penthouse which Biermann called home was perched upon the highest apartment house in the Wilshire district. They rode up from the garage to the top floor in the elevator, and walked to the roof. Biermann opened the door and stepped aside.

"My Jap boy is taking care of some unfinished business of his own. You'll have to mix the drinks, Tom. You know where the junk is. Make yourself at home, Bill. I'll be out in a couple of minutes."

He disappeared into his bedroom. Bardee headed for the butler's pantry and Lennox walked into the library. The room had full-length windows opening on to the narrow terrace. He gazed thoughtfully beyond, and below, where the lights of the city spread out like an immense checker-board. Red and green Neon signs gave the board its touch of color, while in the distance, the hills showed a darkish purple against the lighter sky. The phone on the desk rang sharply. Lennox turned and looked at it as it rang again. Biermann's voice reached him faintly. "Get that, will you, Bill?"

Lennox crossed the room and picked the phone from its cradle. "Hello!"

A man's voice said: "So you're answering the phone, Biermann? Well, this is the last call. Twenty grand, or you take the rap. We've heard enough excuses." The voice was harsh, metallic. Lennox started to say, "But this is—" The click of the receiver at the other end was his only answer. Slowly he replaced the phone and turned around. Tom Bardee was standing in the doorway, a tray of drinks in his hands.

"Someone for Sam?"

Lennox said: "Wrong number. The phone service is lousy." He repeated the lie a moment later when Biermann came into the room, accepted the drink from Bardee and sipped it. "Not bad."

Biermann said lazily: "If Tom's washing-machines ever fail, he would make a swell bartender. I'll back you in a joint, Tom."

Bardee said: "Thanks; but that calls for work, and I never got along with work." He yawned. Biermann walked to the phone and put in a call for New York. Bardee winked at Lennox. "Can you imagine a guy's being married two years and still wasting dough calling his wife on long distance? Childish, I'd say."

Biermann swung around. "Supposing you two buzzards drink your drinks and toddle. *I* have to work tomorrow, if you don't."

They went, with a lot of good-humored protest. Bardee drove Lennox to his apartment and dropped him at the curb. Bill watched the big roadster disappear, walked into the lobby, and called a cab. Twenty minutes later he was riding up in the elevator towards Biermann's apartment. Sam stared at him as he opened the door. "Forget something?"

Lennox shook his head. "I wanted to talk to you. I couldn't while Bardee was around. Shall we go into the library?"

The production manager shut the door slowly and followed his visitor down the hall. Lennox selected his seat so that the illumination from the only light on in the room would shine on Biermann's face. He said, without preamble: "Your father-in-law came to see me tonight."

Biermann was selecting a cigarette from the ornate box on the desk. He did not raise his eyes. "Yes?"

Lennox said: "He was worried, about you."

Biermann looked up. "Worried? About me? But why?"

Lennox said: "That's what Jake didn't know. He knew that something was the matter. He wanted me to find out what."

Biermann smiled a little but his voice had an edge. "I don't see that it's your business."

"It isn't, and I don't give a damn about it, except that Sol Spurck asked me to do it and I'm still working for him. Goldfinch wants me to find out what's the matter so that he can help. I figured that the simplest way was to ask you."

For a moment their eyes fenced. Lennox had the advantage of the light. Biermann said, in a voice which was almost normal: "Jake made a mistake. There's nothing worrying me. Go back and tell him that. Tell him he's crazy."

Lennox shook his head. "I can't." His voice was very dry. "That telephone call that I answered. I said that it was a wrong number. I said that because I did not want to speak before Bardee. It wasn't. Whoever was calling mistook my voice for yours. He said if you don't kick through with twenty grand that you'll take the rap; that this was the last warning."

Biermann was staring at him, the cigarette in his fingers burning unnoticed. "Are you lying, Lennox?" His voice had an unnatural sound.

Lennox said, angrily: "Why the hell should I lie? I'm here to help you, not for yourself, but because your wife is swell people, because she's due back on the Coast, and Jake doesn't want her worried."

Biermann dropped his cigarette into a tray and passed a hand slowly across his eyes. "Sorry."

His voice had a dead quality. "This thing's about got me. That's all."

Lennox's voice changed. "Forget it. I'm here to help. What's the matter! Someone blackmailing you? A woman?"

Biermann said, without looking up: "In a way."

"Guilty?"

The production manager shook his head. "It's a frame."

"Then go to the cops. I've got a little influence downtown, and we can straighten this out. Maybe if we're lucky, we can keep it out of the papers."

Biermann shook his head. "It isn't as simple as that. "His voice held a hopeless note. "They've got me on this; got me cold. If I had the twenty thousand they'd get it, but I haven't. I got hooked in the market six months ago, and it about cleaned me; then you have to keep up a front in this business."

"Better tell me about it," Lennox suggested.

Biermann said: "I've got to tell someone or go crazy. I haven't talked to anyone except Bardee. He advised me to pay. Offered to lend me part of the money."

Lennox shook his head. "If you pay once, they'll be coming back for more. What have they got on you?"

"Kidnaping."

"What do you mean, kidnaping?"

"Just that. They swear that I kidnaped this girl, took her out of the state. That she escaped, and that unless I pay, they'll place the facts in the hands of the District Attorney. You know what that means. The way people feel, I'd be lucky to get off with life."

Lennox whistled. "How much truth is there in the story?"

"Enough so that they can make it stick. I did take this girl to Nevada in my car. Who's going to say that I didn't kidnap her?"

Lennox shrugged. "There are plenty of holes in their story. If she had really been kidnaped, her disappearance would have been reported to the police."

"It was." Biermann rose and began to pace back and forth across the room. "Her brother reported it the morning after we started. That's what makes me know that it was a frame. I didn't see a paper until I got back."

Lennox said: "Where is she now?"

Biermann shrugged. "I don't know. She's still missing, at least as far as the police are concerned. It's all fixed—the story, I mean—in case I don't come across. She'll appear in some little desert town, and say that she escaped and has been hiding. Can't you see? There isn't any way out except to pay, I guess I'll have to get the money from Jake."

Lennox's lips were thin. "Maybe you'll learn not to play around," he said grimly. "I'll try to help, not for you, but because of your wife. Don't do a thing until you hear from me. If I can't make connection, there's time enough to pay then. Now, what is the girl's name? Her brother's name? And the address?" He watched while Biermann went to the desk and wrote down the information, picked up the white slip and handed it to Lennox. Bill stared at it. The names meant nothing to him, the address less. He folded the slip and stuffed it into his breast pocket. Okey! You'll hear from me." As he went down the stairs to the floor below, and waited for the elevator, he buttoned his coat.

It was colder when he emerged from the apartment and stared up and down the dark street. There was no taxi in sight, and he walked towards Wilshire.

4

THE SWITCHBOARD MAN said: "Oh, Mr. Lennox! A woman's been calling you every ten minutes. As he spoke, a tiny light glowed on the board. He plugged in and gave the name of the apartment hotel. "One moment, please." He put his hand over the transmitter. "It's her, for you."

Lennox said: "I'll take it in the booth," and walked around the end of the desk.

He closed the door and said: "Hello!" into the phone.

A girl's voice reached him, a frightened voice. "I've been trying to get you, Mr. Lennox, to warn you. They're going to kill you."

Lennox said, sharply: "Who is it? Who's calling?" He thought that he recognized the voice, but wanted to be sure.

She said: "Laura Sterns. You picked me up behind the theater tonight. They're going to kill you. I—" there was a sharp cry at the other end of the wire. Lennox yelled: "Hello! hello!" He heard the receiver click. The line was dead.

The switchboard operator's face was white when Lennox stepped from the booth. Bill said: "Get me the studio, quick, and this time don't listen in."

Red crept up beneath the boy's skin as he plugged in the outside line. Lennox said into the phone: "Gimme Barney, quick!"

The girl's bored voice reached him across the wire. "Mr. Barnard isn't—" Lennox cut her short.

"This is Bill Lennox, you blond menace. Barney's working

all night. Ring his office."

Barnard said, profanely: "Well, who is it?"

"Lennox," Bill told him. "Listen, Barney. A girl dancer, doubled for Deborah Day in *Dance Team*. Her name is Sterns, Laura Sterns. Look up her address and give it to me. I'm in a hurry."

"What's the matter? Lose your date book?"

Lennox did not trouble to answer. While he waited, he pushed open the booth door and said to the operator: "Get on another line, Sam, and call me a cab."

Barney's voice reached him finally. "She's listed on North Wilton," and gave the number. "I wish you guys would keep track of your own—" Lennox hung up.

As he reached the sidewalk, a cab pulled to the curb. He gave the man the number and climbed in. Fifteen minutes later he was getting out before a modest brick-faced apartment. He paid the driver and walked to the door. There was no lobby, only a small vestibule with brass-bound mail-boxes. Lennox saw the name Sterns on number eighteen. He mounted the carpeted stairs and went along the dimly lighted upper hall. Somewhere in the house a radio played softly. Except for that, everything was in silence. Suite eighteen was at the end, next to the fire-escape. He tried the door and found it locked, knocked sharply, and waited. Nothing happened, and he knocked again, without result.

For a moment he hesitated, looking around, then raised the window at the end of the hall and stepped out on to the iron fire-escape. He shut the window and walked to the end of the little platform. Beyond was the first window of number eighteen, small, dark. He stepped over the rail and leaned far out.

The window was closed and locked. With his free hand he felt in his coat pocket, found a metal cigarette case, and drew it out. With it he broke the glass above the middle sash. It fell with a tinkling noise, and for a moment he stood waiting, listening. Nothing happened.

He replaced the cigarette case in his pocket, clutched the iron rail firmly with his left and leaned far out. His groping fingers touched the lock, but could not turn it. He edged his left hand along the rail towards the brick wall. Below was a concrete driveway, deep in shadow. His groping fingers again touched the lock. This time he had a better purchase. The lock turned finally, and he pulled himself back to the platform, stood for a moment getting his breath, then leaned forward again, trying to raise the lower sash. It stuck, and he swore softly.

There was a gold knife at the end of his watch chain. He loosened it and inserted the blade beneath the window. It moved, then the blade snapped. He dropped the handle into his pocket, worked his fingers into the crack, and raised the sash. For a moment he hung there, panting, one hand still clutching the railing, one foot on the platform. Then he reached out, got his free hand around the edge of the inner sill, let go with his left, and caught a fresh hold as his body swung outward. For seconds he hung there, then slowly began to draw himself up.

He got one knee on the sill, then his feet inside. In another moment he was standing panting in a small and extremely dark closet. A faint odor of moth balls filled the air. Women's clothes hung in a little row. Then his groping hand found the knob, and a moment later he stood in the small entry hall.

The single light burned steadily, unblinkingly. No sound reached Lennox from the room beyond the closed door. After a moment he opened it and peered in. Then he swore and went quickly across the room. Laura Sterns lay on her side at the end of the worn divan, her reddish yellowed hair tousled about the thin face. The pajamas which were her only clothing were torn, exposing a white shoulder, thin, pitiful. Lennox bent above her, noted the red marks at her throat, the bulging, staring eyes, then saw that she lay in a little pool of blood which still seeped from the gaping knife wound below her left breast. He straightened, stared about the room, then pulled out his handkerchief, picked up the receiver of the phone gingerly, and called a number.

After a time, a sleepy voice answered. Lennox said: "Listen, Floyd. This is Lennox. There's a girl dead in her apartment on North Wilton." He gave the number. "Jump into some clothes and get over here. I'll wait."

He hung up and stared down at the frail body, his thin lips twisting cynically. Acting on impulse, he walked into the tiny kitchen and looked into the cupboard. There was little there, the small ice-box held less. He returned to the front room and lit a cigarette. He had smoked three by the time a heavy knock aroused him. He squashed out the butt, rose, and went into the hall.

Detective Captain Floyd Spellman came in, followed by two men in uniform. He nodded to Bill and went over to look at the girl. Then he turned around. "Who is she?"

Bill told him. "And what are you doing here?"

"She called me," Lennox explained. "Said that I was in danger, then she cried out and the line went dead. I called the studio, got her address, and came over. I had to bust a window to get in. This is what I found. Then I called you."

Spellman's eyes were incredulous. "That's some story."

"It happens to be true." Lennox's voice was edged. "The telephone operator listened in on the girl's call. He'll tell you what she said; that she was alive when I talked to her. That is, if you have any ideas in that thick skull of yours about hanging this on me."

Spellman shrugged. "I ain't saying that you had a thing to do with it, am I? Still, you manage to get into more jams than any other bird I know. Come on, Bill! Gimme the low-down. Either you've said too much, or not enough."

Lennox shrugged in turn. "I don't know a thing, Floyd. I picked this kid up tonight. I didn't know her except that she worked on the *Dance Team* set, and she was plenty good. Someone was following her in a car. I thought that it was some stage-door John at the time. I changed my mind later when a wise boy with a gun walked into my apartment and said things."

"What things?" Spellman's voice held interest.

Lennox shook his head. "Nothing that made sense to me. He thought that the kid had told me something, something which it wasn't wise for me to know. He was going to rod me. Then Spurck came in and spoiled the play. I couldn't say anything or the cull would have started shooting. I had to let him walk out."

Spellman made a disgusted face. "The story's lousy. Gets worse all the time."

Lennox said: "If I'd had to make one up, I'd never called you, and that makes sense—even to you. This kid, this little cheap dancer that's been starving herself, knew something big—so big they killed her. It's funny, copper. Here she was, dancing in a prologue, fifteen a week and furnish her own costumes, not sure of work next week nor the week after, broke and honest.

The audience wouldn't believe that. They sat and watched her dance. They never thought of the years of training, hardship, drudgery. They sat there and envied her, envied her freedom, her chance at things, and yet—with all that, she stayed honest, tried to tell me what was up, even when she knew it might mean her death. That's life, copper. That's Hollywood."

Spellman grunted: "I'll begin to think that you were her boy friend."

Lennox spoke angrily. "I hardly knew the little tramp, but I can feel sorry for her, sorry about the chance she deserved and never had. The papers will play this up as a love nest killing. You cops will hunt for the man or the other woman, and the citizens will read about it and smile knowingly. If they were half the people this kid was, this would be a swell place to live." He slammed on his hat.

Spellman said, almost mildly: "Where you going?"

Lennox swore at him. "I'm going to find who killed this kid. If I don't, he'll never be caught. You cops wouldn't think of looking in the right place."

5

LENNOX COMPARED THE address with that of the brother and sister given him by Biermann. The number was correct and he stared at the house, a rather substantial one just south of Pico. Then he went up the walk and rang the bell. A Japanese opened the door slightly and peered out. Lennox shoved the boy aside and went in. The boy stared at him, his slanting eyes widening. His English was correct. Lennox judged him American born. "What's the idea?"

Lennox had him by the front of his white coat. "The idea is that I want to see Mr. Conrick and I don't want an argument."

The boy shook his head. "He didn't come home last night. I don't know where he is."

Lennox stared at him. The yellow face was expressionless, the eyes unwinking. "I'll have a look."

The boy did not answer. Lennox shut the door and shoved the servant ahead of him. "There's a gun in my pocket," he said, grimly. "It goes off easily."

The Japanese said nothing. They went along the hall, Lennox peering into rooms as they passed, then up a wide, old-fashioned stairway. There were three bedrooms. None of them bore signs that it had been occupied on the preceding night. They went back down the stairs and Lennox saw the boy grin as they reached the hallway.

He stood there a moment, undecided. Then a voice behind him said: "I didn't expect you here, Lennox," and he swung about to face the man who had threatened him in his apartment the night before. Bill's eyes got narrow as they saw the gun in the other's hand. "So you're Conrick?"

The man's dark head inclined ever so slightly. "That name suits as well as another. Get his gun, Rocco."

The house-boy's right hand slid in and out of Lennox's pocket. The other patted the trouble-shooter's coat; then he stepped back. Lennox said: "I was pretty dumb, wasn't I? I didn't connect Sterns' killing with Biermann's trouble."

Black eyes studied him. "Are you trying to talk your way out?"

Lennox laughed without mirth. "After all, the joke is on you. If you hadn't come barging into my apartment last night, I never would have connected the two. Sterns didn't talk to me. She didn't tell me a thing."

The man's eyes were unchanged. "So what?"

Lennox let his voice grate. "You spoiled the play, Conrick, when you killed that kid. I couldn't hang the fake kidnaping on you until I located the girl, but I can hang this killing where it belongs and by —— I'm going to do it."

White teeth flashed. "You forget two things, Lennox. You couldn't tell what you know without dragging in Biermann. That's one. The other is that you aren't going to be around to talk." His voice tightened, grew deeper. "I should have rubbed you last night. I didn't, and you almost caused us grief. You won't ag—"

The phone on the little stand rang sharply. Conrick hesitated; the houseboy crossed behind Lennox and picked up the receiver. He listened for a minute, then extended it to his employer. "Her."

Conrick said: "Watch him, Rocco. Let him have it if he moves." He stepped sidewise towards the phone and picked up the receiver. Lennox heard him say. "Hello—yes, kid— No, he hasn't paid yet. Well, I'm doing the best that I can. He'll pay and like it. There isn't any way out— Yeah, she talked. Lennox is here now. You don't need to worry about him. He won't get a chance to rat. I'm telling you—"

Lennox's eyes strayed to the Jap. Rocco stood across the hall, Lennox's own gun in his hand. Bill's eyes focused on the gun and a tiny smile twitched at the corner of his mouth. One eyebrow lifted for an instant; then his face was expressionless as ever. It was a revolver, not an automatic. He remembered something that he had forgotten, something that counted now. The hammer was on an empty cylinder as always, but the next one was empty also. It meant that Rocco would have to pull the trigger three times, that there would be a second, maybe two, before the gun would be spitting death.

He stole a look at Conrick. The man was half turned away from him, his left hand holding the receiver, his right, with the gun, hanging at his side. Even as he looked, Conrick was saying good-by. In another moment it would be too late.

Lennox suddenly sprang towards the house-boy, his right coming up in a half swing for the other's jaw. He saw the boy tense, saw his eyes narrow as he squeezed the trigger; then his fist crashed home, crashed with a force which sent pain shooting up his arm.

Rocco went over as if hit by a club. Lennox never looked at him; he pivoted and leaped at Conrick. The man had been in the act of replacing the receiver on the hook. He dropped it as Lennox sprang, tried to raise his right arm as Lennox's fingers closed about his wrist. He was off balance, trying to turn. For a moment they stood facing each other, the black-haired one attempting to raise his arm, Lennox forcing it down; then Bill's free hand cracked against the man's nose in an overhand swing.

The blow lacked force, but it brought tears to Conrick's eyes. He cursed with surprise and pain, and tried to draw away. Lennox hit him again, driving the lips back against the white teeth, bringing blood. Conrick reached for Bill's throat with clawing fingers. Lennox caught them, twisted them. He let go suddenly, turned sidewise, caught the gun arm with both of his hands, brought it up then down across his knee, sharply. Conrick swore as the gun dropped from his nerveless fingers.

Lennox pushed him away, measured him, and sent over his right. It missed the jaw and cut the cheek above the bone. His left dug its way into the man's stomach, bending him almost double. Lennox said, pantingly: "How do you like it, bum?" and hit him again. Conrick went down in a crumpled, moaning heap. With the toe of his shoe, Lennox prodded the man's side. "Get up and fight, you yellow ——!"

Conrick did not get up. For a moment Lennox stared down at him, then stooped, loosened the man's belt, and fastened his arms. Conrick groaned and opened his eyes. Lennox said: "Come on, where is she?"

The man shook his head. "Go to he —"

Lennox caught his right arm and Conrick cried out: "It's broken, for —— sake, don't."

Lennox grinned, but his eyes weren't smiling. "Come on, where is she?" He twisted the arm again. Beads of perspiration showed on the other's forehead. His face was pain twisted, terrible. "I'll talk, don't."

Lennox didn't release the arm. "Where is she?"

"*Fairway,* five-o-eight. Get a doctor."

Lennox said: "If you're lying, I'll come back and break the other arm."

He turned and looked at the Jap. The boy was still out, his body crumpled against the wall. Lennox picked up his gun and slipped it into his pocket; then he picked up Conrick's automatic and, carrying it with him, went into the kitchen. The automatic he dropped into the garbage pail, found a length of clothesline, and returned to the hall. He dragged Conrick into a room to the right, bound him to a chair, and went back to Rocco. The Jap stirred as Lennox lifted him, said something which Bill did not understand. He carried the boy into the room, bound his wrists and ankles, and laid him on the divan; then went out to the phone and called a cab. While he waited, he went through Conrick's desk. There was nothing in it but unpaid bills; there were plenty of them.

6

THE *FAIRWAY* HAD a uniformed doorman and a desk clerk. Lennox paid no attention to either. He went through the lobby and up in the automatic elevator to the fifth floor. At the door of five-o-eight, he stopped, hesitated a moment, then knocked. After a moment he knocked again. A woman's voice from the other side said: "Who is it?" angrily.

Lennox said: "Package for you, Miss. C.O.D."

The voice said: "What the hell?" The chain rattled, the door opened a crack. Lennox helped it and it went wide, exposing a girl in black pajamas. "Say, where do you get—?" He was inside, closing the door. "Morning, Miss Conrick."

She stared at him, her smoky eyes widening. One long-fingered hand went up, brushing the hair back from her forehead, the reddened nails glittering. "What's the idea of busting in here? Can't a lady have any privacy?"

"A lady can," he told her, his voice sharp, "but you don't count, sweetheart. You're just a girl that gets kidnaped. I'm Bill Lennox."

She caught her lower lip with two white teeth. "So you're Lennox. I've heard of you."

He said, without emotion: "We're wasting time, tramp. Let's go in and telephone."

"Who would we call?" She was still staring at him.

He said: "We might try the cops. I understand they're hunting for you. Too bad the little kidnap story broke down."

"But my brother said—"

Lennox grinned. "Your brother made a mistake. He thought he had things coming his way. He shouldn't have killed—"

"Killed?" Her eyes were very wide now.

"Yeah, Sterns. Your sister, wasn't she?"

The girl shook her head. "Laura dead? No, she wasn't my sister."

It was Lennox's turn to stare. "But Conrick called her that last night. He said that Sterns had threatened her sister, threatened to come to me with the story."

The girl shrugged. "We grew up together. We did a sister act once. We always called her that, but she wasn't, really." She was silent for a moment. "The little fool!" Her voice was bitter. "So she ratted to you. She couldn't keep her nose clean."

Lennox said, softly: "She was too honest, too decent, and she died." He was speaking half to himself. "I wonder why she was coming to me, why she thought that I'd be interested in Biermann?"

The girl shrugged. "Because you're in the movies, because you're the only one she knew that was, because the little fool was half in love with you, with your reputation." She shrugged and turned towards the front room. All life seemed to have gone out of her. Her shoulders drooped, her steps dragged.

Lennox followed her, watched while she crossed the room and found a cigarette; then she turned and looked at him through the smoke. Her eyes were defiant now. Her shoulders straightened. "This is going to look nice in the papers. Have you thought of that? Has Biermann?"

"It's no use, tramp." Lennox was walking towards the phone. "The play's washed up. The papers will carry the story my way. When I get through, Biermann will be something of a hero."

She laughed. "Gawd, that's funny! Sam a hero; the dirty—!"

Her mood shifted and she laid down the cigarette. "Look at me, Bill Lennox. Am I hard to take. Play with me, boy, play. We can grab the dough between us, and scram. I can be nice, plenty nice." Her hand was on his wrist. He shook it off. He wasn't seeing her. He was seeing Laura Sterns, seeing her tiny body, crumpled on the floor. She was not deterred, but stepped closer, her arms slipping about his neck, her fingers locking at the back of his collar, her reddened lips parted, invitingly. He grasped her wrists roughly, pulled the fingers apart, and shoved her away.

"It won't work, tramp. I'm calling the cops."

She gave him a throaty laugh. "It did work, fool! Did you think that I meant it? I was stalling, stalling for time."

A voice from the hall doorway said: "Turn around, Lennox, and let's look at you."

Bill turned slowly. He knew that voice, wasn't surprised when he saw Tom Bardee's big bulk filling the door. Bardee's face wasn't smiling now. His eyes were chips of blue metal, iced, penetrating. Lennox said: "So the washing-machine business isn't paying dividends these days?"

Bardee said across him to the girl: "Where's Conrick?"

She shrugged. "Ask Lennox. He came busting in here ten minutes ago. I knew that you were due, and stalled him."

"All right, Bill." Bardee's voice held no expression. "Where's Conrick."

Contempt showed in Lennox's tone. "Spilling his guts to the cops, Bardee, to save his yellow hide. When you went into the racket, you should have picked a better man."

"Get on the phone," Bardee told the girl, "and call him." She obeyed silently. Finally she turned, fear creeping into her voice.

"No one answers. Rocco should be there, at least."

Lennox laughed. "The Jap went downtown, too. I don't think he'll talk though, if that's any satisfaction. He looked stubborn."

Bardee swore.

"This isn't going to help you, Bill. Your number is up." He moved a step closer. "Why didn't you keep out of this? Why did you have to butt in?" He was working himself into a rage, working towards a point where he could kill. "We get a new racket, a fool-proof racket, and you gum the works. At least you won't be around to see."

Lennox said, dryly: "The doorman saw me come in, so did the clerk. They're going to ask questions, Bardee, questions which you can't answer."

The other laughed, not a nice laugh, but a grating sound which made the short hairs at the back of Lennox's neck prickle. "But still you won't be around to see."

The big man was coming closer. The blue eyes were hardly sane. Lennox read death in their depths, and breathed deeply. Without warning, he sprang. The gun roared, almost in his face. Something struck him, high on the left shoulder, numbing his arm. He ducked and drove head foremost into Bardee's middle.

The big man grunted, tried to press the gun to Lennox's side. Bill had the wrist with his right hand, twisted sidewise, and Bardee went over his outstretched leg, the gun falling to the carpet. Both dived for it. They lay there for a moment, struggling, their breath coming in short, sharp gasps.

Bill saw the girl move around them, saw her catch up a vase and come forward, her eyes intent, staring. His left hand was almost useless. His shoulder felt hot, sticky. He reached out suddenly, caught her ankle, and jerked. She sat down, hard, the vase crashing at her side. Bardee seized the opportunity to get his fingers at Lennox's throat, working their way in beneath the collar. Lennox managed to jerk free, roll over, and come to his feet. Bardee was struggling upward. Without a moment's hesitation, Lennox leaped at him, feet first. The movement would have done credit to a professional wrestler. The heel of his right foot struck Bardee directly in the mouth. He went down, hard, on to his back.

Lennox fell also, beside the girl. He saw her claw-like hand reaching for the gun, caught her wrist, and pulled her back. She fought him like a wild cat, but he got the gun and threw it at the window. It went through the glass with a crash; then he came to his knees and stared at Bardee. The man lay where he had fallen, a slight trickle of blood showing at one corner of his mouth. The girl was a huddled heap, sobbing quietly. Someone pounded on the outside door. Lennox called, "In a minute," and rising unsteadily, he went to the phone. He called the Homicide Bureau and told the story to Spellman, then unfastened the door.

A WHITE-FACED CLERK and angry manager stamped into the room. Lennox hooked his useless left hand into his vest and stared at them sardonically. The manager said: "What's going on here?" and looked open-mouthed at the unconscious Bardee.

Lennox told him in a dozen words. The manager said: "I don't believe it. Why, that's Mr. Bardee."

Lennox's grin widened. "You don't tell me? What are you going to do about it?"

The man said, pompously: "Call the police," and turned towards the phone.

"Too late, sport. I already have. They'll be here in fifteen minutes." Lennox pulled his gun from his pocket and laid it on the stand beside the telephone, then he dialed a number and asked for Biermann. The secretary said that he wasn't in. "This is Lennox of General," Bill told her. "Do you know where I can reach him?"

She said: "I'm sorry, but you can't. He's gone out to the United Airport to meet his wife. She's arriving from the East."

Lennox thanked her and hung up, then called his own studio and asked for Spurck.

Sol said, in an excited voice: "I have been trying to reach you. Where have you been?"

Lennox stared at the phone. "I've been working on that Biermann thing for Goldfinch. What's wrong now?"

"What's wrong? What's wrong? He asks me what's wrong. It's that *Dance Team* picture, y'understand. Such lousiness! Retakes we have to have, and that dancer we can't find?"

"What dancer?"

"The one which doubles for Day. I asked Barney and he said that you know her, that only last night you was asking for her address."

"Well, what about her?"

Spurck was excited. "What about her? What about her? Why, she is the only part of the picture which has guts. Get her, at once, and bring her here. Burton is writing in a part, and we will shoot the last half over with her playing Day's sister, y'understand, instead of just a double."

Lennox's voice was very tired. "Don't you ever read the papers?"

"Huh? The papers? What about the papers?"

"Laura Sterns was killed last night."

"But I tell you, we need her for the picture—"

Lennox said: "You didn't understand me. She was killed last night, murdered, because she was a game little tramp who wouldn't turn chiseler. She knew about Biermann's trouble. She threatened to come and tell me. The gang thought she had, and rubbed her out."

"Such luck!" Spurck's voice was thick. "Out of a million girls which might be killed, she has to be the one."

Lennox said: "I wanted to talk to you, Sol. The kid didn't have any money. She died, trying to do the right thing. I think that you and Goldfinch might see that she gets a decent funeral—"

Spurck was not listening. Lennox knew from the tone of his voice that he had heard very little. "It ain't that I don't sympathize, y'understand, Bill. Talk to me sometime when I ain't busy, but right now we gotta have a dancer with the whole company waiting and expenses—" Lennox hung up and stared moodily at the phone.

"I'm a sap," he muttered. "I forgot for a minute that I was living in Hollywood."

Whatta Guy

Bill Lennox slams lead into the
gears of a big money snatch

1

BILL LENNOX, TROUBLE-SHOOTER for General-Consolidated Studio, sat on the corner of the littered desk and grinned at Ted Babcock, assistant city editor of the Los Angeles *Telegram*. Babcock was tall, with sandy hair and deeply lined face. Lennox knew that he was forty-three, but he looked older as he fumbled in the pocket of his unbuttoned vest, found a stick of gum, and peeled it slowly. Then he looked up. "What's on your mind, Bill?"

Lennox shrugged. The littered room was strangely quiet. The *Telegram* was an afternoon sheet. The final edition had been put to bed. Below, the presses still roared, but here the typewriters were stilled; the men about the copy desk were sliding back, relaxing, and going for their coats. It was five-fifteen. Lennox said: "Thought you might eat with me. I've found a new joint over on Brooklyn Avenue. They've got swell kosher corned beef, and the beer tastes like beer."

Babcock squinted at him. "You must want something?"

Lennox looked pained. "That's what I get for acting human with a gorilla like you—"

The key from the city News Bureau broke into sudden action. The last operator straightened without interest, a cigarette drooping from one corner of his tired mouth. Suddenly he stiffened, straightened. "Babcock! Hey, Chief." His voice carried a note of strain as it came through the open door of the glass partition. It brought Babcock to his feet, started him towards the door.

"What the hell—"

The other's voice shook. "Great God, man! Miriam Ford has been kidnaped."

For an instant nothing in the room moved. Lennox straightened with the rest, his cigarette sending up a tiny curl of smoke about his suddenly narrowed eyes. "Miriam Ford—" One of the battery of phones on Babcock's desk shrilled. Ted crossed the room, caught up the receiver and barked: "City desk. Babcock—Yeah, Hughes—yeah, we just got the flash from the city News Bureau. What the hell do you think you're working on, a police year book? Okey, is this straight, no publicity gag? When? Yeah, yeah! Okey! Hold on—" He swung about. "Pete! Where the hell's Pete?"

"He's gone."

"Find him. He'll be in that beer joint across the street. Mac, take my phone and get this from Hughes, get everything he's got. Where the hell is Lawson? Hey! Get a cab and get out to Ford's estate. Take a photographer with you. Get everything you can and keep calling in. Boy, get down and stop those presses. Get Mike in the composing-room. Tell him to hold his men. I want an extra, a replate. Rip out the front page. Get the file and metal on Ford from the morgue. Get the biggest hunk of metal you can find. Smear Hughes' story around it. What's the matter with you guys? Get the lead out of your pants."

Lennox sensed the thrill as the paper came to life about him. A minute before they were tired men; through, through for the day— Now the room leaped into life, bustled with activity. Babcock said to no one in particular: "Why the hell couldn't this have broken sooner? The biggest story of the year. But if you think I'm going to let the morning's skim the cream with their bull-dogs, you're nuts. Boy! boy! Where the devil is that kid?"

Lennox read the story across Mac's shoulder as the re-write man hammered it out. Babcock was jerking the sheets from the machine and shooting them to the composing-room as soon as they were filled. Miriam Ford had called at Colossal Studio that morning to talk about a proposed picture. She had left the studio at ten-fifteen and had not been seen since. Neither, for that matter, had her bodyguard-chauffeur. At quarter of five Hiram Mullier, her business manager, had received a ransom note. The note had been left by a messenger boy, who claimed that it had been given him by a well-dressed man at the corner of Highland and the Boulevard. Leo Fay, who covered Hollywood for the News Bureau, happened to be in Mullier's office when the note arrived. Hughes had dropped in a few moments later. The note read:

Dear Mullier:

I am being held a prisoner. Do not notify the police or papers, or I shall be in grave danger. Please realize on my securities at once. You will receive instructions later. Whatever happens, don't notify the police.

It was signed Miriam Ford, and the note was in her handwriting.

Lennox crossed the room and went into a phone booth. He called the studio and asked for Spurck. The head of General-Consolidated had already gone, and Lennox called the Beverly-Swiss château, which was Spurck's home.

The other's guttural voice finally reached him across the wire. "Well?"

Lennox said, tensely: "I'm down at the *Telegram* office. A flash just came in that Miriam Ford has been kidnaped."

"Mein Gott!" Spurck's voice seemed to explode from the receiver. No other section feared kidnaping as did Hollywood, no other city took more precaution against it. And now the blow had fallen, not on some semi-obscure leading lady, but on Miriam Ford, darling of the fans, little mother of Hollywood. "I wouldn't believe it."

Lennox said soberly: "I wouldn't either, but I guess it's true."

Spurck moaned into the phone: "For a million, I wouldn't have this happen, y'understand. We gotta do something. Go see Mullier. Tell him that you will help, that I will help, all of us. *Gott soll huten* that she should be hurt."

Lennox said: "I'll be out there in half an hour," and hung up. He left the building, and hailed a cab. "Hollywood and Wilcox, and drive like hell!" he told the driver and settled back on the lumpy leather to think things out.

2

HIRAM MULLIER WAS short, with a rounded body and bandy legs. His head was somewhat egg-shaped, and glistened brightly at the top, fringed by yellowish dun-colored hair. His nose had a pronounced hook, and was too large for the rest of him. Lennox knew that he was smart—smart, and very honest, two unusual traits in the movie village. He said, in a smothered tone: "Thanks, Bill. Thanks for coming."

Lennox nodded. He had just succeeded in shooing the newspapermen from the inner office, and had fastened the door. "Well, Hi?"

Mullier spread his hands. "You know about as much as I do."

Lennox's voice held a hint of impatience. "What in the devil did you let that News Bureau man see that note for?"

Mullier spread his hands defensively. "Could I help it? He was in here when that kid brought it. He was standing there." He indicated a spot on the thick rug a couple of feet from the flat-topped desk. "My secretary brings in the note. I open it, then I say, 'My God,' and sit down hard. The note falls to the floor, and this *schlemiel* picks it up. The first thing I know he is phoning his office."

Lennox whistled softly, without tone. "That makes it bad. The kidnapers will be scared to make a move with the cops crowding around."

Mullier nodded vigorously. "I try and grab the phone from Fay, but he won't let me. In about five minutes, Hughes of the *Telegram* comes in. I'm crazy by that time. Fay tries to keep him from seeing the note, but I think since the Bureau has it, it's better to play with the papers. Honest, Bill, you don't think I would do something which would hurt Miriam? Why, I love her like I love my own *kinder*. I knew her maybe twenty years yet; back when she was making pictures for Triangle, Essanay and Biograph. I would kill myself for her." His brown eyes were moist with emotion. Lennox patted his shoulder.

"I know it, Hi, but there's nothing we can do now. We'll just have to wait." A noise in the outer office interrupted him, and someone knocked heavily on the connecting door. Lennox looked at it angrily, walked to it, and unlocked it. He opened it a crack, then pulled it wider. "It's you, huh?"

Detective Captain Floyd Spellman walked into the room. He nodded curtly; to Lennox and then looked at Mullier. "Okey! Let's hear the story."

Mullier stared at him. "But I told—"

Spellman said, with impatience: "Sure, sure, you told the Precinct man, but I want to hear it. This is big."

Lennox growled at him. "So you want to chisel in, huh? You wouldn't miss the publicity—"

Spellman stared at him. "By the way, what are you doing here?"

Lennox started to answer, stopped; then, in a different voice: "Listen, Floyd. Suppose you forget for the moment that you're a cop and act human. Give us a chance, will you? The note said that if we called the police something would happen to Miriam. The papers got it, or you wouldn't have been called. Lay off. Give us a chance to treat with them."

Spellman said, harshly: "It's the duty—"

Lennox cut in: "Hell! I know that speech. Of course it's the duty of every citizen to help catch snatchers. We all know that, but we also know that a bunch of us in this town love Ford. She's one grand girl. The country loves her, and there's going to be a howl go up at this news. Do you think that the kidnapers will take a chance with the cops around? Come on. Call your men off. Give us twenty-four hours to make contact, to try to find her. After she's safe, I'll be the first to help land these rats. My —— Floyd! Haven't you any feelings?"

The detective shrugged. "What can I do, Bill? If we lay off we catch hell. If we don't, we catch the same. We're in a spot. You know that."

"Not quite as tough a spot as Miriam is in," Lennox told him, softly. "Listen, Floyd. Remember who she is. There isn't a more prominent woman in the country. She grew up with pictures. She started with Pickford, the Talmadge and Gish girls. She still makes a few, and is plenty strong at the box office, but it goes deeper than that. Her whole life is absolutely wrapped up in pictures. She's the little mother of Hollywood."

Spellman nodded. "I know it, Bill, but what can I do?" He spread his hands. "The Chief has ordered a dragnet out. Every man is on duty. They're going to stop every car entering or leaving the city."

Lennox swore and picked up the phone. He called Spurck and talked heatedly with his boss, then hung up. "We might as well eat?"

Mullier choked. "I couldn't, Bill. I can't stand the thought."

3

NANCY HOBBS, STAFF writer for one of the better fan magazines, rose from her seat in the lobby of the apartment hotel which Lennox called home. "Have you heard about Ford, Bill?"

He nodded. "I guess everyone in town has heard by now." His voice was bitter. "It was a tough break that Fay happened to be in Mullier's office."

She said: "I wonder if there's any fresh news?" Her voice had a hushed quality which spoke of fear.

He shook his head and drew a folded extra from beneath his arm. A large picture of Miriam Ford smiled out at them from beneath the heading: "Actress Kidnaped."

He glanced down the column. It gave a résumé of her career, her early pictures, her war work, and her three marriages; pictured the third husband, who was at present in Yucatan, making a picture with native actors in a setting of Mayan ruins. Lennox stared at his long, narrow face. Walter Condrey, director and independent producer, was almost as well known as his famous wife. He'd begun in pictures as a cowboy actor, but had switched to the production end years ago. Lennox wished that he were in Hollywood, wished his help. He liked Condrey, despite the man's bizarre acts and publicity-seeking stunts. He was a smart, level—

The radio music across the lobby stilled as a man's voice cut into the dance program.

"Ladies and Gentlemen: We are interrupting the Carnelle

Coffee hour for an important announcement. You all have heard that Miriam Ford, that beloved actress who has so often entertained us, has been kidnaped. Mr. Mullier, her business manager, has requested our aid, and we are more than glad to put the entire facilities of our nationwide network at his disposal. Mr. Mullier."

Hiram Mullier's voice reached them, broken, almost unrecognizable. "Friends, I have a message for the abductors of Miriam Ford. I hope that they are listening. The note sent me by Miss Ford fell into the hands of reporters by mistake. I am perfectly ready to cooperate with you in any manner which you may designate, if you will only communicate with me.

"The Police Chief has agreed to withdraw his men from the hunt. Please, please, get in touch with either myself or with William Lennox of General-Consolidated Studios, who is assisting me. His phone number is Hillside 1-8590, while mine is Crestview 2-7598. These wires are not tapped, and no calls will be traced. Our addresses are—"

The girl said, in a low voice: "So you're in this, too?"

Lennox nodded soberly. "I only hope that I can help. I've got to get upstairs, kid. There might be a call."

She said: "When you know something—"

He patted her shoulder. "I'll let you know." He turned and went to the desk, conscious that every eye in the lobby was watching him. The clerk said, in an unnatural voice: "This is terrible, Mr. Lennox. To think that Miss Ford—"

Bill nodded. "Right, Sam. Listen! If anyone comes asking for me, send him up and don't be too inquisitive."

He walked to the elevator and rode up to his floor. In the apartment, he dragged a heavy chair close to the stand which bore the phone, and then went towards the kitchenette. The phone rang sharply, shrilly, and he jumped. It rang again before he reached it, and lifted it from its cradle. A man's voice said: "Is this Lennox? Bill Lennox?"

Bill's brows drew together as he said: "Yeah."

"This is Harry Marsh. I just heard the broadcast. I thought maybe I could help."

Lennox's lips were a straight, thin line. "That's nice of you, Harry." His voice held no inflection.

Marsh said: "Can you drop over here later?"

Lennox sounded uncertain. "I've got to stay by the phone, Harry."

There was silence for a moment at the other end of the wire, as if the man were hesitating. "What about my coming up there?"

"Swell! Don't ask at the desk. No use giving the clerk ideas. I'll expect you."

He hung up and stared at the phone. Harry Marsh, night-club owner, ex-gangster, with his finger in the slot machine and pin marble racket. Lennox sat there asking himself questions. Then he rose, went to the kitchenette, and poured himself a drink.

The phone rang again, sharply. He almost ran towards it. A girl's voice said: "Bill, any luck?" It was Nancy Hobbs.

"Don't know yet. What is it, honey?"

She said: "I thought that the cops were called off. There are a couple staked out across the street from your apartment. I thought that you ought to know."

He swore softly into the instrument. "Thanks, pal. You sure?"

"I saw Spellman and another man. They don't know that I saw them."

He said: "I've got a call to make. See you later," and hung up. He dialed the number of Marsh's club and asked for Harry.

A smooth voice said: "He ain't here. Who's calling?"

Lennox hesitated for a moment, then gave his name. The man at the other end of the wire said: "He's on his way over to your joint now. He should be there in about ten minutes."

Lennox thanked him and hung up. He played with the dial of the phone for a minute, then called Mullier. The other's voice was questioning, keen. It lost its eager note when Lennox said:

"This is Bill. Had any luck? Heard anything?"

Mullier sounded old. "Not yet. I was hoping, this call—"

"I thought that the cops had been pulled off."

Mullier said: "They have. The Chief promised."

Lennox grunted. "There are a couple staked out across the street from my joint. Better call Headquarters and find out. We'll never make contact with the boys in blue hanging around." He replaced the phone and went towards the bedroom.

Someone knocked on the door, sharply, insistently. Lennox called: "Come in."

The door opened and a black-haired youth in a double-breasted blue suit slipped through. He nodded to Lennox, crossed the room, and disappeared into the bedroom, made a circuit of the apartment and went to the hall door. His hand was out of sight in his side coat pocket. His movements were assured, businesslike. "Okey."

Someone from the hall answered. The next minute, Marsh was in the room. He was short, inclined towards stoutness. His curly hair was streaked with gray, although Lennox knew that he was not yet thirty. The belted camel's-hair coat covered a tuxedo. His head was bare.

Another man followed him in. Lennox knew him for an ex-fighter, who served Marsh as a bodyguard. He took up a post just inside the door, shot the bolt into place, and let his heavy eyes wander about the room. Marsh stepped forward, ignoring the actions of his companions. "How are you, Bill?" His hand gripped Lennox's and fell away. They measured each other for a moment with their eyes.

Lennox said: "Fine!" He had a sense of detachment, as if he were not part of this scene, but rather a spectator, watching from the sidelines.

Marsh laughed suddenly, an unpleasant sound, not burdened with mirth. "You think I've got her?"

Lennox shook his head slowly. "I'm not thinking, Harry. I'm waiting."

The other nodded slowly. "I believe you. Well, I haven't." His voice seemed extra loud, unnecessarily so. "I'm here to help, to help if you want help."

Lennox said: "We need help, all we can get."

The gangster nodded. "I know it. I'm not trying to kid you, Bill. I've broken some laws. I'll probably break more, but—well, this is going to turn this town wrong side out. It's going to make it tough for all of us. The quicker Miriam Ford is home, the less rumble there's going to be. I'm offering to act as contact man. I don't know who's got her. It's going to be tough. Los Angeles isn't like New York or Chi. There aren't organized gangs here. There are plenty of grafters, but they work alone. It's hard to put the finger on them."

Lennox nodded. "You aren't telling me a thing that I don't know, Marsh. If you can make contact—" He stopped suddenly as someone pounded on the door. Both of Marsh's men stiffened, their hands darting towards their pockets. Marsh's eyes swept towards Lennox, read the surprise in Bill's face.

For a minute there was silence in the room. A heavy voice said: "Open up, Lennox!" It was Spellman's voice.

Bill swore and looked towards Marsh. "I didn't frame this, Harry."

The other nodded. "Okey!" To the man standing beside the door he said: "Open it."

The ex-fighter obeyed, and Spellman shoved his way into the room. Marsh said, in a voice devoid of expression: "Hello, Floyd."

The detective captain nodded shortly. The man with him stayed by the door, his hand in his pocket. Spellman stepped towards the center of the room. "I didn't figure you in this kind of deal, Harry."

Lennox said, angrily, harshly: "Get some brains. Marsh is here to help. I thought that you boys were pulled off. Spurck talked to the Chief and if you don't think that General-Consolidated drags weight in this town—"

Spellman said: "Save it." His voice was harsh, but it had gained an uncertain note.

Lennox said: "For —— sake, start thinking and forget the publicity. If you gum this play for us I'll have your heart if I have to—" His hands made themselves into fists at his side. His face had reddened with anger. Marsh's cool voice recalled him. The gangster was unruffled, unexcited.

"Did you want me, Floyd?"

Lennox found a cigarette, rolled it unconsciously between his thumb and finger, his eyes on their faces.

"Take him down, Spellman, and you'll never take another prisoner."

The big man said, heatedly: "Who's running this department?"

Lennox walked to the phone, called Headquarters, and asked for the night Chief. When he got him, he said half a dozen words, then extended the phone towards Spellman. The detective captain took it unwillingly, his heavy brows drawn together. He listened silently for a moment, then hung up.

No one in the room spoke for a second. Spellman scowled at Lennox. "Okey. You win now, but don't think that I'm going to stop looking just because I can't tag you."

Lennox said: "No one wants you to, you ape. Look, and I hope that you find her. I hope to God someone does."

Marsh and his men waited a few moments, then followed the detective out.

4

LIGHT DUG ITS way through the heavy drapes and aroused Lennox. He straightened in his chair, stretched stiffly, and glanced at the watch on his wrist. It was twenty minutes past seven. He stared at the silent phone, ran his fingers through his hair, and then across the stubble on his chin. He picked up the phone and called Mullier.

A servant answered and said that his master was taking a bath. Lennox asked if there was any news. There wasn't. He hung up, then rang the desk and ordered breakfast. "Send up all the papers," he directed, went into the bathroom, stripped, shaved, and stepped under a shower. The water took the aches from his muscles, revived him.

Someone knocked on the door as he was using a towel. He slipped into a flannel robe and unfastened the door. It was the boy with his breakfast. He looked at the tray distastefully, and picked up the papers. Almost the entire front page of each was given over to the kidnaping. Lennox paid no attention to the mass of misinformation. What caught his eye was the announcement which he had telephoned to the papers the evening before. Under a subhead he read:

"Night-Club Owner Appointed Contact Man. Harry Marsh to serve as Intermediary. William Lennox, an executive of General-Consolidated Studios, announced late last night that Harry Marsh, night-club owner and underworld figure, had been appointed by him as contact man. Lennox refused all information regarding the kidnaping of Miss Ford, and refused to state whether or not he had received any communication from her abductors. Harry Marsh is well known in certain circles of Los Angeles. Although he has never been convicted, it is thought—" There followed a résumé of Marsh's career.

Lennox did not bother to read further. His eye ranged across the page, noted the boxed-in editorial, calling upon the nation to rise against the kidnaping racket, read reports that Miss Ford had been seen as far east as Portland, Me., that two plane pilots were being held by the Salt Lake police on suspicion that they had carried Miss Ford away from Los Angeles, and then, down in the right-hand corner under the head, "Husband Flies to Rescue Wife," he read that Walter Condrey, director and producer, who was in Yucatan making a picture, had been notified of his wife's abduction and was returning to Hollywood by plane.

Lennox grinned without mirth. It was just the sort of thing which Condrey would try, yes, and probably accomplish. The man had a flair for the spectacular, and the luck to carry it through. If he were in Hollywood now—but he wasn't. Lennox rose, went into the kitchenette, found a half-filled bottle of Bacardi, and poured a liberal dose into his coffee.

The phone rang as he was drinking it. He answered, and heard Babcock's voice. "Can't you give me something, Bill, something that's really news?" he pleaded.

Lennox said: "I wish I could," and cut short the other's protests by hanging up. The phone rang again, and Lennox stared at it sourly. It was probably one of the other papers. It might, of course, be Babcock, calling back. He picked it up with his left hand. His right still held the half-empty coffee cup.

A high, thin voice said: "Is this William Lennox?"

Bill stiffened. He set the cup on to the table. It hit the rim of the saucer, and turned over. Lennox paid no attention. Excitement welled up in him. No one ever called him William. His voice was steady when he answered, steady and contained. "What is it?"

The voice persisted. "This is the Lennox that was referred to in last night's broadcast?"

"Yes."

"We, ah, have your goods. It is in splendid shape, and we are ready to make delivery under certain conditions."

"What are they?"

The voice said: "You have full authority to negotiate?"

"You heard the broadcast, didn't you?"

"Certainly. We are merely assuring ourselves. First, get one hundred thousand dollars in fives, tens, and twenties."

Lennox started to say, "Is that all?" then he stopped. "What next?" His voice still hid his surprise.

"Get a car and drive slowly over the pass into San Fernando valley. Follow Ventura Boulevard until you reach the road which comes through Laurel Canyon, turn right and follow this road for seven miles. Take the next cross road to your left and drive five miles, then the road to your right again, and come back towards town any way you like. If you are followed, no contact will be made. Is that clear?"

Lennox said: "Let me get a pencil."

The voice at the other end of the wire was decisive. "Don't write it down. I'll repeat it once more. Memorize it." Lennox listened carefully until the wire went dead, then called Mullier.

The business manager said: "Any news?" His voice held a hopeless quality.

Lennox said: "Yes."

"What?" Mullier seemed suddenly without sufficient breath.

Lennox said: "Get this, Hi. They called me a couple of minutes ago. They want a hundred grand."

"Is that all?" Relief and surprise mingled.

"Yeah. The way I figure it, they're scared. All this publicity has them on the run. They're willing to take a quick profit and scram. Now get this. Get the money, fives, tens, twenties, and for gawd's sake, don't take the numbers. We don't want a hitch of any kind. Send over to the bank for it and watch that no one gets wise, then put it in a plain package and send it over to Nancy Hobbs by ordinary messenger. I don't think that the cops are watching, but we can't take a chance."

"Isn't that risky?" Mullier sounded uncertain.

Lennox said: "Sure, but we've got to take chances. Get it over there as soon as you can."

"All right; but, Bill, where are you going to make contact?"

Lennox lied. "I don't know yet. Leave it to me." He hung up and called the girl. When he had his connection, he said: "Listen, Nance. A messenger will deliver a package to you in a little while. Get your car and drive out to the *White Spot* in Beverly, park in the parking space, and leave the package in the car."

She said: "What is it, Bill?"

"Can't explain now, honey. Do as you're told." He hung up and went into the bedroom.

AN HOUR LATER, Lennox, seated in a rented you-drive-it car, saw the girl swing her coupé into the restaurant's parking space, leave it, and disappear around the corner. There was an empty space beside the coupé. Lennox pulled into it, saw the newspaper-wrapped package on the seat of the girl's car. It took only a moment to transfer it to his own, and then he was pulling away, with the package at his side.

He went across La Brea to the Boulevard, right to Highland, and left, past the entrance to the Bowl, and out into the pass. There was a heavy stream of traffic on Ventura. Lennox drove slowly, his eyes straight ahead, but he raised them occasionally to the rear-view mirror.

As nearly as he could judge, he had not been followed. The only things which did not pass him were the heavy gravel trucks on the extreme right of the wide pavement. He passed Universal City and kept steadily on. At the Laurel Canyon road, he turned right, his eyes dropping to the speedometer, noting the mileage. For seven miles he drove, holding the car at twenty. Hardly a machine passed him, going either way. He was certain now that he was not followed.

When he had traversed seven miles, he looked for the next cross road. It was a broad strip of macadam without a car in sight. He had gone perhaps three miles on it when he saw a car in the rear-view mirror. It was coming fast, a light road-ster, swaying from one side of the road to the other. It passed him at a terrific rate, and he saw, as it flashed by, that it held two men. For perhaps five minutes it was in sight, ahead on the deserted road; then it was gone in the haze of distance. He passed a dirt road leading off to the left, and stiffened as he saw a long, black car parked in the shelter of some trees. The car pulled on to the road behind him, pulled up beside his car, and Lennox saw three men, two in front, one in back. Their faces were covered with handkerchiefs and their hats pulled low above their eyes. The man beside the driver held a subma-chine-gun, pointed at Lennox.

"Keep driving, buddy, slow."

Bill let his speed lessen until he was doing about ten miles an hour. The black car slackened, keeping abreast. "Toss it over," the man with the gun told him, harshly.

"What about Miss—"

For answer the man in the back seat raised a woman's form from the car's floor. She was bound hand and foot, and a scarf of some kind was wrapped about her mouth and the lower half of her face. Her hair, however, was uncovered, and Lennox recognized the reddish brown bob, the darker eyebrows. "Toss it over." The gun moved menacingly.

Lennox said: "It's pretty heavy," and kicked his clutch out. The car lost speed. He picked up the package, weighing it in his hands. "How do I know that you'll play square with me?"

The man with the gun laughed. "A lot of comeback you'd have if I sprayed you with this. Let's see the dough."

Lennox's car had almost halted. He extended the package with both hands. The man in back let the girl go and leaned out. He took the money from Lennox. The man with the gun said: "Stay here." The black car pulled twenty feet ahead. The rear door opened, and the woman's limp form was lifted out on to the road's shoulder. For a moment Lennox was seized with the conviction that she was dead; then he saw one shoul-der move slightly. The man with the gun stepped out. The gun broke into rattling sound, and both front tires of Lennox's car went flat. "That will hold you." The gunman swung into his place, the black car moved away, fast. Lennox saw that its plates were plastered with mud.

He ran towards the woman and knelt at her side, his fingers fumbling at the knot which held the scarf gag in place. He had trouble with the knot and was forced to use his knife; then he swore as he unwrapped the scarf. It was a pretty face, an almost beautiful face, but it was not the face of Miriam Ford.

He stared down at her for a moment. Her eyes were closed and her breath came heavily. He shook her, and she groaned. Then his knife severed the ropes which bound her arms and legs. She groaned again, her eyes still closed. Lennox slapped her, sharply, but not too hard. The eyelids fluttered, came open, stared at him without understanding. He said, harshly: "Come on! Snap out of it. Who are you?"

Fear came into her eyes. "I don't— I don't understand."

He said, ruefully: "I don't either, but I know someone pulled a fast one. Can you walk?"

She tried to get to her feet, failed, and Lennox picked her up and carried her to the car. He looked up and down the road, but there was nothing in sight. Then he looked at his front tires. They had been cut to ribbons. He got the jack, raised them, and pulled them from the rims. Then he climbed in, leaving the ruined tires where they lay, and started the motor. It was almost two miles to the first house. He made it as fast as he could, dashed through the gate and up to the front door. "Telephone," he panted to the heavy woman who answered his knock.

He brushed by her without waiting for permission and called the operator. "Let me talk to Police Headquarters, L.A., then get me the station at Van Nuys, North Hollywood, or wherever else they have them out here. Come on. Snap it up!"

He caught Spellman in his office. The detective captain said:

"So you're asking for help, smart boy?" There was satisfaction in his voice.

Lennox swore at him. "They got away in a Packard sedan, thirty. The license plates were gummed with mud, but they'll probably ditch the car anyway. Their scout car was a Ford roadster, thirty-two or three. The license began with 2H. That's all I got."

"And they got a hundred grand." Spellman's voice was mocking. "After this, don't be so ready to tie the can to the cops."

Lennox said: "Shut up, and get the alarm out. I'm coming in now."

"I'll be waiting, sweetheart."

The trouble-shooter did not bother to answer. He hung up, then called the operator. "Never mind those other calls. They're sending out the flash from downtown." He hung up again and turned around. The heavy woman was watching him with unconcealed interest. She said: "My, to think—"

Lennox did not wait. He laid a half dollar on the table and went through the door. The girl was still seated in the car where he had left her. He got in, kicked the motor into life, and then looked at her. It was evident that she had been made up heavily. Her eyebrows showed it, as did her eyes. She looked at him, her thick-lipped mouth trembling, started to say something, then didn't. The car went into motion, the rims making noise on the road. At the first garage, Lennox bought two tires. The mechanic looked at the battered rims and shook his head.

Lennox said: "Fix them somehow so I can get into town," and turned to the girl. "Now, just who the devil are you, and what were you doing in that car?"

5

SPELLMAN WAS WAITING in front of Lennox's apartment when Bill brought the car to the curb. A department Buick with the radio going was parked across the street, three men in it.

Lennox said, before he got out: "Any news?"

The big detective shook his head. "They found the Packard two miles from Van Nuys. It was hot."

Lennox nodded heavily and looked at the girl. "This is my hundred-grand baby. She hasn't much tongue. Claims that she was grabbed on Selma last night, and don't know what it's all about. Claims that she's an extra. I'm going to check with the casting bureau."

Spellman was staring at the girl. He said, softly: "Save yourself the trouble, Bill. I know her."

Lennox widened his eyes. "Okey, Slew-foot. Who is she?"

"Wash that gold out of her hair and she'd be Marie Bigelow, Harry Marsh's moll."

Lennox said something sharply, under his breath, and looked at the girl. She returned the look, fear gone from her eyes, defiance taking its place. "What about it?"

Spellman said: "Isn't this swell? Isn't this just too swell? Lennox won't play with the cops, but he will play with the gangsters. He takes a hundred grand for a ride, and comes back with a helluva story and a gangster's moll."

Bill eased himself from the car. "Just what do you mean by that, Floyd?"

The heavy shoulders moved up and down slightly. "I may not mean anything; I may mean a lot." His big hand fastened on the girl's wrist. "Come on, you."

She said, defiantly: "Try to take me."

Spellman grinned at her. "Try?" One hand opened the door, the other yanked her forth. She clawed at him like a wild-cat, and Lennox saw long, red marks appear on the leathery cheek. "You little devil!" Spellman gathered her up in his arms and carried her across the street towards the squad car. Over his shoulder he said: "I'm leaving two men to watch you, Lennox. Chief's orders. The moratorium is over."

Lennox did not bother to look at him. He went through the door and towards the desk. From one of the booths at the right of the switchboard, he called Mullier, and told the business manager what had happened. The other moaned into the phone: "Whatta we do now?"

Lennox said: "I don't know. I should have guessed that this was a plant, but I didn't get wise. I was so sure that the girl was Ford. Now I'm not even sure that the muggs were the kidnapers at all. Maybe they were some wise boys, trying to chisel in."

"But Marsh's girl?"

"I'm going to try to get into touch with Harry now. There's something fishy about this whole set-up. I'm going to try to find out what it is."

He rang off and called Marsh's club. The gangster wasn't there, but Lennox got the address of the man's apartment. Bill went out, got into the car, and drove out to the apartment.

A heavy man with wide shoulders turned around from one of the windows as Lennox followed the Filipino houseboy into the room. "Harry will be out in a minute, Lennox. I'm Tempke."

Lennox shook hands. He knew that Tempke was Marsh's lieutenant, in charge of the slot machine and pin marble rackets. He'd never met the man before. Marsh came through the door, said: "Hello, Al," to Tempke, and nodded to Lennox. "I haven't been able to make contact yet, Bill. There are all kind of rumors floating about town."

Tempke laughed without mirth. "I even heard this morning that she'd been taken across the Line into Mexico."

Lennox said: "And I handed out one hundred grand and didn't get her."

"You what?"

He told them exactly what had happened. Marsh said: "I wish you had called me. I'd have had you covered, and the monkeys wouldn't have known it. Who was the girl?"

Lennox was watching Marsh with narrow eyes. "Marie Bigelow."

For an instant the name did not seem to register, then Marsh's face whitened. "Not, not—"

Lennox nodded. He was certain of the other's surprise, or was he? Marsh's face had shown little except for a change in color. "I didn't know who she was when I brought her in. She wouldn't tell me anything. Spellman recognized her."

Marsh said, tunelessly: "Where is she now?"

Lennox said: "Spellman took her downtown. I thought that you ought to know."

The night-club owner nodded. "Thanks, Bill." His voice still lacked tone. He walked to the phone, called his lawyer, and gave some curt instructions. Tempke said: "What did these monkeys look like?"

Lennox shrugged. "There were five of them. The Packard

was hot. They had a Ford roadster for a scout car. Maybe they used it for the getaway, maybe they used another. I couldn't see them."

Tempke said, complainingly: "Something's gotta be done. Things are getting outta hand." He crossed the room and picked up his hat. "I'll go out and see what I can hear."

Marsh hung up and turned around. "Call back in an hour. I may want you." The other nodded and went out. Marsh said to Lennox: "Do you think that it was the kidnapers or some chiselers?"

Lennox shrugged. "I don't know. I'm guessing that it was chiselers, but they picked on your girl—"

Marsh said: "To make it tough for both of us. It's going to look swell in the papers, isn't it?"

Lennox said: "To hell with that. If they'd find Ford, I wouldn't care. I'm beginning to think that we won't hear from her, that she's dead."

6

HEADLINES ALMOST FILLED the front pages of the evening papers. A picture of Miriam Ford with her husband and a caption, *"Condrey flies to wife's aid."* A picture of Lennox, snapped as he emerged from Marsh's apartment. Headlines, but no real news of Ford. The actress was still missing and no one had been found who had seen her from the time she had driven away from Colossal Studio. One paper hinted strongly that Lennox knew much more than he had told, and that his association with Marsh should be investigated by the police. A group of producers, headed by Spurck, offered a reward of fifty thousand for information which would lead to the safe return of Miss Ford.

An item on the second page caught Lennox's eye. Three men, reputed to be local gangsters, had been shot to death late that afternoon in a dive on Central in what police believed to be an outbreak of gang war. All three had records, and two were wanted in connection with a downtown robbery. Lennox turned over to the comic page, tried the sport section, and then threw the paper to the floor. The inactivity irked him. He rose and walked twice about the apartment. Someone knocked on the door. He crossed the room and jerked it open, savagely. Spellman came in. The detective's heavy face looked tired and he sank into a chair without bothering to remove his coat. "Heard anything?"

Lennox shook his head. "Not a murmur. Have you?"

The other said: "Marsh's dame is out. We couldn't shake her

story and her lawyer kept buzzing around."

"Maybe it was on the level."

Spellman narrowed his eyes. "Maybe it was. Have you told all you know, Bill?"

Lennox spread his hands. "Would I be sitting here if I knew things? It's funny you boys don't at least turn up Ford's car."

Spellman shrugged. "It's tucked away in some private garage on some alley. Probably the garage owner wouldn't know it if he saw it. By the way, a flash just came in that Condrey's plane is down somewhere. They haven't heard from it for hours."

Lennox whistled. "Looks like the whole family will go out at once—" He broke off as the phone rang shrilly.

Spellman said, eagerly: "That might be the kidnapers."

"More likely some half-baked reporter." Bill crossed to the stand and picked it up. "Hello."

A smooth, almost liquid voice said: "Mr. Lennox?"

Bill said, sourly: "What do you want?"

"Merely a little news for you, my friend." The voice had a foreign sound, but there was little accent. "I am calling for Miss Ford."

"What? Is she all right?" He was conscious that Spellman had come out of his chair and was crossing the room.

"Is it—?"

Lennox nodded silently.

The detective said, in a whisper: "Stall him as long as you can. I'm hunting another phone." He whirled and was gone.

The voice in the phone said: "Are you alone?"

Lennox heard the door close behind the departing detective and said: "Yes." The other laughed with easy mirth. "I only called to tell you that we received the hundred thousand which you so recklessly paid out this morning, and will consider it the first payment."

"The first payment, but you—"

"You mistake, my friend," the oily voice continued. "It was not to us you paid the money. It was to some other men, other men who made the mistake of thinking they could cut in on our game. We learned who they were. Three of them are dead, and the money passed to our possession. Surely you would not insult Miss Ford by thinking that we valued her at so small a sum as one hundred thousand."

"You say three men are dead?" Lennox was stalling now, trying to give Spellman time to trace the call. The twenty-four hours given the kidnapers in the broadcast were up.

The man at the other end said: "Maybe you read about them in the papers. That's what happens to people who cross us, Lennox."

Bill said: "But Miss Ford. Tell me what we have to do?"

"You'll hear later." The voice was mocking now.

Lennox said: "Wait," but the wire was already dead. He replaced the receiver and sat back. Spellman appeared several minutes later. The detective shrugged.

"No luck. The call came from a pay station on Broadway, but our man was gone before we got there. Why didn't you hold him?"

Lennox said: "I tried to, we—" The phone rang again and he caught it up eagerly, listened for a moment, and held it towards Spellman. "For you," he said.

The detective took it, listened for a minute, said: "I'll be right down," and hung up. "They've got Ford's chauffeur," he told Lennox. "Come on."

7

THE MAN WAS a wreck. His features had been battered until they were hardly recognizable. One eye was puffed closed and a long, narrow cut went diagonally across the right cheek. The once smart whipcord of his uniform was grimy and torn, and the left arm dangled awkwardly at his side. A patrol car had picked him up on Maple between Tenth and Eleventh and taken him to Georgia Street Hospital.

The doctor said; "You can't question him now, man, he might die while you're talking."

Spellman said, grimly: "That's just why I am going to question him. Can't you give him a shot that will bring him to?"

The other hesitated, raised his eyebrows, and shrugged. A nurse, with the assistance of an orderly, was undressing him. The doctor said: "I doubt if I can revive him, but I'll try." He tried, and failed. The chauffeur died within twenty minutes.

Spellman did not trouble to hide his chagrin. He said to Lennox, as they stood on the curb beside the patrol car: "I've got men out combing all the private garages. They could work from now until next Yom Kippur and still not cover half of them, but we gotta do something. I've got every stool in town out, but they're either scared or they can't find out a thing."

Lennox suggested: "Work on that Central Avenue killing. If the kidnapers did that, it might furnish you a clue."

He turned just as a cab pulled up behind the squad car and walked towards it, gave the driver the address of Marsh's club, and climbed in.

The cab stopped at a traffic light on Eighth, and Lennox bought an extra. A black headline screamed: "Producer Missing. Condrey Lost on Way to Help Wife." The driver turned around and said:

"Any news about Ford, governor?"

Lennox told him that there was no news, and the cab moved on. At the club, Lennox got out, paid his driver, showed his card to the doorman, and mounted the heavily carpeted stairs. The supper room was packed. Evidently Marsh's connection with the Ford case was attracting custom. Lennox nodded to a director, checked his hat, went along the hall to a door at the rear, and slipped through.

There was an iron door beyond, halfway down the passage, but it stood wide and there was no guard in sight. He followed the passage, turned to the right, and went through an arch into the main gambling room. There was a crowd about the roulette layout in the center, with a smaller crowd at the crap table. The other wheels weren't running. Lennox saw Tempke across the room, his big shoulders filling a dinner coat.

Marsh's lieutenant nodded as Lennox reached his side. "Any news?"

Lennox said: "I was just about to ask you that. Where's Harry?"

The other shrugged. "He's around somewhere. Haven't you heard a thing?" The man's eyes seemed to be probing, trying to reach Lennox's mind.

Bill said: "Those gangsters that were killed on Central. Know anything about them?"

Tempke stared at him, then he turned. "Let's get out of here so we can talk." He turned and led the way diagonally across the room, through a door behind the cashier's cage, and down a short passage into a small office. "Now, what did you mean by that last crack?"

Lennox had found a cigarette and was rolling it in his fingers. "I asked, because the kidnapers, the real ones, called me tonight and claimed to have killed those muggs."

"The hell you say!" The other's voice had lost its softness.

Lennox said: "I came over to ask Harry what he knew about those guys."

Tempke was silent for a moment. "I don't think that he knows a thing. They were a bunch of cheap grafters. I wouldn't have thought that they had the guts to stand you up for that hundred grand. They sure got out of line. I'm almost glad that the real kidnapers took it away from them."

Lennox didn't say anything. His eyes were narrow, thoughtful, as he put the cigarette into his mouth and lit it. A noise at the door made him turn as Harry Marsh appeared. The night-club owner looked tired, and his usually untroubled face showed lines. "Any news?"

Lennox shook his head. "I thought that you might have some."

The other dropped heavily into the chair at his desk. "No, nothing." He was silent for a moment. "Condrey's been found. At least it just came over the radio."

"Where was he?"

"Don't know. He's hurt, I guess, but he's coming on, they say, across Mexico. He should get here some time tomorrow."

Lennox nodded, his eyes on the other. "I did hear from the kidnapers. I forgot that when I said that there was no news."

The man at the desk stiffened. "You did? When?"

Lennox told him, watching Marsh closely. There was no change of expression. He said to Tempke: "Go and get what you can on those muggs that got rubbed out. It might lead somewhere."

The big man nodded and moved towards the door. When he had gone Lennox said: "Think I'll be moving myself. If you find out anything, give me a ring."

He went through the gambling room, pausing for a moment to speak to a red-haired girl at the crap table. She was winning and a little drunk. "Bill, darling, have they heard anything about Miriam?" Her voice was high and other sounds in the room died. Even the croupiers seemed to be waiting for his answer.

He said: "Nothing yet."

She held his arm. "But this is awful. They might snatch any of us."

He loosened the reddened nails. "Some of you, I wouldn't care." He moved away as a man across the room laughed.

ON THE SIDEWALK below, he walked towards the row of cabs and got into the last one. To the driver, he handed a folded bill. "A big man will be out in a minute. I don't know whether he'll have his own car or will use a cab. Either way, follow, and don't lose him—yeah, and God help you if he thinks he's being followed."

The cabman looked uncertain, started to say something, and then glanced at the bill. It was a twenty, and he changed his mind. Lennox settled far back into the seat, his hat drawn low, his face hidden, obscured by shadow. He sat there almost five minutes. He began to think that the other had left the club ahead of him, when he saw the bulky shoulders of Tempke appear in the lighted doorway.

A dark sedan which was parked across the street came to life. Its motor raced as it moved away from the curb and turned in the middle of the block. A moment later it drew up before the doorway. In the light, Lennox recognized the ex-fighter who served Marsh as a bodyguard, behind the wheel. Tempke crossed the sidewalk and climbed in. The sedan went west, turned left at the first corner, and left again at the next. The cab's motor raced as it took up pursuit, but the taillight of the other car was fading into the distance.

Lennox leaned forward, urging his driver on. The man did not take his eyes from the road. "We're doing sixty-five. Whatta yuh think this is—an airplane?"

A traffic light helped them, holding the sedan for a moment. Traffic increased as they neared the city, and the driver of the other car slowed his pace. Lennox settled back with a sigh of relief. They swerved right and went crosstown for several blocks, then left. The sedan was perhaps three blocks ahead, weaving in and out of the late traffic, still going fast, but not at the terrific rate it had held earlier. Suddenly it pulled over towards the curb. Lennox, bending forward, said: "Keep going." As they flashed by, he had a glimpse of Tempke talking to the driver. The cabman looked about inquiringly. Lennox said: "Next street to your right," and looked back at the empty apartment house just beyond which the sedan was parked.

Brakes squealed protestingly as the cabman pressed the foot-pedal. The tires screamed as they made the turn. "Where next?" The cab was rolling down the dark side street, losing momentum.

Lennox said: "Next street to the right and stop before you reach the corner."

The driver obeyed. He looked at his passenger thoughtfully as Lennox opened the door and swung out. "Okey. That's all." Bill watched the taxi disappear, then walked rapidly around the block. The sedan was gone.

He cursed under his breath. It had not entered his head that the sedan would not be there. Perhaps Tempke had only stopped for a moment. Lennox had had a clear view of him and the driver, but at best he had been playing a hunch.

He fumbled in his coat pocket, found a cigarette, and lit it. As he threw away the match, he glanced idly at the empty apartment. It was unfinished, its windows, black oblongs staring out like so many eyes. There were five identically such houses in town; started by the Seaboard Mortgage Company, it stood, an unfinished monument to investors' hopes and investors' losses. The company had failed with the depression; the receivers would not, or could not, liquidate the properties.

Lennox looked up and down, hoping for a cruising cab. There was none in sight. He looked again at the apartment building, speculating how much it had cost, how much it would cost to finish. Suddenly he stiffened. A ray of light flashed for a moment from an upper window and was gone. He stared at the window, not believing his eyes. Then the flash came again; not from the same window, but from another to the right of the first. Lennox muttered something to himself.

It might be tramps, it might not be. He moved to the apartment's front door and found it barred with planks. Whistling tonelessly, he walked to the corner and down the side street, looking for open windows. There was none. An alley opened behind the house. Lennox turned into this, looking for a fire-escape. It was dark here, and he could not see well. High above his head the fog drifted, making a ceiling for the city, reflecting the lights from a cushion of dull gray, but shutting out both moon and stars. He moved along the building's rear wall, feeling his way.

Suddenly it seemed that the ground gave beneath him and he fell heavily, wrenching an ankle. He struggled to his feet and struck a match on his thumbnail. He had fallen into the concrete runway which led downward to the basement garage. The match burnt his fingers and he dropped it, found another and lit it. By the uncertain flame he saw a jagged tear in the knee of his pants, with blood showing through, but he hardly noticed, for he had seen something else. The garage door was planked over, as was the front, but on the other side, one plank had slipped, leaving a dark opening, perhaps a foot wide.

He dropped the match and moved along the runway, feeling the wooden door as he went until his fingers found the opening. The planks were of two-foot width, and this one moved beneath his hand. It was secured at the top, but not at the bottom, and swung loosely on its fastening.

Lennox pushed it farther aside and wormed through the opening. It had been dark in the alley, but it was black inside the building; the darkness seemed heavy, oppressive, bearing in upon him with untold warnings. He found another match, scratched it upon the wood, and held it above his head. He stood in what was to be an immense garage. Rows of pillars formed stalls which at some future date would house the finest products of motordom, but now it was a dark, damp, desolate room with long shadows and large patches of gloom.

Lennox had no idea where the stairs were. He wasn't even certain that there were stairs. The match burned down and he lit another, moving across the room towards the front of the building. Again the flame was close to his fingers and he dropped the match, moving ahead in the smothering darkness. He bumped into a concrete post, felt his way around it, and went on until his groping fingers touched the wall. He went along it, searching for a door, failed to find one, and turned back. Finally his fingers encountered wood. He stopped and reached into his pocket. There were three matches left. He lit one and studied the planks which barred his progress.

There was nothing particularly interesting about them, but there was about the new hasp and padlock which held the door in place. The lock was new, so new that there was still a tiny scrap of paper stuck to it, oiled brown paper in which it had been wrapped. The match flickered, and he was again in darkness. He cursed, fingered the lock and drew his keys from his pocket. None of them fitted. He brought out his knife and tried the screws which held the hasp. One came easily; on the second he broke the point of the blade, but it came finally. He stopped and wiped the sweat from his forehead. It wasn't hot in the basement, but an inner excitement filled him.

The last screw gave, and he pulled the door towards him. The hasp, still held by the lock, blocked his efforts, but he managed to get his fingers into the crack and pull. It gave suddenly, hitting him in the face, bringing tears to his eyes. He swore as he stepped back, swung the door out of the way, and felt for another match.

He was in a smaller room now. He did not try to guess its use, did not care. What interested him was something in the corner, something covered with canvas. He crossed the room hurriedly, yet carefully, for the tiny flame was flickering, and he was forced to stop just short of his goal and nurse it back into life. Then he raised one corner of the canvas, his pulses racing. He had guessed what the covering concealed before he reached it, but he wanted to be sure. For a moment he stared at the radiator of Miriam Ford's foreign-built car, then dropped the canvas. A voice behind him said: "Turn around; let's have a look at you." Lennox dropped the match to the concrete floor.

8

A FLASHLIGHT STABBED a beam through the darkness, blinding him. Tempke's voice said: "Keep your hand away from that pocket."

Lennox obeyed, blinking at the light. His hands came up, almost level with his shoulders. Tempke's voice was complaining. "I always hated nosy punks. Turn around."

Bill obeyed, felt the man's hand run over his pockets. He was seized with an impulse to turn, to smash his fist into the other's face, but he merely said: "What a swell hide-out this is!"

Tempke had stepped back. "I don't see how you found it." His tone was still complaining, as if he considered Lennox's presence a personal affront.

Bill managed to laugh. "I followed you," he told the other. "It wasn't so tough."

"Which doesn't buy you anything but trouble," the gangster warned him. "You don't think you're going out of here to tell the world about it?"

Lennox was silent for a moment. "And you don't think that I was screwy enough to walk into this joint alone?"

The other made a harsh sound, intended for a laugh. "If you hadn't, you wouldn't be telling me about it. You came in here alone because that's the only way you know to play it. You like trouble. You trust yourself and you don't trust the cops, but I don't see how you got wise."

Lennox grinned, this time with amusement. "You made a couple of breaks, Tempke. Tonight when I was talking about the kidnapers calling me and bragging that they'd rubbed out those muggs on Central, you spoke about the kidnapers having got back the hundred grand from the dead gangsters. I hadn't said anything about that when I told you. I hadn't told anyone. Of course, you might have guessed, but it made me suspicious, that and the fact that those men were rubbed out before the news that I'd paid the hundred grand got into the papers. The only people that I had told that outside of the cops were you and Marsh."

Tempke said, from behind the light: "Smart guy, aren't you?"

Lennox said, without emotion: "Not too smart. I fell for Marsh's play, hard. I suppose Harry was planning to come to me when the publicity died down and claim that he'd finally established contact?"

Tempke said: "Marsh, oh—" His voice had a funny sound.

Lennox went on: "And all the time I suppose you'd have kept Ford upstairs while they searched the country for her. Not such a bad idea."

"I think it's swell." There was pride in the man's voice. "And don't think that because you nosed in, there'll be any change. You'll be missing in the morning, and there will be plenty of people who'll figure that you went south with that hundred grand. Come on, wise boy. We've got stairs to climb."

Lennox said, coolly: "If my number is up, I might as well take it down here. I never liked stairs."

The other laughed. "You're game." There was a hint of admiration in his voice. "Who knows? You might come out of this jam yet if you use your head and play ball. I'm almost glad that you stumbled in." He flashed the light a little to the right. "This way."

Lennox hesitated, then obeyed. They crossed the room and went out through another door. Stairs led upward around an unfinished elevator cage. Lennox went up slowly. The ankle which he had hurt in his fall was bothering him. The man behind him said: "Snap it up, cull. You've got fourteen floors yet."

Lennox said: "Who carries up all the groceries?"

Tempke chuckled. "Don't let that worry you. You won't eat many." They climbed in silence for three floors. Lennox asked: "How'd you happen to think of this joint?"

The other said: "I didn't. Some of the boys have been using it for a hideaway for months. This Ford play framed itself. You'll never guess how we got her inside without being seen."

Lennox told him: "I wouldn't even try. How'd you work it?"

"Ran her car into a garage and got it into a big van. The chauffeur was in on the play but he got cold feet. Maybe the cops will get something out of him, but I doubt it. He didn't know much."

Lennox did not answer. He was thinking of the battered face he had seen at Georgia Street Receiving Hospital. They reached the top at last, and Tempke indicated a door. "Open it."

Lennox obeyed, and stepped through into a furnished apartment. He looked around in surprise. The windows were covered with heavy drapes to keep the light from showing through. There were a divan, three chairs, and a cheap rug. Tempke said: "What do you think of the joint?"

Another man came through the door from what was apparently the kitchen. He stared at Lennox with evident surprise, then looked at Tempke. "Who in hell is this?"

The gangster said: "I found him poking around Ford's car

and thought that since he'd seen so much, he'd better see the works. This is the bird that you've been reading about in the papers. The famous Bill Lennox. Lennox, meet Pete."

The man grinned, showing broken, discolored teeth. "Swell to know you." Lennox didn't say anything; he was looking around. "Where's Miss Ford?"

"Impatient, ain't you?" There was a jeer in Tempke's voice. "Sorry, but I'm afraid that we can't let you see her, Bill. You know too much. You might tell her things, and then when we turn her loose, she might talk."

Relief was in Lennox's voice. For a moment he had feared that the actress wasn't here, that she might be dead. "Okey! What next?"

The door behind him opened and another man came in from the hall. He was carrying a tray with some dirty dishes. He stopped and stared at Lennox, then at Tempke. "Who's this?" His voice was heavy, anger-filled.

Tempke explained. The other said, harshly: "You damned fool! What if he did see the car. What did you bring him up here for?"

Tempke's voice changed. "I'm still giving orders around here, Mike. Don't forget that."

"But it's a screwy play." The other showed no signs of backing down.

"Is it?" The big man's voice was like a whip. "Listen, you. I framed this thing, planned it, and carried it off. You haven't lost anything by following me, have you?"

The other set the tray on the table. "Not yet." His eyes were on Tempke's face. "But I still think that it was a dumb play."

For a moment Bill thought that Marsh's lieutenant was about

to strike the man, then Tempke relaxed, and the tension went out of the room as the big man laughed. "Okey, smart guy! Listen to this. Lennox is going to call Mullier. He's going to tell the kike that he's made contact, that he knows who has Ford, and that it takes five hundred grand to get her back."

"But!" the other man's voice was uncertain now, thoughtful.

Tempke said: "There aren't any buts. It's air-tight. Lennox tells Mullier to get the money tomorrow morning and to send it over to his apartment. I'm there, waiting for it. If there's a slip and the cops see me, why, I'm merely Marsh's lieutenant, working with Lennox. I'm there because my pal Bill asked me to be. I'm helping, and I don't know a thing."

"So what?"

"So I get the dough, you fool. We wait for night, take Ford out in her own car and park it on some side street, her in it, bound and fixed so she won't yell. Someone will find her there. It's perfect."

"And Lennox?"

Tempke looked at Bill speculatively. "That depends on how good a boy he is. We'll leave him here, tied up. When we get out of the country, we might send a message to the cops; that is, if he does exactly what we tell him and doesn't make any funny moves. He will, too. This guy is screwy. He thinks more of Ford than he does of himself. If he gets her free, he won't care so much what happens to him, will you, Bill?"

Lennox said: "I doubt if Mullier can raise that much."

The gangster laughed. "Don't be an egg. Everyone in Hollywood, yeah, and half the fans in the country would kick in to help. Of course he can raise that much. Come on. Get on the phone and call him."

Lennox raised his eyebrows. "Phone?"

Tempke laughed. "This is one instrument that the company isn't collecting from. It's an extension from a phone in a house around the corner. Are you going to call him?"

Lennox said: "And if I don't?"

The man's face got ugly. "I won't threaten you, Bill, but something might happen to Miss Ford."

Lennox looked at him. "Let's quit stalling, Tempke. I paid a hundred grand and didn't get a thing. How do I know that this isn't another stall? How do I know that you've really got her?"

"You saw the car, didn't you?"

"Yeah, I saw the car, but—well—how do I know that she isn't dead?"

For an instant there was silence in the room as the three gangsters looked at each other, then Tempke said: "Take him up there, Mike, but don't speak to her, Lennox. Whatever you do, don't speak to her."

The one called Mike muttered: "I don't like it. I tell you, I don't like it."

Tempke said, harshly: "Shut up, and do as you're told. Go on, Lennox."

The trouble-shooter looked at Mike. The squat gangster took a snub-nosed automatic from his pocket and waved it towards the door. "Okey, let's go." There was a flashlight in his other hand.

They went into the bare, unfinished hall. Mike growled: "To the right, and no funny moves. This baby makes a hell of a hole."

The light flashed around Lennox, showing him the way. He went along the hall to the far end. Concrete steps led upward. He began to climb, hearing Mike close behind him. The impulse to leap backward, downward, upon the man was strong. It was the thought of Miriam Ford that deterred him, not fear for his own safety.

At the top of the stairs a heavy fire door barred his path, and Lennox paused. Mike said: "Go on, push it open." Lennox pushed, and stepped on to the flat roof. The gangster followed, shutting off his light as he emerged. About and below them, the lights of the city stretched out in what seemed an unending checker-board, broken here and there by red neon-signs. Above, the fog made a gray arc, reflecting the lights. A penthouse loomed directly ahead, and Lennox walked towards it. No light showed from within; no sound came. It seemed deserted, barren. The door was fastened on the outside by a piece of chain slipped through the handles, and secured by a padlock. The gangster handed Lennox a key and stood back while Bill unfastened the door and pushed it open. They stepped into an entry hall, and Mike flashed on his light.

"Hey, Miss Ford!"

From within a woman's voice said: "What is it?" and Lennox tensed as he recognized the voice.

The gangster said: "A friend to see you." His voice was sardonic.

There was movement somewhere in the penthouse, someone feeling the way along the rough, unfinished wall. Then a door opened, and Miriam Ford stood in the entry. Her hair was mussed, tangled rather, giving her an odd appearance; and a streak of dirt showed on her forehead.

"Bill Lennox!" It was a gasp of mingled surprise and relief.

The gangster said: "The boy friend merely wanted to be sure that you were here. Come on, Lennox!"

She said: "Bill! Bill! Get me out of here."

He stared at her without speaking, then he nodded his head. Mike said: "Come on!" His voice was rough.

The actress stepped forward. "Please let me talk to him for a minute." Her voice broke. "Have they found Walter? It—it came over their radio tonight that he was lost."

Bill nodded without speaking. The gangster touched his arm. "Come on, you. Beat it!"

The woman said: "Please, oh, please, leave the light. This darkness is terrible."

Mike laughed. "And have you flashing it around? Not much, sister. Pipe down, and you may not have to spend another night here."

Hope leaped into her eyes. "Then, then—" But the gangster had Lennox's arm and was forcing him from the hallway. He re-fastened the door and they went down the stairs. At the bottom Tempke met them. "Satisfied?" he asked Lennox.

Bill nodded: "Where's the phone?"

"In the apartment." Tempke led the way, Mike bringing up the rear. "And listen, monkey. One funny word, and not only do you get hurt, but they'll never find Ford."

Lennox nodded and picked up the phone. He dialed Mullier's number and waited. The houseman's voice said: "Mr. Mullier has retired. Who's calling?"

Lennox told him and the man's voice changed. "Is there any news, sir?"

The gun pressed into Lennox's back. He said: "Call Mr. Mullier. He will tell you." He waited impatiently until the business manager's voice reached him. "Listen, Hi. I made contact. Yeah, I'm sure this time. I've seen Miss Ford."

The other's voice trembled with suppressed excitement. "How—how is she?"

"Pretty nervous, but she seems all right otherwise. Now get this. They want five hundred grand. Yeah, a half million. I know, but what can we do? Well, get it, in as small bills as possible. What? No, they won't take securities. I know it, but you'll have to do it somehow. Yeah, send it over to my apartment. No, I won't be there, but I'll have a man there to receive it, and whatever you do, don't let the cops or papers know." He hung up before the other finished protesting.

Tempke said: "That was swell."

A voice behind him said: "What in hell is going on here?" Harry Marsh stood in the doorway.

FOR A MOMENT nothing in the room moved. Tempke's voice was dry, flat. "Why, Harry?"

Marsh's eyes were on Lennox, on the gun which Mike still held pressed to the trouble-shooter's back. They swung slightly to take in Tempke and the other gangster. "So."

Tempke's voice was too loud. "So what?" His hand was close to the opening in his coat, close to the shoulder holster.

Marsh said: "So that's the way it is. You thought that you'd run a little business of your own, using me for a front. This was the reason you advised me to offer my services as contact man. Well, you ought to know me better, Tempke. Where's Miss Ford?"

Lennox answered: "She's upstairs, Harry. So you weren't in on this play, after all?"

Marsh's eyes went across him. "Thanks for thinking that I was that kind of rat. I wasn't in on the play, and there isn't any play. Mike, go up and let Miss Ford out."

Tempke's voice cut like a knife. "Keep out of this, Harry."

The racketeer laughed. "How can I keep out of it when you drag me in? Don't get ideas, Tempke. You can't buck me, and you know it. Mike, did you hear me?"

The gangster moved uncertainly. The gun came away from Lennox's back. Tempke said: "Stay where you are, Mike." He was facing Marsh, his hand close to the edge of the coat. Keep out of this, Harry. You—"

Marsh said: "Rat!" and his hand darted towards his coat pocket. It never got there. Tempke shot him where he stood, the sound echoing hollowly from the unfinished walls. Lennox did not see Marsh fall. He moved instinctively, without conscious thought. The fingers of his left hand closed on Mike's wrist, just above the gun. His right fist smashed into the man's face, knocking him backward against the wall. Lennox brought up his knee sharply, twisting Mike across it, forcing the gun from his hand.

Tempke swung about, snapping a shot at Lennox. It struck the wall above the trouble-shooter's head. Bill caught the gun, but couldn't get it up. Tempke fired again, and something like a knife struck Lennox's leg. He gathered the half-conscious Mike in his arms and half threw him at Tempke. They went down together. The third man had his gun out, but his first shot went wild. Lennox dived for the open hall-door, went through it, and came up against the wall, hard. A bullet followed him, missing by inches. He raced down the dark corridor, up the steps, and onto the roof. The lock on the penthouse door stopped him for a moment.

He reversed the gun in his hand, and struck the lock with the butt. It flew apart, and he pulled the door open. "Miriam! Miriam!"

"What? What is it?" She sounded startled in the darkness. He was fumbling at the door he had closed behind him. There was a little knob which controlled the bolt on the inside. He turned it as steps sounded on the roof outside. "It's Bill Lennox."

She cried: "Those shots—are you hurt?"

He told her: "No," as he felt her hand on his arm, "but I'm afraid we're in a jam."

She said: "You're sure that you aren't hurt?"

He did not bother to answer the question. "That door won't hold them long," he growled. Then he was out of the entry hall, groping his way through the penthouse. On the other side was a tiny terrace, walled in on both sides, that looked out across the roof of another building, far below. The door on to the terrace was locked and bolted, but a little light came through the glass. He pulled off his coat, wrapped it quickly about his arm and shoved his fist through the glass.

Noise from the other side of the roof reached him, Tempke's voice, calling his name. Lennox paid no attention. He worked the glass from the frame and climbed through. The terrace was small, a dozen feet long and only half that wide. It was ten stories down to the other roof. He peered at it, then turned and crawled back through the broken door. The actress was beside him in the darkness, her fingers on his arm. Her voice had gained calm. "What are you going to do?"

He said: "I don't suppose that there's any rope around here?"

"No-o," slowly, then, "There's the blankets on my cot."

"How many? Where are they—" Someone pounded heavily

on the outer door and Lennox crossed to the entry hall and sent a bullet crashing through the wood. "That will hold them for a minute," he told her as the pounding ceased suddenly. "Where are those blankets?"

She was already getting them. He had admired her in the past, but he admired her more now. No questions, no hysterics, only action. He gathered them from her arms and carried them to the terrace door, shoving them through. He lifted her easily in his arms, and put her through the opening, feet first. She landed on the pile of blankets. A moment later he was at her side. His leg ached, but he had too much on his mind to give it thought. Swiftly he knotted the corners of the blankets together.

"Listen." His voice was tense as the hammering on the door recommenced. "I'm going to lower you to the window of the next floor. When you get down to the sill, kick the glass out if it's locked, then crawl in. There are stairs leading to the garage. There's an opening at the back. Tempke's men are too busy trying to get in here to be down there."

He pulled one end of the improvised rope around her, beneath her arms and knotted it in place.

She said: "I'm not going to leave you here. They'll kill you."

He lied to her. "I'll be all right, but hurry. I'll tie the rope to something and let myself down, but don't wait for me. When you reach the next floor, start running and don't stop until you find a cop."

He fastened the other end of the blanket rope beneath his arms and lowered her over the edge. For a moment her white face was level with his, then she was gone. He strained backwards, playing out the knotted blankets slowly, not daring to look over the edge for fear that he would lose his balance. The blankets had a tendency to slip through his sweaty palms. It seemed an eternity since she had disappeared over the concrete railing before the faint tinkle of falling glass made sound. Her voice called: "Okey!" and he peered over the edge to see her head extending from the window below.

"Come on."

He said fiercely: "Don't wait. Go for help." He made it an appeal, knowing that otherwise she would wait.

The head disappeared. Lennox slipped the blanket from about him and let it fall to the roof far below. There was nothing to which he could have fastened the end, had he so intended, but he had not given that plan a moment's consideration. He had to stay here, to keep the gangsters' attention while Ford made her escape.

He turned and crawled back through the broken door into the dark of the penthouse. His hand went into his pocket and came out with the gun as he moved across the living-room towards the entry hall. The pain in his leg was worse now, sending sharp knife thrusts up into his thigh. Before he reached the hall, the outer door crashed inward, and Tempke's voice called:

"All right, Lennox! Come out, and we won't hurt Miss Ford."

For answer, Lennox fired through the opening. His only object was to gain time, to keep the gangsters from discovering that the actress was gone until she should be clear of the building. A gun crashed outside and Tempke swore. His voice sounded hoarse, muffled, as it reached Lennox. "Fool! Cut the noise."

There was a snarling return, and Lennox grinned in the darkness. Evidently Tempke still hoped that the shots had not attracted attention to the empty apartment. "Maybe this will help," he muttered, and, raising the gun, fired again. There was silence for perhaps a minute, then something moved in the lighter oblong of the broken doorway. Lennox squeezed on the trigger, and was answered by a slight click. He squeezed again with no better result. Silently he cursed himself. The gun was empty. He had counted on at least five shots. There had been only three in the magazine.

For a moment he stayed where he was, his mind numbed by this sudden knowledge; then he reversed the gun and moved through the dark towards the door. As he did so, a light flashed suddenly in his face. He hurled the gun at the light, heard the impact as it struck, and leaped forward himself. The next instant his clawing fingers fastened in a man's coat, and they went down together.

He sensed, without knowing how, that it was Tempke. The gangster was striking at his face with the gun barrel. It found its mark twice, sending jarring pain through him, but he hung on, trying to work his fingers to the other's throat. The gun struck again on the bridge of his nose, flattening it, blinding him. He tried to roll free, failed, then someone was playing a flashlight upon his back, and everything went black.

9

SPELLMAN CAME INTO the hospital room, seeming to fill it with his bulk, and stared down at Lennox's bandaged face. "What a swell picture you'd make! Spurck'll probably use you!"

Bill tried to grin, but a strip of adhesive tape kept his upper lip from moving. "Hello, copper!" His voice sounded muffled. "What happened after the earthquake?"

Spellman said: "I don't know how much you remember, but Marsh's men came up just as you were knocked out. Tempke took a shot at them, but they burnt him."

Lennox said: "How'd they happen to be there? I've been wondering about that."

Spellman shrugged. "That ex-fighter, who was Marsh's body-guard, got suspicious of Tempke. He acted as his chauffeur a lot, and he started wondering why Al was hanging around this empty apartment. He knew that it had been used for a hide-out, but that didn't explain Tempke's actions; so after he dropped him last night, he went back to the club and told Marsh.

"Harry was suspicious then himself. He got another of the boys and they piled into the car. When they got outside the apartment, he insisted on going up alone. The two waited for him in the car. They didn't hear the shot which killed Marsh. It was inside. But they did hear the shooting on the roof. They piled out and went around back. On the way up, they met Ford coming down; they recognized her and the driver stayed with her while the ex-pug went up and got Tempke and the other man."

Again Lennox's lip twitched. "That's tough, Floyd. All the excitement and you didn't get a chance to break into the publicity."

Again the detective shrugged, grinning slightly, himself. "Don't brag, mugg; you didn't either. Condrey took it away from you."

"Condrey?"

"Yeah. That guy is like a cat. Nine lives. His plane was forced down somewhere in Mexico. He got a busted arm. Then he grabbed a worn-out car from a ranch and drove to where some Mexican had an old crate he was playing with. Condrey flew it to the nearest airport; flew it himself, with a broken arm. Then he got a real plane and came on in. He landed at the station just as the call came in from the man on the beat who heard the last shooting, rode out to the apartment with me in the squad car, and was there in time for his wife to faint in his arms. He sure picks his moments. They got half a page with that picture. It made a swell fadeout. If I didn't know better, I'd think that Condrey staged the whole thing. Whatta guy."

www.ingramcontent.com/pod-product-compliance
Lightning Source LLC
Chambersburg PA
CBHW031204020726
47499CB00002B/483